SYMPHONY ROAD

SYMPHONY ROAD

A SHANE CLEARY MYSTERY

BY

GABRIEL VALJAN

First published by Level Best Books 2021

This novel is entirely a work of fiction. The names, characters and incidents portrayed in it are the work of the author's imagination. Any resemblance to actual persons, living or dead, events or localities is entirely coincidental.

First edition

ISBN: 978-1-953789-07-5

This book was professionally typeset on Reedsy.
Find out more at reedsy.com

Contents

Praise for the Shane Cleary Mysteries

"Robert B. Parker would stand and cheer, and George V. Higgins would join the ovation. This is a terrific book—tough, smart, spare, and authentic. Gabriel Valjan is a true talent—impressive and skilled—providing knock-out prose, a fine-tuned sense of place and sleekly wry style."—Hank Phillippi Ryan, nationally bestselling author of *The Murder List*

"Say hello to Shane Cleary, a down-on-his luck private detective walking the streets of dirty old Boston, circa 1975. So come for the twisting plot and suspense, stay for the style."—William Martin, *New York Times* bestselling author of *Back Bay* **and** *Bound for Gold*

"Valjan paints the town, and all the colors are noir."—Tom Straw, *New York Times* bestselling author, as Richard Castle

"Fans of Robert B. Parker's Spenser and Dennis Lehane's Patrick Kenzie will love Shane Cleary. Gabriel Valjan has created a fascinating new PI character who prowls the tough streets of '70s Boston in this compelling hard-boiled mystery. *Dirty Old Town* is fast, fun and first-rate!"—R.G. Belsky, author of the award-winning Clare Carlson mystery series

"*Dirty Old Town* hits every pitch out of the park: it's smart, funny and consistently surprising. A great read!"—Dennis Palumbo, author of the Daniel Rinaldi Mysteries

Characters

Jimmy C: Arsonist.

Bill: Friend of Shane, an Army veteran, and a Boston Police Department officer.

Delilah: Shane's cat.

Mr. B: Mafia don.

Tony Two-Times: Bodyguard and associate of Mr. B.

Delano 'Professor' Lindsey: Shane's former teacher.

John: Bar and pool hall owner, and husband of Sylvia, and Shane's friend.

Sylvia: Owner of Sister Sylvia, a soul food restaurant in Dorchester, and John's wife.

Vanessa: John's niece, visiting from Canada.

Saul Fiedermann: Jeweler on the first floor of Shane's office building.

Richard Case: Shane's writer friend.

Nikos: A South End luncheonette and property owner.

JC: Jean-Claude Toussaint, a former doctor in Haiti, and an orderly at City Hospital.

Sal: Driver and Mr. B's protégé.

Isabella Rivera: The woman in Apartment 418, in Park Plaza.

Toni Ruiz: Resident at Park Plaza

Kiernan: Boston Police Department officer.

O'Mara: Boston Police Department officer, and Kiernan's partner.

'The Syrian': Boston slumlord aka Sharif Faisal.

Mr. Pinto: Middle man between Shane and the Boston Police Department Commissioner.

'Shadow': Assistant to the Boston Police Department Commissioner.

Larry: Arsonist.

Jerry: Addict and petty thief.

Chapter One: Devil's Moan

Two things you don't do in Boston: side with the Yankees or double-cross Jimmy C. No matter how good the odds were from the bookie, don't, and no matter how much was in your favor, how stitched up your plan was to get away with it, you won't.

Not when it came to Jimmy. Ever.

When yet another apartment building on Symphony Road went up in flames one night in March, nobody thought of another suspect. Nobody knew the exact time the fire started, but the building went up or down fast, depending on your perspective. Frequent fires on that street, in that part of Boston, earned it the nickname The Devil's Moan.

Firemen sorted through the smoldering ruin and found what they expected: evidence of arson. They also found what they didn't expect: a body.

Jimmy was a torch, a professional firebug. In the dispatches between the Fire and Police Departments, the PD discovered the complex was slated for repairs. The landlord was in Key West for the winter before it was winter, a snowbird. The signs and stickers, the permits, like the rest of the structure, were ashes. "A total loss." The black coats spoke to the blue shirts and the blue shirts paid Jimmy a visit all because someone had it in for him, which is why, later that night, he was arrested.

Someone else picked up the phone and called me.

"Jimmy's been pinched."

"Arson?"

The sound of a solitary typewriter I heard clacking in the background was likely the song of a hooker or a john being processed.

"I'm not a lawyer, Bill. Do you have any idea what time it is?"

"Four-thirty, and he asked for you."

"Find him a lawyer first, and he'll get him sprung, and I'll talk to him then."

"He won't make bail, Shane. Not this time, not with homicide on the sheet."

"Homicide?" That woke me up, and helped me see through the darkness better than my cat Delilah. "I don't get it. Jimmy's always been careful."

"Not careful enough. The body is in the morgue at City."

"Homicide, huh, and he asked for me?"

Click. The line went dead.

Bill calling me about Boston's best arsonist was the least of my problems. The cops, Boston's finest, hated me. Once upon a time I was a cop until I lifted a leg on the Blue Wall and testified against one of them, which is to say, all of them. Shane Cleary wouldn't nickel-plate his shield.

Delilah stared at me.

"How about it, girl? Blink once for Yes, and two for No. Should I help Jimmy?"

Her green eyes blinked. Once.

"This isn't going to end well, is it?"

Twice she blinked and added a silent yawn. I saw incisors bared and a long pink tongue. To be certain, to banish the Delphic Oracle's ambiguity, I asked her, "Want some breakfast?"

She blinked once and hopped off the bed.

Hat on my head and light blazer on, with feet out the door, I was thinking two things—no, three things—as I took the steep flight of stairs down to Union Park. First: Mrs. F, the landlady, ought to do something about these steps. They were small enough for her ballerina feet, but impossible for normal hooves. Even that fat Corgi of hers had to sidestep his way down to the street. Second: the fedora on my head reminded me of Jimmy. The hat, the kind I imagined Phillip Marlowe wearing, had been a gift, a way of paying the bill for information.

The third thing. Jimmy was known as Jimmy C. The letter itself inspired fear and mystery, neither of which Jimmy cared to dispel. Jimmy had a rep for carrying a meat cleaver. Jimmy the Cleaver. I knew better. Jimmy's last name was Constantino. Bill hadn't mentioned whether carrying a concealed weapon was another charge on Jimmy's sheet.

Jimmy managed what some people would call an antique shop but he preferred to call a nostalgia shop. His true skill, however, was as an artisan of the flame. Jimmy was Boston's open secret in plain sight. He had no record; he was untraceable, a consummate professional, and meticulous as a watchmaker. Fire chiefs and insurance investigators wasted many an hour trying to find the matchstick and haystack, and came up with nothing.

Which is why Jimmy C in the can didn't add up. Set aside Bill's comment that Jimmy had asked for me, I wondered about this convenient phone call. Bill had acquired his post and a promotion in Vice thanks to Mr. B, the last of the dons in Boston's Italian North End, so it stood to reason the mafioso was behind the phone call.

Sure, Jimmy worked for the mob on occasion, but rescuing a pinch from doing a stint in Walpole wasn't their way of settling issues. Those guys didn't believe in do-overs on their playground. Mr. B, if he had hired a torch, wouldn't want attention directed his way. As for shoddy work, no excuses were allowed. Like the brat neither seen nor heard, Mr. B didn't leave bodies. Jimmy would've and should've disappeared if he had screwed up the job.

The Boston PD, the nation's oldest police department, had a station house on Berkeley Street. Jimmy would be held there until he was transferred to Chucky's Place, the Suffolk County Jail on Charles Street, where he'd wait for his arraignment. At this hour, the buses slept and hacks weren't roaming the streets for fares, so I walked. A fast gait would deter muggers, prostitutes, and winos. I decided against wearing my sidearm, despite the valid licenses as a PI and for a concealed carry. I wasn't about to give the desk sergeant sprinkles with his morning donut.

I went to cross the street when the wheels of a black Cadillac sped up and bristled over tempered glass from a recent smash-and-grab. The brake lights pulsed red, and a thick door opened. A big hulk stepped out, and the car wobbled. The man reached into his pocket. I thought this was it. My

3

obituary was in tomorrow's paper, written in past tense and in the smallest and dullest typeface, Helvetica, because nothing else said boring better.

Click. Click. "I can never get this fucking thing to light."

It was Tony Two-Times, Mr. B's no-neck side man. His nickname came from his habit of clicking his lighter twice. "Mr. B wants a word."

"Allow me." I grabbed the Bic. The orange flame jumped on my first try and roasted the end of his Marlboro Red. "You really oughta quit."

"Thanks for the health advice. Get in."

Tony nudged me into the backseat. I became the meat in the sandwich between him and Mr. B. There was no need for introductions. The chauffeur was nothing more than a back of a head and a pair of hands on the wheel. The car moved and Mr. B contemplated the night life outside the window.

"I heard you're on your way to the police station to help your friend."

"News travels fast on Thursday night. Did Bill tell you before or after he called me?"

"I'm here on another matter."

The cloud of smoke made me cough. Tony Two-Times was halfway to the filter. The chauffeur cracked the window a smidge for ventilation. As I expected, the radio played Sinatra and there were plans for a detour. A string of red and green lights stared back at us through a clean windshield.

"A kid I know is missing," Mr. B said.

"Kids go missing all the time."

"This kid is special."

"Has a Missing Persons Report been filed?"

The look from Mr. B prompted regret. "We do things my way. Understood?"

We stopped at a light. A long-legged working girl with a chinchilla wrap crossed the street. She approached the car to recite the menu and her prices, but one look at us and she kept walking.

"Is this kid one of your own?"

The old man's hand strummed leather. The missing pinky unnerved me. I've seen my share of trauma in Vietnam: shattered bones, intestines hanging out of a man, but missing parts made me queasy. The car moved and Mr. B

4

continued the narrative.

"Kid's a real pain in my ass, which is what you'd expect from a teenager, but he's not in the rackets, if that's what you're wondering. This should be easy money for you."

Money never came easy. As soon as it was in my hand, it went to the landlady, or the vet, or the utilities, or inside the refrigerator. I'd allow Mr. B his slow revelation of facts. Mr. B mentioned the kid's gender when he said "he's not in the rackets." This detail had already made the case easier for me. A boy was stupider, easier to find and catch. Finding a teenage girl—that took something special, like pulling the wings off of an angel.

"He's a good kid. No troubles with the law, good in school, excellent grades and all, but his mother seems to think he needed to work off some of that rebellious energy kids get. You know how it is."

I didn't. The last of my teen years were spent in rice paddies, in a hundred-seventeen-degree weather—and that was before summer—trying to distinguish friendlies from enemies in a jungle on the other side of the planet. And then there were the firefights, screams, and all the dead bodies.

"Does this kid have a girlfriend?" I asked.

Mr. B said nothing.

"A boyfriend then?" That question made Mr. B twist his head and Tony Two-Times elbowed me hard. "I've got to ask. Kids these days. You know, drugs, sex, and rock' n roll."

"The kid isn't like your friend Bill, Mr. Cleary."

The mister before Cleary was a first. The ribs ached. I caught a flash of the driver's eyes in the rearview mirror. Mr. B conveyed specifics such as height and weight, build, the last known place the kid was seen, the usual hangouts and habits. This kid was All-American, too vanilla, and Mr. B had to know it. Still, this kid was vestal purity compared to Mr. B, who had run gin during Prohibition, killed his first man during the Depression, and became a made-man before *Leave It to Beaver* aired its first episode on television.

The car came to a stop. The driver put an emphasis on the brakes. We sat in silence. The locks shot up. Not quite the sound of a bolt-action rifle, but close. Mr. B extended his hand for a handshake. I took it. No choice there. This was B's way of saying his word was his bond and whatever I discovered during the course of my investigation stayed between us, the Father, the Son and the Holy Ghost.

"I've got to ask," I said.

"I'll pay you whatever you want."

"It's not that," I said, feeling Tony Two-Times' breath on the back of my neck. "Did you hire Jimmy C to do a job lately?"

"I did not."

"And Bill called me, just like that?" I knew better than to snap my fingers. Tony would grab my hand and crush my knuckles like a bag of peanuts. A massive paw on the shoulder told me it was time to vacate the premises, but then Mr. B did the tailor's touch, a light hand to my elbow. "Jimmy is queer like your friend, right?"

"What has that got to do with anything?"

"When it comes to friends, you forgive certain habits, like I allow this idiot over here to smoke those stupid cigarettes. *Capisci?*"

"Yeah, I understand."

"Good. Now, screw off."

I climbed over Tony Two-Times to leave the car. Door handle in my grip, I leaned forward to ask one last thing, "You know about Jimmy's predicament?"

"Ironic, isn't it?" Mr. B said.

"What is?"

"I know everything in this town, except where my grandnephew is. Now, shut the door."

The door clapped shut. I heard bolts hammer down and lock. There was a brief sight of silhouettes behind glass before the car left the curb. I had two cases before breakfast, one in front of me, and the other one, behind me in the precinct house. There was no need for me to turn around. No need either, to read the sign overhead.

The limestone building loomed large in my memory. Two lanterns glowed and the entrance, double doors of polished brass, were as tall and heavy as I remembered them. It was late March and I wasn't Caesar but it sure as hell felt like the Ides of March as I walked up those marble steps.

Chapter Two: Take-Out

The station house on Berkeley Street was once seven stories of ill repute, full of flappers and bathtub gin. When Prohibition ended, architects etched City of Boston Police Department Headquarters above a row of shields. The one thing cops and citizens shared in common, then and now, was everyone had to climb the same five steps and open one of two doors, each large enough for Goliath, and walk across an alabaster floor.

A patrol cop from the overnight shift drifted past me. Ahead of me was a high counter of solid oak, behind which the desk sergeant sat. The tall and thick cop thumbed through the ledger for the night's haul. He licked a stub of a pencil between scribbles. Duffy looked once. He looked twice and dropped his pencil.

"Feck me, if it ain't the Prodigal Son. You've got Irish courage."

"You've dropped your pencil."

"And you've been dropped on your head coming in here."

The ledger forgotten and closed, Sergeant Duffy rested his mitts in front of him. Beefy hands with liver spots, Duffy had not changed in years. His sidewalls and dome were shaved down to fuzz, so it was a guess whether it'd grow back in a dull shade of gray or red.

"So, what can I do you for?" he asked and I gave him Jimmy's Christian name.

A cluster of rookies rang through a set of doors behind Duffy, mouths emptying stories from the night's beat. I've heard them all. Like eyeballing the pimp as you rotate his stable of girls from one street to the next to give

8

the walkway some rest; or making house calls, where the husband and wife were intent on the "for worse" part of their vows. He hits her. A week later, she pours boiling water on him while he's asleep.

An older cop in the herd spotted me and tapped his buddy's shoulder. Duffy's tack with me changed. The scent in the air wasn't Old Spice. Duffy had a face to save and a role to play.

"Are you his lawyer?" he asked me.

"Look what we've got here, boys."

My eyes locked on Duffy, the gatekeeper. I ignored the veteran cop and his pal. A desk sergeant's word was God in the station and God chose silence. An officer approached. Hang air fresheners from his earlobes and he'd still reek of stale sweat and Chinese take-out from an all-nighter in a squad car, the AC cranked up.

"Shane Cleary went to night school and got himself a law degree...a mouthpiece, huh?"

A small burst of laughter erupted from the recruits. These young men lived for crumbs from their training officers. I remembered life as a rookie cop and the stiff walk that came with unbroken gunleather. The lead cop, inches from my face, came into focus. I recognized his mug. We boxed more than once in the gym and I dropped him every time. His partner with a name plate that said O'Mara stood behind him. Lo Mein breath moved in.

"Officer Kiernan," I said, and nodded to his partner. "O'Mara."

"Heard you lick a stamp and the school sends you a law degree these days," Kiernan said and inched closer, "but you know what? You've got to bend over to pass the bar. Think you can do that?"

"Pass the bar, sure, I'm flexible."

"Now, why is that?"

"I learned from the best."

"Did you now? Learned it from being a rat?"

"No, your sister taught me."

He lunged, but the choirboys around him reeled him in. I gave him the same look I had the last time I'd laid him out on the canvas. If he dared try anything he'd have his nose on the other side of his skull.

9

"Knock it off," Duffy yelled. "Get the hell out of my house, the lot of you, before I write you up."

The small pack migrated to the front doors. Now and then, one of them would glance over his shoulder to remind me they had tribal memory. Next time, the eyes said.

"You have the gift wherever you go, Cleary. What do you want with Constantino?"

"He's a client. I'm a private investigator."

"So I've heard," Duffy said and picked up his pencil. "Carrying?"

I was right not to bring my snub-nose because I'd have to surrender it. I wouldn't put it past the boys in Ballistics to test-fire my .38 for future reference. I opened the jacket and did the slow circle. "Want me to show you my socks, squat and cough, Sarge?"

"Shanty Irish is what you are, Cleary," he said as he picked up the phone. "I'll let you in, but make it quick. The two officers with your guy don't know who you are, but there are guys around who do. I'd move fast, if I were you."

A thick finger turned the rotary dial and Duffy tucked his chin in and mumbled a few words. He put the receiver down. Somebody would come and escort me to Jimmy. We communed in silence. This imposed quiet time signaled the end of the round of hospitality from Duffy. Hard hallways awaited me.

I wasn't Bernstein or Woodward, but my little exposé of corruption that kicked me off the force was as loud as the backfire of the buses used to integrate the schools in South Boston. Nobody from Berkeley Street to Beacon Hill wanted to know about cops on the take, or about the murder of a Black kid. I had stepped up and crossed the line to do right by my badge and the vow I took, and all that got me kicked to the curb. Boston was a town that neither forgets nor forgives.

The station smelled of all the dirty mornings and dirtier nights. One of the double doors swung open. I glimpsed a payphone behind the cop. The phone was high on the wall, the cord twisted. The twelve steel buttons on that phone didn't dial freedom or justice for the poor. Most collars couldn't make bail and sat in the clink until their court appearance. Most lawyers refused their cases because they couldn't pay. The Public Defender's Office was understaffed and overworked, and slower than the time it took to make Indian pudding. Ma Bell ate all their dimes and all their dreams, too.

A fresh-faced boot introduced himself. "This way," he said, and we proceeded down the corridor together. One year out from the academy, a soft soap. The giveaway was the long sleeves and the starch in his shirt and pants. This early in his career, he sat on the edge of his bed every night and polished his badge.

"Somebody will be right with you," he said while we walked.

I entered a room with a window, cameras in the corners, and fluorescent rods overhead. The single chair and no clock on the wall hinted of Purgatory.

Five minutes.

Ten minutes.

I stood at ease. I had plenty of experience with that stance, thanks to Uncle Sam. I played their mind game. I stared at the door. I counted on detectives behind the treated glass. They'll come and they'll have a script. The question was whether the plot was cooked to high drama or horror show.

The doorknob clicked and two suits off the rack at Filene's Basement downtown appeared. Tie, black and knotted perfectly, and pressed white shirt walked in first. His sidekick followed him. Same black tie, but his knot, a simple four-in-hand, looked as if it had been looped and pulled through with broken fingers and his shirt was wrinkled, ironed by elephants.

"Sergeant said you wanted to see James Constantino."

"I did and I do."

"May we ask why you wish to speak with him?"

"Professional matter."

I played the part. Minimalistic answers to these boys left little to twist and use against Jimmy or me. No introductions, no names from them, also told me this meeting never happened. Their word against mine, and I'd better have patience for Jimmy's sake. Sloppy Cop left the room, leaving his partner with me for a staring contest.

"He's in for arson."

"So I was told."

"And homicide."

"So I heard."

"I'd advise him to take a plea deal and save everyone a lot of time." The tall and neat detective decided to do the walk-and-talk to show I was in his house and he made the rules. "When I arrested Jimmy, do you know what he said to me?"

"Knowing Jimmy, he probably said fuck you."

"That's exactly right. He said fuck you. Nice guy, your client Jimmy. I didn't quote him in the report, so you could say I cut him some slack. Heat of the moment."

To thank him, or agree with him would give him a lever. I said nothing.

"Now, let's get to the point, shall we? Jimmy is a pyro. You know it and I know it."

He touched his chin. I knew this trick, too. Semantics.

"Excuse me, alleged arsonist," he said. "Imagine how it'll play for Jimmy when the DA explains to a jury how a person dies in a fire, how he smells his own flesh cooking, and how he'll start coughing and sputtering and gasping for air before he chokes to death." He stepped close enough that I could smell Maxwell House on his breath. "Not a whole lot of sympathy. I'd love to be there, right up in his face and ask Jimmy who's fucked now?"

The detective's dark brown eyes drilled into me.

"I'm curious, Detective," I said. "Did the coroner's report come in?"

"It's coming."

"I'll take that as a no then. I thought you might know something about the deceased in the building since you keep repeating *he*." I raised a finger. "That brings up another small matter. Neither of us knows whether *he* was already dead or not when the building burned down, do we? And one other thing, did you find any traces of accelerant on Jimmy?"

The detective leaned forward. "What's your point?"

I stepped right up and delivered. "It's called presumption of innocence."

The door opened. Partner Slipshod returned. He let the door yawn close. Since Jimmy wasn't with him, I assumed the next stop was holding.

Wrong.

A brief walk, two doors down, I met a proper interrogation room. The sloppy little man eased the door open for me to see Jimmy inside what cops called the box. My escort whispered, "I'll give you two some privacy."

Straight out of the latest research from the psychologists, the room boasted four sharp corners, smooth surfaces and edges. Accommodations included an uncomfortable hardwood chair for Jimmy, its back to the door for the element of surprise. The light fixture hung low and bright, its glare relentless to blind the eyes or toast the top of the head. I walked towards the empty chair. I ran my hand along the tabletop. Jimmy came into view, handcuffed to an eyelet in front of him. His eyes glanced sideways, to a glass window, to remind me there were eavesdroppers. I gave him the slightest nod.

Jimmy had one look: composed menace. Hair short, shirt tailored, and slacks pressed. The cops had confiscated his wristwatch, belt and shoelaces. The harsh lighting did him no favors. His high cheekbones, long face, hooded eyelids and dark eyes telegraphed violence.

The bruise on his cheek was as purple as raw steak. The left eye would close up soon. His knuckles were scraped and bloodied. He had gotten a few in. Lawyers used the Socratic method. Boston cops used the Ground and Pound, familiar to Marines.

"Haven't had much sleep, have you?"

Jimmy smirked. "What can I say? Hard mattress, harder pillow, and then somebody wanted to dance, but you know how it is in the dark. Clang, clang, bang, bang, and nobody heard a thing."

I toured the room. I stopped by the glass and breathed on it and did the car-washer's oval with my sleeve for the eyes and ears on the other side of the divide.

"Give a statement, Jimmy?"

"Only thing I told them is I didn't want to talk to them. It's my legal right, but that's when the music started. I didn't give them my name, but they pillaged my place, like the Huns they are, and found a Social Security card and used that for identification. I'm law-abiding. I pay my taxes. I look both ways when I cross the street and I don't run red lights."

"A Social Security card doesn't constitute a positive ID, and you don't drive, Jimmy."

"I don't do a lot of things."

"About that profanity with the arresting officer; talk to me about it."

"Is he calling that resisting arrest?" Jimmy tried to move, but the handcuffs reminded him he was tethered. "I told him off. So what?"

We had guests and I wanted a show, and Jimmy caught on. "You're a bachelor," I said.

"I live alone, yeah, so what?"

Symphony Road wasn't far from Jimmy's nostalgia shop, though his apartment in Bay Village placed him far from the scene. The cops, I figured, would argue Jimmy placed a timer in the building. I'd let Jimmy talk and they listened.

"One of the cops when they collared me smelled of take-out. I like take-out, too, but I'm particular about how I want my food prepared." I saw Jimmy's long index finger tapping the table. "None of that MSG garbage. Who needs filler and the migraine later, right? And I like my boneless ribs with a generous side of duck sauce or—"

"Hot mustard." I thought I understood Jimmy's code.

"Clears out your sinuses in a flash, and I like vinegar on my fried rice. But, you know what's better? Middle Eastern food. Try it sometime."

The door swung open and the shorter detective barged in with the rookie I'd met earlier, and an old friend behind them. I recognized him from the small scar on his cheek. We encountered each other while I was on a case. I said nothing and he stood there with a smile.

He could've made me. He could've told the other cops in the room I wasn't Jimmy's lawyer, but he wouldn't because then he'd have to discuss our unfortunate history. I worked a missing person case last year for Bill, and Scarface here surfaced like pond scum. He moonlighted as hired muscle and as a bagman for unnamed clients.

I looked to Jimmy and his eyes avoided me. I understood now what played as music to the tango Jimmy described moments earlier, the dance that left him with a bruised cheek and a case of red eye. The title to their duet was called Payback. Scarface led and Jimmy kept up. It was a simple case of revenge. Jimmy saved me that day from Scarface when he put a meat cleaver to the cop's throat.

The tall cop from earlier loped in like a Bullmastiff, anxious for his chew toy. He pointed an accusatory finger at me. "You're no lawyer, you son of a bitch."

"Never said I was," I answered.

His partner behind Jimmy fanned a weathered phonebook. I could tell from the frayed edges it wasn't tired from frequent calls to psychics in Kenmore Square. Jimmy took one look and sighed. "Fuck me, my day gets better."

"You're Shane Cleary," the rookie said. "I heard about you. You testified against good cops."

I bit my tongue for Jimmy's sake. Those good cops this newbie admired dished out beat-downs for kickbacks from the Irish mob, and looked the other way when some Hispanic kid fell down a flight of stairs, in their version of Slip and Fall.

Scarface nodded, gave the go-ahead to the squat detective. The little guy let Jimmy have it with the phone book. The freshman cop went to say something, and I grabbed his arm and shook my head. He had to learn the ways of the world and see it with his own eyes. We watched the hobbit wallop Jimmy.

Some cops weren't imaginative. A phone book was tiresome on the arms. A newspaper rolled into a club did a better job, and served a purpose after the fact. You can read it. Jimmy accepted the blows to the head and shoulders and didn't utter a sound.

The tall detective visited me. He balled his fist. "Get the hell out of here, before I—"

"Before you what," another voice said. A three-piece suit stood in the doorway looking as if the law firm he represented had three or more names on their shingle, and he was a partner, or damn close to it. For a lawyer who'd fallen out of bed this early in the morning for a case, he sported nice threads. His tie costs more than what most cops made in a week. "I'd like a word with my client, please."

I said to the tall detective with the fist, "You know what?"

"What?"

"You can't even do wrong right."

"What the hell does that mean?" he asked.

"Beat a confession out of a suspect, and you use a phonebook? Amateur move. Didn't they teach you not to leave marks?" I walked past him and clipped him with my shoulder.

"And who are you?" the lawyer asked me.

I fished out a business card and he read it. "Shane Cleary, Private Investigator."

I made to leave. Jimmy's arson and homicide, the hunt for a mobster's missing relative, and this unwanted run-in with my exes in uniform required a serious dose of aspirin.

"Shane?"

I turned to Jimmy. His good eye focused on me. "Don't forget take-out."

"Chinese, no MSG, ribs, hot mustard, and…oh, almost forgot to ask, like Lo Mein?"

"I hate Lo Mein."

"Yeah, me too. I'll try Middle Eastern instead."

Jimmy rocked in the chair. The look on his face chilled me.

Chapter Three: Copyright

Night turned into day and what I needed was breakfast. What I had were clues. I could try and solve both walking down Stuart Street to the South Street Diner. The farther and farther I marched away from Police Headquarters, the more I appreciated the honest air, the full-throated cries of cars on the street. Every car horn sounded different, from a honk to a beep to a squeal. Bostonians went to bed angry, slept angry, and woke up and drove angry. Theirs was a sincerity I enjoyed at the intersections of whatever life threw at me.

Some people might think Jimmy shouldn't have said what he said to the arresting officer, that he deserved the tune-up he received but, right or wrong, Jimmy was a fighter and wouldn't lie down like a dog. The son of Greek immigrants, Jimmy's flip remark to the cop came from the orneriness deep in the bones and marrow of this city. Back in the day Brahmins wore powdered wigs, Blacks and Irish used the backdoor, and the Italians, not the last on an endless list, dug the city's ditches, but nothing stopped freedom of speech. The city may've changed, but not Yankee honesty.

Across the street the old theatre district faded into sad, prim Victorian niceness, while another venue reared gaudy and lit up like a young girl who didn't understand makeup. Entertainment changed and the clientele varied. It's *Playboy of the Western World* at the Puritan one day, *The Sound of Music* at the Gary another, but walk down to where Stuart became Kneeland and porn played at the Pilgrim.

Take-out was Jimmy's way of saying what he couldn't say without incriminating himself. This fire on Symphony Road wasn't his style, and the one thing I learned from Jimmy was that every arsonist, every guy on either side of the white line, had their way of doing things. Call it a Signature, but Jimmy style wasn't the screaming John Hancock for everyone to see. He was subtle and sophisticated. He used traditional ingredients such as trash, storage stuff, the kind of kindling you'd expect to find somewhere in a building. Whoever might suggest timers were used on Symphony Road read too many Ian Fleming novels. Jimmy, like his ancient forebears, was resourceful.

He'd catch himself a mouse, tie a tampon to its tail and light it. The MO was rather ingenious because mice were indigenous to Symphony Road near the Fens, which was swampland, notorious for vermin and hustlers. Jimmy hated rodents. He explained to me rats had burrowed into the timbers of ships during the Middle Ages, and destroyed a third of Europe's population with the plague. He never mentioned fleas, the real culprit behind the Black Death. In the right location, with the right décor, he said, a tampon, a match, and Mickey Mouse with his ass on fire did the job.

No MSG and *hot mustard* were code. His words had me itchy as a wool sweater on a hot day. *Lo Mein* and *Middle Eastern*. I had a name for Lo Mein, Kiernan, and an idea about *Middle Eastern*, but nothing in my mental Rolodex connected the two men together.

Breakfast beckoned. I walked into the diner. The smell of eggs and sausages on the grill taunted me. The number of octane knocks in the house coffee matched the number of times the bell above the door rang before it stopped. Day or night, around the clock, whether the hard hats from the construction site called it The South Street Diner, or the posh late-night crowd in their tuxedos referred to it as the Blue Diner, the menu was one of the most reliable in Boston. My head said "Eat for a long day," my heart said "Eat Healthy," and the stomach said "The hell with it." Bacon sizzled, music to my depraved soul.

A sharp whistle and a hand raised above the heads of customers called me. I walked the aisle, turned this and that way through waitresses and customers. One of the girls, whom I should have called after our date but had forgotten to, shot me a sour look. Another did a fly-by, close enough I could smell Ivory Snow on her uniform.

"Good to see you, my boy. Please, take a seat and join me."

Delano "The Professor" Lindsey was once my teacher, what the Brits called a schoolmaster, but to me he was the father, uncle, and older brother I never had. Something was off. He had his usual Breakfast Special No. 2, but no book nearby. Accustomed to the man with a fork in one hand, a book in the other, he seemed like a nun or priest without a crucifix.

Literature kept Lindsey buoyant in the world, especially after he'd been bounced out of academe for allegedly sleeping with a student. The professor taught me the art of the deep-read at St. Wystan's and kept me plied with books while I bounced around foster care after my parents died. There was one mystery about Delano Lindsey I never could solve, though. Was he related to *those* Delanos of Hyde Park?

"Surprised seeing you here," I said, as I hung my coat on the back of my chair.

He didn't say a word. I thought since it was a Friday morning, the professor was celebrating another week, another paycheck from steady employment. The waitress arrived with coffee. I placed an order for a stuffed omelet, bacon on the side. The crabbed expression on his face worried me.

"Thought you would be at John and Sylvia's for breakfast," I said. "No, let me guess, you criticized Sylvia's gravy biscuits." Lindsey often offered unedited reviews tableside, and his foot went where his fork should.

John owned a bar in Central Square. His wife, Sylvia, ran an eatery and the professor and I were so fond of her soul food that she joked we must've been black in a past life. Lindsey loved her biscuits and he'd fight to the death for the last one.

"Drink some of your coffee first and I'll tell you," he said.

My lips were about to kiss the rim when Gloria, the waitress I'd forgotten to call, placed my breakfast on the table. The heavy plate slapped the tabletop to announce her disappointment in me. I crossed my legs should she stop later to give me a refill of the diner's bottomless coffee.

"John and Sylvia have a niece visiting from Canada," the professor announced.

"Didn't know they had a niece, or relatives in Canada, for that matter."

"The girl is John's sister's daughter and a teenager."

"Nice to know, but that doesn't explain why you're sitting here."

Too preoccupied and enamored with the silky eggs, velvety cheese, and the crisped bacon, I savored the first bite of the day while Lindsey talked.

"The girl's name is Vanessa," the professor said, as he looked through the window near us. Clean glass and noisy traffic, Bostonians on the hoof to corporate offices and cubicles or whatever paid the rent. His voice, in a tone I imagined Cotton Mather used when he'd discovered a witch in his congregation, transmitted fear. "Vanessa is trouble."

"Most teenagers are. Exactly how old is this trouble?"

"Does it matter? She's the worst kind there is," he said, and I waited for his drawing of a forked tail and pitchfork. The professor didn't disappoint.

"I mean, she's pleasant, polite, and intelligent. She let me borrow her edition of *Things Fall Apart*. Have you read it?" I said that I had not. "Nigerian author Chinua Achebe. She reads in French, which I should have expected since she is from Canada and...what?"

"Vanessa has brains. I get it, Professor, but what is it about her that bothers you?"

"She does things for a reaction."

"Ah, a girl on the brink of womanhood," I said and raised my coffee mug. "Let's hope none of the women-libbers heard me. I'll find myself tarred and feathered."

"You think this is funny but I'm serious, Shane. The girl is dangerous."

"Relax, Professor. One sex doesn't own the copyright on bad behavior. Still haven't answered me. How old is she?"

"Old enough to know what she's doing. I made myself scarce after their latest quarrel."

"Who was fighting with Lolita...John or Sylvia?" I asked.

"Sylvia, and her name is Vanessa."

I've witnessed rows between John and Sylvia. John ranted and raved fire and brimstone. Sylvia would stand there, calm as an iceberg and with a stare as cold as the one that'd sunk the Titanic. Water in whatever form trumped

20

fire. Every time.

"Wise of you then, to leave the scene," I said. "It's a family matter, John's house, Sylvia's rules, and never shall the twain meet."

"What twain?"

"Two women in the same kitchen."

The professor didn't find my quip amusing. Finished with my meal, I turned my head both ways in search of a refill. Gloria across the way stood there, pot in hand, and caught my request and squinted. Folgers Instant might be the wiser choice. I had some in my office.

"Forget the family drama, Professor. I've got a proposition for you."

The last time I discussed a case with Lindsey, he took the initiative and almost got us both killed. A fast elevator, a steady hand, and a thick book tucked inside his coat caught the bullet intended for one of us.

"Sure, what is it?" he said and pushed his dish away.

The professor had graduated from the copy center at a newspaper on Harrison Ave to assistant to the Assistant Copy Editor. His job included a modest desk, and paid the man enough that he wasn't eating Ramen noodles six days a week. With his smarts he should earn more, but ours is a disposable society once the hair turns gray. The professor possessed an agile mind, patience, and the skills to teach people how to actually think for themselves, but instead he wasted red ink on the absence of the present subjunctive in modern English.

"There was a fire on Symphony Road," I told him. "Your paper probably covered it. Your place archives past issues on microfilm, right?"

He was intrigued enough not to correct me and say microfiche.

"You suspect a slumlord?"

"If there's one to be found."

I detailed the work-order for him.

"Research any residential fires, the landlords for those razed properties, and the insurance companies that covered the damages. Straightforward stuff, I hope. And pay particular attention to the names of recurring cops, firemen, and insurance adjusters."

"You mean establish a pattern?"

Like I said, Lindsey learned fast. We talked shop enough that he understood how a PI thought and approached work. It didn't require a doctorate, but there's a lot to be said for intellectual curiosity, which I always thought was the true sign of intelligence, and not some number from an IQ test.

"That too, and include anyone and anything else you find intriguing about the property that burned down on Symphony Road," I said as I put on my coat and grabbed his check. A few steps away from our table, I realized I'd forgotten my hat and one last question. "Where do I find you?"

"John and Sylvia's. Where else?"

I nudged his shoulder. "Good to know, and forget about Vanessa, okay?"

I walked towards the till. Gloria was in my peripheral vision. Steamed about the phone call that never happened, I was grateful she didn't still have that pot of coffee in her hand. This Gloria might reenact the scene of Lee Marvin throwing the pot of boiling coffee into Gloria Grahame's face in *Big Heat* with me.

At the cash register, I expected her to hammer the keys there, as if they were my head, until the drawer coughed open and the bell chimed. I'd hand her money and she'd give me change with a poisonous smile.

We met, we exchanged polite words, and we endured our little détente. Pinball machines made a quieter sound than the register did when she thrust her hip against it.

"Have yourself a nice day, sir," she said.

I had been relegated to oblivion with the impersonal Sir.

Nerves dialed up from the coffee earlier, I forgot about the Folgers at my office. I didn't, however, forget the need to get my .38 under my arm, or my suspicion about what Jimmy meant when he said "Middle Eastern."

Boston's most notorious landlord.

Chapter Four: Puzzle Pieces

The diner behind me, I made my way down the pavement when someone in a white hat from a construction site interrupted the sidewalk for me.

"Kneeland Street is closed, Mister," he said.

PI or not, I could've concluded that without him. Hercules without earplugs behind him did the work of a chain gang with the jackhammer in his hands. A crew of blue hats around the metallic clatter busied themselves with destruction and restoration. While one guy shoveled chunks of the broken street into a wheelbarrow, another carted the debris away, and the smallest guy on the team was spreading tar from a wagon with a brush.

The pungent odor of asphalt reminded me of driveways and playgrounds, of hot summer days with my parents at Pleasure Island, the amusement park north of Boston. Memories swept in blue and bright green, of the sounds of firecrackers and lawnmowers, of thunder and lightning, and then there was the cold wind that blew in with Cat, who broke my heart.

"You deaf or what?"

Hard eyes, a face smacked twice with Brut cologne, his words stung my ears.

"Go find yourself an alternate route." His white shirt cuff almost grazed my ear. "Take Lincoln Street to wherever."

I readjusted my route to my office and took his advice. Lincoln Street took me past the old Albany Building and a new parking structure. The sight of the building stirred an unexpected memory. My father collected postcards from the nineteenth century and had a few that featured the Albany. Back then, it was a hotel for bankers and businessmen on weekdays and for tourists who came into Boston on trains into South Station on weekends. Inside the building today, engineers and technicians test chips for faulty diodes and live to please their managers and company shareholders.

The nearby parking structure was three tiers of cement, parked cars, and hookers and their johns who tested the limits of claustrophobia and suspension systems all hours of the day and night. I turned onto Beach Street to cut through Chinatown and the Combat Zone to Washington Street.

Chinatown was cluttered with low-rent apartments and crowded side streets. Restaurants and shops choked Beach Street. A world within worlds and a city within a city, the Asian population here was second only to New York's Chinatown. Discrimination had forced Boston's Asians to form their own neighborhood. Bostonians, whether they'd admit it or not, believed in the saying "To each their own, and they should know their place."

Here, the Japanese and Vietnamese coexisted with a minestrone soup of dialects of Cantonese, Mandarin, Fuzhou, and Shanghainese Chinese. Ahead of me, the lights above the Hong Kong Low and Dragoon Restaurants were silent by day, red and blue and garish as any Vegas sign at night.

Old ladies outside their shops eyed me with suspicion. I was a white devil, a *gweilo*. To them, a round eye was nothing but a dollar sign. He was good for his money for a meal from a wok from one of their kitchens, better for his lust in their massage parlors, and best for his greed in any one of their hundreds of hidden gambling dens in their Chinatown.

I walked Beach Street. Across the street, a koi swam inside of a tank in the window. In front of a butcher's shop ahead, a kid in a blood-stained apron stood in the middle of the street. He'd already worked a couple of hours and was finishing his shift watering down the road with a spitting hose aimed at the curb. The stench of wet feathers couldn't disappear fast enough down the sewer. With concentration, he split his attention between the cigarette stuck to his lip and directing the last of the slaughter down the drain to Boston Harbor.

A right onto Washington Street reacquainted me with the part of the Combat Zone closest to Downtown Crossing, where puritanical shoppers averted their eyes from seeing the flesh trade. I was standing where many considered the divide between Them and Us, between decency and smut, civilization and the barbarians. Each year, cops and politicians wrung their worried little hands and lobbied for laws harsher than Hammurabi's to reset the boundary.

I overheard a conversation, the kind you won't find in Human Resources. The pimp, in his leather jacket, ashen turtleneck and tight slacks, was arguing with his girl. Money changed hands. His angry voice moved his moustache and the unlit cigarillo between his lips. Unhappy with her take from the night, he threatened her with mediation, the two-fisted kind. The sister would have none of it.

She worked overnight in a pair of low-rise jeans that hit the hips several inches below her belly button and not far from the feature attraction. Their conversation see-sawed back and forth. She pined and whined for a breakfast of cognac and scrambled eggs at her girlfriend's studio apartment. He insulted her.

"You call this hustling to meet quota?" He held up her roll of green. "Hell, my granny takes home more from Social Insecurity than you do with your hooha."

The Zone ate people alive. This is where you'll find every kind of hustler for every kink, a pimp for every persuasion, and winos on the hunt for a nip in any of the numerous alleyways.

Cinderella here was what cops called likely, as in likely to be beaten, stabbed and robbed, and that's if she's lucky; likely as in likely to be ignored and dead in the ER at Tufts Medical Center, not far from where she was bickering with her Daddy, because "She's just a hooker and got what she deserved." I've heard cops, doctors, and nurses say that a thousand times, in one form or another, as if *she* was never someone's aunt, mother, or sister.

Some northern steps later, I heard a whistle. I ignored it, along with the roadside chatter and distractions, thinking it wasn't for me. I heard it again and glanced to the street. The man inside the car, whom I mistook for a wolf on the prowl, pointed ahead where he wanted to speak with me. Some car, too. A Ford Pinto.

Compact and designed for the proletariat short on money and green as a mango, the vehicle was squarish in the front and the rear suddenly dropped off, as if someone chopped off the ass end of the car. The punchline to a popular joke about the car was that the Ford Pinto killed more people than Charlie Manson, and I had no reason to doubt it. This Ford Pinto coughed its way to the curb. He lowered his window and I ducked my head down.

"Get in the car, Officer Cleary."

"Nobody calls me that."

"I just did. Now, get in."

He flipped open a billfold. I saw a flash of gold, but he flicked it closed before I could catch the name or identify the agency. Whatever he was and whomever he represented seemed low-budget because my new friend hadn't dressed for success in decades. Rumpled brown suit and wrinkled shirt, the workingman's noose around his neck earned him one point for effort. The only credibility Mr. Anonymous here possessed was the authority behind his voice. I assessed the ride, the same way working girls did on this street.

"Step inside, Officer Cleary. We need to talk."

I opened the door and sat inside. "Talk about what?"

"I have a proposition for you."

"Two men alone in a car, in this neighborhood, is a proposition."

"I'm here with a proposal then, Officer Cleary."

"Stop calling me that. Nobody calls me Officer Cleary. I'm not a cop. I'm a PI."

"Once a cop, always a cop."

"Who are you?"

"The instinct never leaves you really. A private investigator and a cop differ by degree."

"Really?" I said. "What instinct might that be and remind me again, who are you?"

"The instinct to right wrongs. The savior complex is a blessing and a curse."

"Look," I said, and pointed northward. "Want to hire me? My office is in the Jewelers Building on Washington Street. My name is on the directory, or ask for me at the front desk. Now, if you'll excuse me, I have things to do."

I flung the door open, about to bolt.

"I work for the commissioner."

"You work for the commissioner?" I said.

"I do."

"And this proposition is from the commissioner, the man himself? Not for nothing," I said and eased my door shut. "The man didn't exactly go to bat for me during the Douglas case, and he didn't stop his boys from putting extra starch in their uniforms on my account. You know that, right?"

I leveled a stare that required sunscreen with UV protection. I testified against a cop who'd shot and killed a black kid in a hallway in South Boston. Douglas lost his shield, served time and I became a pariah, and now this guy wanted to dangle a job in front of me?

He fixed his gaze on his windshield. He offered me a cigarette from a green soft pack. Salem's. Menthols. I declined. He fixed the cigarette to his lip but didn't light it. He said nothing for a long minute while his fingers drummed the wheel. "This proposition—"

"This proposition, what?"

"It's a case," he said, and reached down on his left, deep into the car door. His hand surfaced with a large envelope, pregnant with paperwork. He let it rest between him and the steering wheel.

"What kind of case?" I asked.

"A chance to collar bad guys."

"Again, what kind of case?"

"The kind that rights wrongs and provides answers."

Mr. Pinto was all sales pitch and I had had it with him. My hand on the door, ready to leave again, his hand seized my wrist. "The commissioner will make it worth your while."

"Worth my while, how?"

He touched the oversized envelope in his lap with his left hand. "Investigate this closed case, and no matter how it turns out, he'll make sure you get your pension." He smiled the smile politicians use, and I wanted him to writhe on his own hook for using retirement money as bait, money I might never live to see and enjoy when I'm old and grey, close to dreaming the dead man's sleep. I corkscrewed myself in the seat to face him. I looked at the envelope. He grinned. This worm knew if I reached for the envelope it was a commitment, so I stalled him.

"I don't get it," I said. "You come at me without a name to go with your face, come at me with a closed file and you swing faraway money in front of me. If this case is off the books, then the money you promise is also off the books, and this whole thing has a skunk sitting on top of it. Am I wrong?" I held up my hand before he could answer. "Shut up and hear me out—"

"Your skepticism is understandable, Officer Cleary."

"I told you not to call me that, and who are you? As for skepticism, it's more like cynicism. The Commissioner has what, two-thousand men in uniform working the line?"

"More or less," he said.

"And in that vast number there are detectives he could've assigned this case, but the commissioner goes offshore, off book, and hands me this file... why?"

"Luisa Ramírez. Remember her?"

Names and cases I worked or heard about spun like a Ferris wheel inside my head. Her name sounded familiar, but the reason why eluded me, stuck to the tip of my tongue like a wet stamp. I gave up and admitted defeat. "Enlighten me," I said.

"Community activist who advocated for better housing conditions, amongst other things. She made herself a target for every shady landlord out there, and a pain in the ass for about every agency in the Commonwealth. She had brains, a heart of gold, and a smart mouth until she was found dead in Park Plaza. OD'd."

He slid his thick envelope under a paperback on the leather between us. The title of the book was *The Dwarf*. He saw I'd noticed and said, "Man who wrote it died two years ago. You should give it a shot. I heard you like to read. The author was famous for allegories. I enjoyed it because I feel a personal connection to the story."

"How do you know I like to read?"

"I know a lot of things about you, Shane Cleary."

I picked up the book, considered the cover art and read the author's first name to myself. The umlaut made me think of Lindsey. He'd know how to pronounce it, whereas I'd butcher it. "Pär Lagerkvist," I said and returned the book to its place. "Swedish name. What's the personal connection?"

"I make sure what the commissioner wants done gets gone, like the dwarf in the story. So, will you take the file on Luisa Ramírez?"

The man handed me the envelope. "The commissioner believes this woman's death wasn't an overdose. All he asks is that you look into it and you shine a light on whatever you find."

"Maybe it was an accidental overdose," I said.

"She had a drug problem. Past tense."

"She might've relapsed."

"The commissioner doesn't think so."

"Okay." I nodded, digesting the man's words. "To beat the drum again, why me?"

"Because you can go places others can't." The man in the lousy clothes looked at me. "The commissioner trusts few people. A handful, to be exact, and work this case right, and he might add you to his Shadow Company."

"Shadow Company? Sounds like something you'd expect to hear in Vietnam."

"Amusing, but we're civilians now." His eyes darted to the parcel in my hand and then back at me. "There's a phone number on a card inside the envelope. The person you'll talk to is another civilian. He'll vouch for me and he'll explain the rest to you when you call him from your office."

I went to open the envelope but his hand covered mine. He said I should read the contents at my office. Like a kid told he couldn't open his Christmas presents, I huffed. I capitulated though, and said I'd take the case. I told him that I needed time to review the paperwork inside the envelope before I called his friend. I asked him how to contact him if I needed help, or had questions.

"You're on your own on this, I'm afraid. The call to the man on the card is a one-time deal, a way for you to confirm I'm on the up-and-up."

"Like I said, what if I need help?"

"I'd suggest you use your friend Bill." He wiggled his fingers. "Hand me one of your business cards, just in case."

I dipped my hand inside my jacket. "Number is an answering service," I said. "You know Bill?"

"I know about Bill. I also know about you and Mr. B in the North End and his lieutenant, Tony-Two Times, and I know about your professor friend and his backstory, along with John and Silvia. Did I forget anyone?"

"Brayton and Catherine Braddock. I worked a case—"

"Ah, the blackmail case last year. Bray is dangerous because he was born with too much money, and she's fatal because she knows what it's like not to have money. Word of advice, friend. Stay away from her, and keep your zipper zipped." His friendly operator voice then dropped like ice into a martini shaker. "Now, get out of my car, but I insist you take the book with you." He picked up his copy of *The Dwarf* and handed it to me.

"You insist?"

"You might learn something about human nature."

I pointed to the street in front of us. "You could at least drive me. My office is—"

"Outta the car, Cleary. You have your envelope and a book."

"Like I have time to read," I said.

"Make the time."

I scooted out, with the two items tight to my chest, but kept my other hand on the door for one last word. His hand on the gear stick, I asked one last time. "Who the hell are you?"

"The guy who has kept you alive all these years."

He said it with all the charm of Cary Grant, and angled his green crate into traffic for the escape. I watched the backend of the car flee from me, and I remembered why the Pinto was a dangerous automobile: the gas tank faced the rear.

I'd caught another case, understood the Pinto as a metaphor for my life, and hoped this unexpected gig wouldn't explode in my face.

Chapter Five: Three Cases

The Swede's book was hot in my hand but the thick parcel was hotter. Where Washington Street met Temple Place, I dipped into Kresge's to chew up some time, possibly sling another cup of coffee and prioritize my caseload.

Case one: Mr. B.

Question marks lingered around his relative's disappearance. The easiest explanation was the kid had himself a lost weekend of crazy stupid fun, time had run away from him, and the kid was too afraid, too embarrassed, or both, to come home. If his grandnephew had wandered off the villa, he'd pay for it. If, however, someone had poached the kid, that someone would pay for it. If some grave misfortune had befallen the kid, someone would pay for it.

The don's concept of power, essential as a One A Day vitamin, was never let any misdeed go unpunished. Ever. Mr. B, like most Sicilian mafiosi, possessed patience with a capital P. If he wanted you dead, you were dead. Maybe not today, maybe not tomorrow, but one day.

I'd decided I could work the pedals and give him an honest song, a progress note here, a phrase there, as I investigated the case of the missing nephew. I'd marshal whatever evidence I found, be it circumstantial or as hardcore as anything in the Combat Zone, and give it to him straight.

Case two: Jimmy.

Jimmy was Greek and as vulnerable as Achilles and his heel. This arrest, his one and only, tagged him for arson, and it would haunt him to his last breath. Any future fire in Boston, Jimmy would be the first stop for the cops, the fire department, and insurance investigators. He needed to alibi out, with something stronger than a Brinks armored truck. One way or another, now and forevermore, the fire he so loved had touched him and burned him this time.

Case three: Luisa Ramírez.

I stopped at Kresge's to review the file from Pinto. The office could wait. Pinto expected me to call the number on the card, and that conversation would start the clock on a closed case. Pinto claimed the person on the other side of the conversation would corroborate everything I'd been told about the commissioner and my pension. I accepted the job, but I wasn't anxious to call the man. I wasn't Wile E. Coyote after the Road Runner. Pinto and Shadow Squad could wait.

Pinto flattered me with words from the commissioner. The first man in law enforcement in the Commonwealth of Massachusetts believed in my character and integrity, enough so I might merit admission to his Shadow Squad. I suppose this band of brothers upheld the BPD's motto: *Sicut patribus sit deus nobis*, or "God be with us as He was with our fathers."

This was Boston, God wasn't with me, and my father was dead.

The first floor of Kresge's returned memories of me with my mother. We would shop Filene's and Jordan Marsh, and stop here for lunch or a treat. On my left when I walked in, there was a dining area. Two rotisseries stations, about half a football field apart, competed against each other for customers. The standoff was chickens rubbed with paprika, thyme, and garlic on one end, and glazed hams with brown sugar, cinnamon and cloves, and honey on a rotating spit on the other.

My mother and I would sit at the counter. Waitresses in pink uniforms and matching caps worked the crowds. I disliked hot dogs, as did my mother, so we'd order burgers with fries and Vanilla Cokes. On a warm day, we'd argue over whether to split a hot fudge sundae or that other treat indigenous to New England, the frappe. No Bostonian called a frappe a milkshake or a grinder a submarine sandwich. My mother didn't care for banana splits, like the gaggle of girls I saw at the counter. These kids were on vacation. It was hard to call it Spring Break when Boston weather could offer up all four seasons in one day.

If my mother were here, she'd have words with them about their choices in fashion. Most of the girls were wearing coveralls, with ruffled bibs and sleeves, and flared bottoms. I can picture her telling these late-morning debutantes that a young lady should wear something more appropriate in public. Overalls were for yardwork or time under the car in the garage.

A young girl walked past me. Farrah Fawcett hair, satin jacket, and cords. Mother insisted corduroys were not jeans, and clothes should contrast colors and not textures. Farrah's girlfriend, a Dorothy Hamill knockoff, strutted alongside her in leather pants and velour top. I counted the bounces in her wedge-cut hairstyle as she walked away from me. As for clothes, her top and bottom were so tight I could read two MADE IN USA tags.

Near the hams, a herd of boys and girls in jeans flirted with each other. My mother would have been aghast that people would pay sixty-five dollars for a pair of Mackeens in New York's version of a Newbury Street boutique, or drop fifty bucks on Calvin Klein's at Bloomingdale's. Levi denims with five pockets suited her fine around the house. Nobody, she'd remind you, needed raw, rinsed, or stone washed jeans. If Levi 501s and copper rivets were good enough for gold miners in California, then they should suffice for the current generation.

She wasn't all sticks and moss, though. She'd spare the young girl I saw by herself, the quiet one with the gypsy look and big hooped earrings because I think, if she was alive, my mother would've appreciated Stevie Nicks.

High school boys congregated near the bottom of the stairs up to the second floor. Years before they dared to cop a feel, they'd chosen the safer course and fake-shopped, turning the carousels of comic books, guilty of the lesser charge of stolen glances. Boys mature more slowly than girls and their clothes proved it. In tight jeans and white shirts, they were poor imitations of James Dean or Marlon Brando. The only difference was that their hair was longer.

Upstairs there was a toy section, a smaller dining area, and phone booths. A student scribbled in her notebook, the air hockey game breathed cold air and the puck shivered, and a waitress contemplated her next victim, the hangnail on her wedding finger.

I had two calls to make. The first one was to Lindsey. I needed his professorial guidance on the Swedish author. Pinto had given me the book for a reason and I wanted to know what he had meant when he said that he was like the dwarf. Lindsey read books and studied every line, as if the author and God wrestled over every word.

I had completed three tours in Latin and Classical Literature with him. Lindsey prized concision and elegance in an author. As for students, he disliked the superficial gloss, like the time we were reading *The Aeneid* in class. Virgil's most famous line, *"Timeo Danaos et dona ferentes,"* had been paraphrased as "Beware of Greeks bearing gifts." Lindsey bristled and said our translation lacked refinement.

"Poets load each word with purpose and intention," he said. He asked us to revisit the famous quote. Easy enough, we thought. Either the poet or some medieval monk had written *et* when they should've written *etiam.* Lindsey proved us wrong.

"The conjunction is there for a reason, used as an archaism," he said. We stared at each other, lost, until he explained. "The correct translation is 'I fear the Danaans, even those bearing gifts.' Virgil warned us to fear all Greeks whether they're bearing gifts or not. It's called nuance and fidelity to the text, gentlemen."

I stepped into a phone booth and pulled the accordion door closed. I dropped coins in the slot, heard the chimes, pressed the squares to Lindsey's work number and waited for the connection to the newspaper on Harrison Ave.

While the line rang, I perused the graffiti. Some smart aleck had spoofed President Ford's call to "Whip Inflation Now." The ad men on Fifth Avenue had spackled the acronym WIN everywhere. WIN appeared on red buttons, on bags, as earrings and needlework, on sweaters and lapel pins. This joker flipped WIN upside down, so viewers read NIM. "Need Immediate Money."

A voice, dry from years of cigarettes and bourbon, answered the phone on the fifth ring. I asked for Delano Lindsey. The phone hit the desk and

34

bounced. I pulled the receiver away before my eardrum bled. Instead of tedious hold music, a chorus of typewriters serenaded me with their rhythm of clickety clacks and soft bells. Footsteps, and then a scratch, a scrape a hundred times louder, announced the professor. I said a fast hello and rushed to the point.

"*The Dwarf*. Swedish author and Nobel Laureate. Pear Lagerkvist. What can you tell me about the story?"

Lindsey sighed. "First of all, it's pronounced Par, as in on par, not as pear the fruit."

"But there's an umlaut."

"Forget the umlaut." He repeated the author's name. "As for your question about the story, why don't you read the book. I hated Cliff's Notes as an instructor, or when a student thought a movie was equivalent to reading a book. You'd think if students had the time to watch a movie, they could read the book."

"Was there a movie?"

"No. What is it that you want, Mr. Cleary?"

Not Shane, but Mister Cleary, and he used his teacher's voice. I treaded with caution.

"If someone were to tell you they felt a personal connection to this story and the dwarf, what would you think?"

"I'd run like hell. The dwarf is evil, my boy."

"Okay, he's a bad guy."

"More like Milton's Satan chained to the lake of fire. Here's your synopsis. The main character is twenty-six inches tall and does whatever his prince asks of him. Succinct enough?"

"But Pär Lagerkvist wrote allegories, right?"

I made sure to pronounce the first name correctly.

"He did. I'll save you the history lecture on how schizophrenic Sweden was during World War II, so think of the dwarf as a necessary evil in the world, someone who gets things done without asking questions. Remind you of anyone we know?"

The professor didn't have to pick up the chalk to write the name Tony Two-

Times on the chalkboard. The man in the lousy car had declared himself, like a tourist through customs at Logan Airport. Pinto did whatever the commissioner desired and his boss would disavow it. If the commissioner was his prince, then I needed to worry about the man whose number I had on a card.

"You've been a big help, Professor. I should let you go."

Lindsey had hustled the job scene with every temporary agency in Boston. I didn't want to jeopardize his paycheck. "Wait," he said.

"Listening."

"If someone said he sees himself in the dwarf, I'd worry."

"Evil, right. I got it, Professor."

"No, you don't. The dwarf's true nature was evil. I can't emphasize that enough. You have to understand that he can't help but act any other way. He's incapable of morality, other than blind obedience to his master, the prince. The dwarf is a fictional character, but your friend isn't, and he is making a choice. Free will, remember?"

"I get it. Run away," I said, and hung up.

It figured. Everything in this town came with a hidden price tag. I had no luck, other than bad luck. I already had one Greek, Jimmy, and I didn't need anybody bearing more gifts. And yet they kept coming. The man in the beater car offered me a deal. The commissioner offered me my pension. What the man on the phone call later had to offer was a matter of revelation in the fullness of time. All I was missing now was the fourth horseman of the apocalypse.

I found a table in a corner and flagged a waitress. I wanted a whiskey. Neat. Water back. I order a cup of coffee instead. Black.

After she left, I opened the case file on the deceased community activist, Luisa Ramírez. The discovery of a dead body was one of the most serious matters a cop will face, the Mount Greylock of paperwork and procedures. I located the police report. The narrative was cold and objective, as in date, time and place. The biographical details, however, punched me the way typewriter keys struck the page.

Thirty years old. Two years older than me. Hispanic.

Hispanic was a recent term. Up to 1970, a Cuban, Mexican, and a Puerto Rican would've been listed as "White" on all state and federal paperwork. Many states and cities were slow to adopt the classification. Not Massachusetts. Not Boston.

A copy of the Medical Examiner's report stated overdose and cited heroin as the drug of choice. The ME had originally thought DEATH BY MISADVENTURE but revised his findings to **SUICIDE**.

There were photos, three of them, that displayed the death scene from different angles. A dead person never looks the way they do in life. The file included a small 4 x 6 Kodak print, an unexpected surprise.

Dark hair, brown eyes, an attractive face. The post-mortem photo showed her sitting on a tattered couch, head back in fatal ecstasy, a latex tourniquet around her left arm. The needle was visible. The needle looked as fresh as a hypodermic in a doctor's office or from a hospital's supply room. It was the first discrepancy for me.

Shooters reused syringes and the barrels brown out with repeated use. Experienced users swapped out needles but kept the barrels. Seasoned junkies jerry-rigged tampons or cigarette butts to filter out impurities while they cooked their fix on a spoon. Not the case here. A polished spoon, a fresh tealight, and a spent book of matches lay at her feet. The scene suggested OD 101 and not an experienced user.

While I didn't have a closeup of her left arm, there were no signs of frequent use, or past use. No track marks. No collapsed veins. Intravenous drug users hide their addiction by wearing long sleeves. Ms. Ramírez's dress sleeves stopped above the elbow, the hemline above her knees.

Not to say there weren't any scars elsewhere on her body. Addicts were clever about access. I've heard of injections done in the groin, or between the toes. I reread the ME's Report. "No scars noted." I was told she had a history with drugs. Neither the report nor any of the pages here detailed which drugs.

I was more disturbed by things I didn't see. There was no suicide note. I shuffled the paperwork and discovered the deceased left one sister, an Antonia R. Ruiz. Address unknown.

Intrigued and interested, the items for suspicious overdose added up but the bell didn't ring and the drawer didn't open up. The few pictures and all the typed pages didn't make the sale for me.

Addicts were desperate people. Junkies were a shell of their former selves. Shake them hard enough and they disintegrated into dust. Luisa looked healthy, what clinicians call "well nourished." Her dress appeared neat and maintained. Her hair and makeup were in order. This was a woman who cared about her appearance and not a mangy alley cat. She could've walked off of a page in a fashion magazine.

Everything suggested a hot shot, a dose with the right grade of poison to put her to sleep for good. Snort or shoot it, the purity of heroin on the street varied. Luisa had scored a bad batch, and I wondered whether there'd been a cluster of deaths from the same lot. I could find no chemical analysis on the heroin in her system, within the syringe, or from any residue on the spoon in the ME's report.

I never worked Narcotics, but I was familiar with the drug. Jazz musicians enjoyed heroin when pot used to be called reefer. Heroin enjoyed a renaissance with Vietnam veterans. Smack was as Asian as Fu Manchu and, in recent years, Mexico was more than our neighbor south of the border. Mexico exported pot first, and then heroin. Narcs called it Pancho Villa's Revenge.

Nobody cared about heroin until white kids started dying. Cops cracked down on Kensington Avenue in Philadelphia. Movies such as *Panic in Needle Park* and *French Connection* put the sordid mess in New York on the screen. South Boston and my own South End saw its share of Liquid Sky, but it was the mill town sisters, as in Lawrence, Lowell, and Lynn, where it occupied law enforcement the most. The L Sisters broke keys of heroin down for distribution throughout New England. Dealers would dilute the ride on the Horse with everything from baking soda to baby powder. How and what they used to cut the drug would change its color, from Snow to Brown Sugar.

The police report said Luisa died in an abandoned apartment. Park Plaza wasn't a dive; it was a latrine. Vermin, most of them human, thrived off the poor and elderly residents there. Park Plaza was public housing, a turnstile for addicts, drug dealers, and prostitutes and their johns. Developers earmarked the place for "renewal," but community board activists, such as Luisa, jammed them up. Until I could prove otherwise, Luisa was there doing what community activists did best, knocking on doors and talking sense into people's heads about their rights.

Last in the dossier on Luisa Ramírez from Pinto were two newspaper articles, joined by a paperclip. I loosened the fastener with care, aware of the paper's fragility and how clip left rust on the page. The first item belonged to the *Boston Herald American*, the second, from the *Boston Globe*, and they both covered the same subject: a clash between Luisa and redevelopment authorities at a town meeting. Same date, too, and that's where the similarity ended.

The *Herald* had not bothered to include a picture of her, whereas the *Globe* had. I counted ten adjectives in the two brief columns in the *Herald*, and none of them were flattering. The *Boston Globe* used more positive language. What told these twins of journalism apart were the Biblical allusions, Judith versus Holofernes in the *Herald*, and David against Goliath in the *Globe*. Politics aside, the comparisons set the tone. Gentile or Jew, Catholic or Protestant, every schoolkid knew David was the underdog and used a slingshot against the Philistine and, while they might not know Judith, the implication was that Luisa was a devious and deadlier because Judith had used a sword to decapitate a powerful man.

Enough. I slid the paperwork into the envelope. I finished the coffee and threw a dollar bill down on the table for a tip. I needed my change for the second phone call. A call on a public payphone costs twenty cents, thanks to inflation and our president, Gerry Ford.

Inside the booth, the halo of light overhead flickered. I looked up at the coil and tried not to think that God wasn't playing me. The receiver against my ear, I dropped FDR twice into the slot. I pulled out the card. Mr. Pinto had written the numbers as legibly as a schoolteacher. I punched in the number.

There were phone calls and emotions. The IRS. Fear and dread. The call from the doctor with test results. Anxiety and dread. Those calls, you received news. They talked, you listened. This was a call where I talked and somebody listened. A person picked up on the first ring.

"Officer Cleary."

"I prefer Shane. And you are?"

"My name is unimportant. Your call is. Am I correct in that you have accepted our case on the community activist?"

"I was instructed to confirm terms with you. I was also told this is a one-time conversation."

"Correct. Work the case to the best of your ability, and you will be paid into a pension account in your name. If you decide to work future cases for us, money will be deposited into the same retirement account. You'll receive periodic financial statements in the mail, like every government employee. Satisfactory?"

"A pension, in my name?"

"In your name. Satisfied?"

"Yes." My yes flowed, fast and smooth as whiskey. I didn't want any dead space in this conversation. I had to ask. "How do I communicate my findings?"

"Don't concern yourself with that, Mr. Cleary. I've got eyes and ears. I'll know."

"Your Shadow Squad, I presume, just like Chief Parker in LA?"

"Something like that," he said.

"You know your history."

The man's voice wasn't monotone, but it hadn't quavered at the mention of the hardliner William Parker of the Los Angeles Police Department. LA's Intelligence Squad predated Internal Affairs, predated Parker himself, until he formed his own squad, the Hat Squad. These men brought brass knuckles to everything they did, from carrying wise guys out of the City of Angels to getting corrupt cops to confess to the 5Ws of Who, What, When, Where, and Why, and like the vowel y, sometimes How.

"And you must know my history with the BPD," I said. "There are men on the force who want me dead. How do I know I'm safe?"

"Nobody is ever safe, Mr. Cleary. You can walk past The Hancock and a windowpane can fall down on your head, and you'd never know it. It's an existential question."

"Philosophy aside, people want me dead."

"And yet you live and breathe," he said. "Ever wonder why that is? Some men on the force is not all men. There are good men who believe you made the right call with Officer Douglas."

"And you count the commissioner and yourself among them?"

"We are talking, are we not? The commissioner and I are two very different men. He's tall and outgoing and dresses modern. I'm quiet and reserved, and prefer the traditional suit and tie. Make no mistake about it, we are both in agreement on one thing, and one thing alone."

His words hovered. He wanted me to act the part of Prufrock and ask the "overwhelming question." I wouldn't. He wanted me to utter some cliché about justice, about corruption, about cleaning house or clearing the deck. I didn't.

"One thing. Know what it is, Mr. Cleary?"

"Haven't a clue," I said. "I'm talking to a man whose name I don't know."

"The one thing the Commissioner and I agree on is that we are outsiders. You are an outsider, Shane."

"I'm an outsider because of what I did. What did you two do? The Commissioner is the commissioner, and you are whatever you are."

"I'm his shadow."

"Like the old radio program? Being the top cop's right hand makes you an outsider? I'm not sure I can relate to—what is it called? Your existential crisis."

"The Commissioner is Italian, and I'm Jewish. Outsiders."

"And I'm Irish, in an Irish town, and without a shamrock to show for it."

"But you're a civilian, on the outside like me, which gives us an advantage."

"Some advantage, provided the cops don't pop me."

"Let me worry about them," he said.

"Forgive me if have my doubts."

"You're in a position of power, whether you see it or not, Mr. Cleary."

"And what power is that?"

"You refuse to be corrupted. Few men can say that for themselves. You also have integrity. You continue as a PI, when there are better ways to make a living, because you remain a cop, even after you've been cut from the fold."

"And what's your power, other than the Commissioner by your side?"

Without a beat, he answered. "People talk, I communicate."

The cold voice continued and carried ice with it.

"The thing about cops," he said, "is they're either pet rocks or social workers with a gun. You are neither. Enjoy the rest of your day, Mr. Cleary."

I hung up. Not a single window pane, no five-hundred pounds of blue glass had fallen on my head. The circle of light above my head didn't shine any brighter either.

Chapter Six: A Mad Minute

I stood in front of my office on Washington Street. The Province Building or The Pro was home to seven stories of human vanity, and my humble roost was on the top floor. Here were jewelers, sellers and resellers, repairmen and watchmen, and craftsmen of the sales gimmick. Inside most shops there were row after row of diamonds under glass, other precious gems, trinkets, and ornaments in every size for every budget made from every conceivable ore since the time of Babylon.

This building was money, made money, and people with money who like making more of it were keen on security. This made my office as safe as the Boston Five bank next door and the Federal Reserve near South Station. The Pro was the pearl, the best policed stack of Art Deco architecture in the city.

I stepped up to the desk and expected to find Sean, the usual concierge. Instead, a sad fellow with bloodhound eyes and a long face greeted me. Sean was a model employee, a real fixture. The man never missed a day of work until today. If it snowed, Sean was out there at dawn's early light, throwing salt on the sidewalk in front of him so he could make it into work on time.

I headed for the elevator and glanced through the clear glass of my first-floor neighbor, Saul Fiedermann, and saw him standing at the counter, the phone next to him. He lifted a chin when he saw me. I did the same. Saul had vouched for me as a tenant. I've also handled situations for him.

As I walked to the elevator, I could hear the new guy at the desk dialing the phone behind me. His fingers were pulling numbers on the rotary dial faster than grandma at the slots. I stepped into the elevator and faced the entrance. Sure as Adam in the garden, the guy had the phone to his ear and was mouthing short syllables. He looked like he was trying hard not to look like he was looking, but his nose was pointed my way. I let the doors close, the chimes ring, and counted the lights to the top floor.

Out of the gilded doors before they gaped their widest, I ran down the hallway to my office door. I slid on the waxed floors but caught the doorknob fast enough to steady the key into the lock. Once inside, I dialed Saul and prayed to our God in common he'd answer on the first or second ring. I heard the voice.

"Saul, Shane here. Listen carefully. Look, but don't look through your window to the front desk and tell me if you see someone suspicious walking in."

"I don't see any…wait, someone just came to the concierge desk."

"Did he sign in?"

"Doesn't look like it." The way his voice dropped, I could tell Saul had put his head down and was talking into his chest. "What do you want me to do?"

"Go to the display board down the hall near the elevators and fuss with the lettering. I want to know what floor this guy is visiting, but put one of the girls on before you do that for me."

Saul had faith not to ask questions. I knew he carried keys to open the message board near the elevator. The bulletin board there was like the one used in churches for telling the congregation which book and what chapter and verse they'd need for mass. Saul advertised sales there. The mysterious guy should already be inside the elevator when Saul faked an edit.

"Top floor," the girl said. I hung up.

A hunch was the butterfly in the stomach that won't stop beating her wings. I used another key and unlocked the drawer and ignored my usual revolver. I removed the Highway Patrolman I'd received in trade for services rendered. I strapped on the shoulder holster. A .357 wasn't my preferred sidearm or cartridge, but something told me I needed something stronger for a housewarming present for my guest. I waited with gratitude for Saul's friendship.

He was good to me. Saul not only arranged for the office, he'd negotiated an adjoining room, activated by a secret trigger and accessible through a communicating door. My office before it was an office had been a makeshift bachelor pad for wayward artisans of timepieces and baubles downstairs. I could push in the panel and close it behind me without the wallpaper losing its seam. The room had disused filing cabinets, a closet for a change of clothes and a convenient Murphy bed for a catnap. With the hidden panel behind me, I cat-burgled my way to a second door, with a view to the hallway. I kept myself flush to the wall and waited.

One thing I learned in Vietnam was patience. Nothing exercised virtue more than sitting under a canopy of dense foliage, mosquitoes buzzing around both ears, ants crawling up your legs, and being unable to say a word because an enemy patrol was yards away. You don't hear or feel a damn thing except for the sound of your own heartbeat. I counted down my days then, like I was counting seconds now.

Head and shoulders appeared, stopped, and my new friend looked all around for witnesses. Best guess was that he would either shoulder the door or drop into a squat and pick the lock. He dropped.

I raised the .357 near my ear. Two things the movies always get wrong. No fool cocks the hammer. A reliable trigger and a good finger did all the work. As for picking a lock, I knew guys who bought headstones thinking they can do the jimmy with a bobby pin. I tried not to smile as he worked the lock and I heard tentative scratches. My hand dropped to the doorknob, ready to turn it, when I remembered the weirdest detail. A door at home opens inward, while doors in public buildings open outward. Change of plans and he was about to experience a mad minute.

I tucked the Smith & Wesson into my holster. I flung the door open and rushed him. He tried to stand up. I parted his jacket and pulled his sleeves down hard. It was a cheap trick to render his arms useless. With him pinned against the wall, I worked whatever flesh I could take with my fists. I connected a stomach to a kidney and salted his ribs.

He pulled a lineman's move, something from his Pop Warner days, and grabbed one cheek and a hamstring for a line drive into the opposite wall. I smashed into the wall, air ironed out of my lungs and I slid down, back bruised. He pivoted for an escape, a sprint down the hall for the stairwell.

I caught a heel with a hand and half of my face. Argyle socks and an exposed ankle had me thinking Dick Butkus and biting him, but he twisted and scuttled backwards crab-like and my face received his footprint. We wrestled some, exchanging blows. There was no referee, no long count, and we weren't Boy Scouts about fighting fair. A thrown elbow, a handful of hair, a thumb into an eye, we went at it.

"Who sent you?" I asked through clenched teeth.

He gurgled something unintelligible.

I'd swear I thought the man's eye would pop out of the socket, wet sucking sound and all. I threw a body blow, using everything I had in my hip, and I heard ribs splinter, followed by the whelp of a wounded animal. I shouldn't have, but I did. I lashed out, a right hook to his jaw and knocked him out cold.

There's nothing noble about pilfering a man's pockets. I found a .22 on his person, demure and ladylike for a night on the town. Make fun of the caliber all you wanted, but the choice of pistol said he worked up close and personal. Possible hitter. I reached in for a wallet and found none. The fingertips sensed something else and I dug deeper, mined that pocket, and came up with a calling card.

My own.

I didn't hand them out like some jailhouse lawyer. I was thinking of the select few who'd have my card. A Rasta minstrel, also a vet, had one, in case he got jammed up, but I didn't see how these two would cross paths. John and Sylvia knew how to get a hold of me. Ditto for the professor. The only newsflash across the brain pan was Cat, my ex. There was a suspect.

I worked a blackmail case for her and her husband, Bray. I'd done him wrong twice: first by sleeping with his wife, though in all fairness she had done all the work; second, giving him a legal headache, when I exposed his business deals, but that was du jour for Boston, and the man had both enough money and connections to receive a slap on the wrist from the judge. The last recipient of a Shane Cleary calling card was Jimmy's lawyer, which didn't make sense, but what did? Law firms hired their own investigators, often former cops with the know-how to squeeze all the letters of the law.

The only other person with my business card was Pinto.

I dragged my unconscious guest to the stairwell and called Saul to have him get one of his Hasidic boys to remove the unwanted guest from the premises the non-Kosher way. I wasn't sure what to do about the concierge.

I needed a change of clothes and to pretty myself up after my sparring session. I'd tip my hat to the hit man for the workout. We went the distance, like a Vegas fight, under the lights, and there was sweat and some blood. I noticed something else.

A small leather wallet dangled beneath my doorknob. I recognized it as a professional kit for picking locks, the kind of rig the G-men at Quantico kept tabs on. This set of tools always reminded me of the dentist. A pick-kit consisted of nine pieces of stainless steel and there were names for each item—balls, diamonds, hooks, and rakes—suggested torture. I removed the toolset from my door, and went inside.

I called my Answering Service. Dorothy picked up mid-ring.

"Mercury Answering Service. This is Dot speaking."

"Shane Cleary. Hello, Dot. Any messages."

"Hold one moment."

The line went dead in my ear. Odd, how Dot was short for Dorothy. I met her once, when I hired the service. I expected a little old lady, but Dorothy was as buxom as Jayne Mansfield. Dorothy was a Midwestern girl. Her mother was also named Dorothy. Another Midwestern tradition, I was told. When I asked her how people distinguished her from her mother, the answer flew faster than a seagull at Revere Beach. "Dot 1 and Dot 2."

"Two messages, Mr. Cleary." She said Caller One left a number and a brief message. She mentioned the time, date, and message verbatim per company policy. "He said Tony, but refused to give last name."

"That's okay, Dot," I said as I scribbled the number. Tony Two-Times wanted an update. "And the second caller?"

"A Mr. Pinto, and he'd like to meet with you." Dot told me the caller's specified date, day, and location, but no number. "He was insistent that you'd meet him near the ducks. He said 5pm, Monday. I told him that there were numerous ducks in the Boston Garden, and that he should be more specific, but all he said was "Near the ducks. I'm sorry, Mr. Cleary."

"No need to apologize, Dot. Some people are built one way, and Mr. Pinto is one of them. Thank you."

I hung up the phone, and dialed Tony Two-Times.

The line rang ten times before the North End's version of Stanley Kowalski with a thick Jersey accent answered. He sounded as if I'd interrupted his dinner with Stella.

"I'd like to speak with Tony. Tell him it's Shane Cleary, please."

"Rahgarding?"

"Returning his call."

He told me to hold myself. The soundtrack behind him suggested an Italian restaurant before peak hours. There was quiet, and there was the distant sound of Connie Francis's "Who's Sorry Now?" playing, which I think is the theme song for the mafia.

"Tony speaking."

"Returning your call."

"Any news on the thing?"

I gave him the address of a friend, Nikos's, and told him I'd meet him Saturday. "On the street, in front of my friend's place," I said.

"Greek. Is the food any good?" Tony asked.

"This isn't a date, Tony."

"It's warm out."

There was a non sequitur. "Then don't wear a coat. Bye."

Chapter Seven: On the case with Case

The high-speed conversation inside my head was a car against the guardrail, all sparks until I pumped the brakes, slowed everything down to a complete stop and looked both ways. I had to decide here and now, left or right, Truth or Fiction, merge and proceed with caution.

My visit to Police Headquarters reacquainted me with Officer Kiernan. His love of Chinese food was as passionate as the hatred he nursed for me, a hatred that dated back to the Academy. Kiernan had wanted to be a Statie, but he wasn't tall enough or bright enough.

The Massachusetts State Police has minimums for height, test scores, and weight. I made the cut but turned them down. Kiernan came up short in triplicate and resented me. He took up boxing, a sport I liked and excelled at, to drop weight. His coach built up his body and his mind until Kiernan started believing his own hype. Then he met me in the ring.

I left the force, he stayed on the job. Other than the incremental bumps in pay, he never rose in rank because he failed the exams. There's no shame in walking a beat. A flatfoot saw the good and the bad on the job. Sights, sounds, and opportunities presented lessons never to be forgotten.

Temptation found Kiernan. Temptation finds every cop. Think of it as mom's cookies pulled out of the oven. She says they needed to rest and cool off. Same thing happens to cops. Break a fence, it's hot merchandise; raid a den and bust a pimp and there's a jackpot of drugs and the great green god himself, money. At some point or another, a cop starts to think nobody'll notice if one cookie went missing.

It's a Rolex one day. The next time, a working girl dipped her head below the dashboard in exchange for a break. A group of cops might decide on a five-finger discount with money that should be vouchered into evidence. Then there's the boys club, the social pressure, the "I scratch your back. You scratch mine." Nobody likes or trusts a virtuous cop. That New York cop, Frank Serpico, the one they made a movie about? Too much virtue.

The story was as ancient as Rome. Delano explained it to me by way of the Gracchi Brothers, Tiberius and Gaius, who some have compared to John and Robert Kennedy. They were two idealistic brothers, who pushed hard for social reforms and they both met unfortunate ends. Tiberius was beaten to death with chairs, whereas JFK went to Dallas. Gaius fell on his own sword instead of confronting a crowd, armed with clubs. Robert Kennedy was told a shortcut through a hotel kitchen was safer than the throng of photographers and newsmen waiting for him. Righteousness and truth may prevail, but they are often buried first, together and forever.

Temptations.

Kiernan was on the take. The Puritans feared the Devil walked among them. He did. They just weren't paranoid enough. He does. Everywhere.

My hunch about the concierge saved me from an untimely demise at worse, a beating at best. Intuition can't go before the law. Swear all you want on a Bible to "solemnly swear that you will tell the truth, the whole truth, and nothing but the truth, so help you God," but the law was about language, about ideals and principles inside fat, thick books that required a priesthood of paralegals, lawyers, and judges to interpret it for us. I needed something better than instinct about Officer Kiernan.

The whole truth will choke a man to death in this town. I'd settle for a slice of it. See, if a cop wanted a hint of that truth, he'll go to his CI, his confidential informant, and he'll make of the information what he will. A snitch lies to save his own ass, or he wants revenge on someone. If I wanted an honest slice, I had to riff on the idea of a CI.

I needed information. I needed facts and someone with no incentive to lie to me.

Crosswinds Irish Pub on Beacon Street in Back Bay was two rooms, private booths, and safe because there was only one way in and out of the joint.

Mirrors above and around the bar afforded me the panoramic view I needed and wanted. There I'd meet my writer friend, my informant.

Richard Case was, and is, as his last name suggested, a handful, but he had the ear for conversations, the cadence and authentic lingo of the beat cop, the desk-jockey cop, and the world-weary detective. A novelist was a professional eavesdropper. Dick didn't embellish or embroider his threads. I counted on his intelligence the way a judge relied on his stenographer.

The Irish flag outside rippled in the breeze. The lettering on the sign mimicked medieval script. I walked in. The lighting was low, intimate, and at this time of day, devoid of cops.

Dick sat at his usual station. He hadn't seen me walking towards him. Dick once cut an impressive figure, tall, but now he was gaunt and ashen. Before him were the usual temple offerings of a tall glass of Jim Beam and a smaller glass of water. The waitress spotted me and I let her know my intentions. The gals here were protective of the man. Dick was a regular, a misunderstood legend, though I doubt any of these women read his books.

I had read all of them. Not uplifting stuff, but it was honest, good work, and I suspect more autobiography than fiction. Dick didn't shelve literary prizes on the mantlepiece but he did win unanimous praise. He knew everybody who was somebody and they all knew Dick Case, the talented chronicler of postwar ennui in the suburbs.

Dick had a talent for words. Dick had craft. Dick also had the gift for self-destruction. He smoked and drank, and drank and smoked around the clock.

He saw me at last. "You're fucked, aren't you?"

"Not yet."

"There's still time."

I pointed to the vacant seat across from him. "May I?"

Dick raised a hand and his serving wench (his words) rushed over. "Two Fisherman's Platters and Beam and some water for my friend here."

One didn't argue with the king in his court. The waitress, a slender thing, spoke with a kind voice, but suffered from the working-class curse of a nice figure paired with a hard face. Terrible and harsh to say, I know, but a diet of coffee and cigarettes, living above or below relatives like some stackable washer and dryer, and life painted the face.

She returned with two glasses for me. I had to drink or Dick would be offended. I placed my fedora on the far end of the table.

"Still wearing the white hat?"

"Gray, if you haven't noticed."

"You'll always wear the white hat, Cleary."

Dick used last names. He said it established distance and a boundary. He used to write speeches for politicians and government officials, like the Attorney General. It was never Bobby, always Mr. Kennedy.

"What brings you here?" Dick asked.

"I'm screwed and I need help."

"Story of your life. You oughta be double-jointed by now."

"I need help."

"Help? Look at me," Dick said. "Do I look like the expert on how to un-fuck your life?"

Two platters arrived. Crosswinds offered the usual pub grub of fried grease and the Fisherman's were no exception. I didn't question the mystery of seafood hidden inside the beer batter.

"There was another fire on Symphony Road," I said to unspool the thread. "The professor is digging into other fires, into property deeds, or whatever else he can find, but I was wondering whether you've heard anything here."

"It don't take a pair of ears in this place to tell you The Syrian was probably behind it. You should know how that scumlord operates."

"Clever combination of words there. Scum instead of slum, but the thing is, knowing is one thing; proving it is another. The landlord is—"

He eyed my glass. "Something wrong with Jim Beam?"

First, I sipped to appease him and then answered. "A connection to The Syrian is tenuous. The landlord for the pile of ashes on Symphony Road is in Florida."

"How convenient," Dick said.

"There was a body inside the building."

"Yeah, I read that in the newspaper," Dick said without looking up. He gulped some whiskey, hit the halfway mark on his glass and dumped water into it and stirred it with a finger. His beard had gotten grayer since I'd last seen him. The feral Santa Clause look became him. For a drunk, he had neither bloodshot eyes nor the red nose. "Read the crispy critter was male, but not much else for details," Dick said.

"Hear whether this man was already dead, or dumped there?"

"Nope, but I do know your friends in uniform have an oversized hard-on for you and your client, Jimmy. Those boys will move fast to nail him because nobody likes a case of blue balls, pun intended."

"They're not my friends."

"It's called sarcasm and situational irony, Cleary."

Dick jawed a mouthful of fish and chips.

"Any money behind their enthusiasm to make the charges stick?" I asked, my hand on my Jim Beam.

"Forget you've lived your whole life in this town, and not some convent?"

I deserved that answer for being naïve. Dick had eaten a bird's portion of food and pushed his plate forward. Alcoholics were rail-thin for a reason. I watched him pull in his Jim Beam for comfort. The more Dick drank, the more inventive he became with profanity, especially the f-word.

He may look the portrait of total dissipation, but Richard Case still wrote three or four hours a day. Some people would call him a functional alcoholic. Dick confessed to me he didn't like to write and reading gave him little pleasure. I'd asked why he bothered and he told me he wrote because he was good at it. He knew he was good at it. There had been no bluster or ego when he said it either. His problem was people. Dick was like Cassandra of Greek mythology in drag, incapable of telling a lie. For her honesty, the Greeks pitched her off the highest cliff. Dick exiled himself from society before the same happened to him.

"I'd like to hear your theory on how this went down," I said.

"Property is wealth, right? The Founding Fathers knew that before the ink was dry on the Declaration of Independence. These days, with inflation and all, it costs more to repair a building than what it is worth."

"And?"

"Easier and cheaper to burn the damn thing to the ground and build a new one. You save money that way and make more money, if you resell it later. The land is more valuable than the building on it. Nonetheless, when you build a new shack, the Assessor's Office reappraises the property, inks in a higher property value in his ledger. More value, more taxes, and it's all hocus-pocus from there."

"The real magic is before all that happens," I said.

"And after," Dick said. "The house burns down, the owner screams Loss. The insurance company pays out. The builder needs permits and the city has fees, and construction has to keep to a schedule and you see where I'm going with this?" He inhaled another mouthful. "And the Wheel of Dharma turns round and around."

"Corruption and kickback city. If everyone profits, why screw the man with the match?"

"Haven't a clue there, Cleary." Dick worked some fish with a fork. "The Syrian is a bastard. He'd sell his own mother for a glass of water on a hot summer day. Simplest answer to me is he had a score to settle."

"And the cops?"

"Money to be made." Dick rubbed two fingers together. "Contributions to the Policeman's Ball. Ask yourself, How many cops dance?"

Dick's outlook on life would've driven the chipper poet Walt Whitman to take a letter-opener to his veins, or a header off the Tobin Bridge, if he lived in Boston. I still needed leverage, something Dick heard as a barfly. I worked an idea.

"If I mention a name, nod if he's in league with The Syrian."

"In league?" Dick laughed. "You've been reading Sherlock Holmes or what?" He leaned forward. "Look, there's more than one cop in on this arson scam, you know that, Cleary. Nothing has changed. Remember that old frog expression?"

"French?"

"Let me see if I can get this right. Ah, '*Plus ça change, plus c'est la même chose.*'" His eyebrow arched for emphasis. "Know what it means?"

"Yeah, I do. The more things change, the more they stay the same."

54

"There you have it." Dick clapped his hands together. "That's the truth about this town without the fortune cookie. Cops, politicians, judge and jury, poodle and caboodle." Dick grinned and curled his fingers around his Jim Beam. "The thing you can't forget, though, is any cop in this for money is the little man. He's nothing more than a moving part, replaceable, and if he thinks otherwise, then he's an ignorant and greedy piglet."

"Sounds like Kiernan. You know the name, don't you?"

"I do," Dick said. "The man is a rectal birth, but in this matter of Symphony Road, a cog who probably think he's a big wheel, and that's what makes him dangerous, Cleary."

I grabbed the hat to initiate my departure. "Written anything lately?"

"Have a book out in August."

I fixed my hat to my head. "Congratulations."

"Critics panned my last one, but this time, they're mad as squirrels about it. I'm the captain of American letters, they say, and here I am in a bar and I rent an apartment upstairs. All that means to me is home is one drink away."

"This book, what is it about?"

"Two sisters. Despair, divorce, and disappointment. The usual. How is Delano? I like the old codger, even if I'm suspicious of man who never drinks. Know an antonym for teetotalers like him?"

"Yeah, I do. Bibulous."

That reminded me. I owed Lindsey a phone call.

Chapter Eight: Boston City

On the corner of East Springfield Street and Harrison Avenue, there's a two-faced luncheonette, where I told Tony Two-Times I'd meet him on the street when I returned his call. By two-faced, the door from one street looked into a deli where the hungry and lonely could buy coffee at the counter if they were low on change, a grinder if they were flush with payday cash, and at another door and street there was a separate room where Nikos the owner and his wife sold ice cream to the kids during the summer.

He served customers, he saved money, and he acquired real estate. Nikos should've retired but didn't because that would mean he'd be alone with his thoughts. He worked and collected the rents from several properties. These days, Nikos spent his time thinking of all those children in the South End, of the son he lost in Vietnam and the wife to cancer, and reading poetry and philosophy.

He's thinner now. The widower's life had stolen the tire around his midsection. When we last spoke, Nikos talked about some writer named Panagoulis who, he claimed, had written lines of poetry in his own blood while incarcerated for trying to assassinate a dictator in Greece.

I wasn't there to sit on one of the red stools, or ask him why he changed the icons of the Greek Orthodox Church every month in his small restaurant. I wasn't there to ask him why he kept a wedding egg in a large cup, or why he hadn't replaced the crippled door or the crooked blinds in the window. I was there because of Tony and because City Hospital was across the street.

Nikos owned a vintage phone booth that was nothing more than a glorified closet. I turned my back to the world, dimes in hand and dropped them into the slot. I ignored the conversation between Nikos and a customer. The resident with the stethoscope around his neck had come in late for lunch and asked for a steak sandwich. Nikos negotiated him down to hot dog because he didn't want to cook. A voice answered.

"Got anything for me, Professor?"

"I do, but I can't talk now."

"I have another request." Lindsey said nothing, so I put my order across the deli counter into the pit. "Please find me any pictures you can on Luisa Ramírez. Luisa is spelled L-U-"

"I know how to spell, Shane. A tilde on the i in Ramírez, correct?"

"That's right," I said. "Now, about that progress report?"

"We'll discuss it tonight at John's. I'll tell Sylvia to set an extra place."

"A headline, please."

"It'll have to wait."

"All words, a carriage return and no bell, and you can't tell me anything?"

He hung up first this time. I was disappointed, and not by his lack of manners. Lindsey's voice sounded fertile with information. I depressed the tongue on the phone and readied the next two dimes when the door snapped opened. I turned around.

Tony Two-Times. I had told him to meet me on the street. For a man of his size, he was capable of stealth. He stepped inside the booth. I raised the receiver above my head to make room for the two of us. We were packed in tighter than sardines in a Steinbeck novel. "What's the idea?" I asked.

"Who were you talking to?"

"An editor at a paper. Why?"

"Mr. B wants a status report."

Three days out from the initial assignment, and my mafioso was antsy for developments. Tony reached into his jacket. His hand came out with a crushed pack of cigarettes. I shifted again when he groped his pocket for the lighter. His teeth pulled a cigarette from the pack. His other hand offered me the lighter. "Light me."

"Kind of cramped in here, don't you think?"

"Faster you are with the report, the faster I'm outta here. Now, light me."

On the first click, I lit his cigarette. I waited. He inhaled. Like a dragon, two long plumes of smoke escaped from his nostrils. Beads for eyes stared at me. I coughed.

"Hold your breath, if the smoke bothers you."

"Makes it hard to talk, doesn't it?"

"Then listen to me, and listen good." He stuck two fat fingers inside my shirt collar. He didn't have to do much else. The pressure against both carotid and jugular made it difficult to breathe. "Mr. B wants an update on the thing he talked to you about."

"You mean the kid?"

"Isn't that what I just said? Whataya got?"

"Still working on it."

His fingers moved and my Adam's apple was grateful. "Look, Cleary, I like you, but I don't got all day. Now, give me something to bring to the old man, or I put this cigarette out in your eye. Nothing personal." He placed the orange end of the cancer stick near my eyelashes. "Give me something. Any news not fit to print is still news."

"Back the hell off, and get that thing away from my face."

"Okay, I will because we're friends," he said. "What have you got?"

"On the level?"

"On the level."

"I've got to rule something out first. If it's bad news, I'll tell your boss myself."

Those dark eyes stared at me. He took in smoke and blew it away from me.

"Shit," he said, after the sigh with smoke. "Sounds like you're expecting bad news." He shook that large head and small brain of his. "I don't want to be the one to tell Mr. B bad news. Business is one thing, but this is his own flesh and blood. Here's what I'll do. I'll tell the man you're still investigating. How's that sound?"

"Great. Now, may I have some privacy? I'm working here."

"Nice office. Did you relocate?" Tony's free hand migrated south and returned north with a dime. "Here's ten cents for hurt feelings." He lifted his chin. "I like the hat. Stay classy."

"Hard to," I said, "when a phone call costs twenty cents."

Tony backed out of the phone booth. Nikos was buffing the counter with a cloth. I stiffed the door's crease straight, turned my back, and dialed the number and hoped for the familiar voice. Three rings later, he answered.

"Shane here and I need a favor, JC."

"Where are you?"

"Nikos's."

"Meet me near the ambulances in five."

"Will do."

I stepped out of the phone booth. I survived an inning with Tony Two-Times. I was batting .500. Only problem was Nikos the umpire. He waved me over.

"Don't have time, Nikos," I said.

He indicated the red stool. "Sit, please."

Nikos reached under the counter. Had John done that, I'd expect a sawed-off shotgun. Nikos placed a cold bottle of Coke and used an opener to pop the bottlecap. Fizz escaped and bubbles blistered to the surface of the dark liquid inside while outside, the thick glass sweated. Nikos pushed it forward. My hand accepted it.

"I don't need to know what kind of trouble you're in."

"No trouble, Nikos."

"Do you owe money?"

"No."

"If it's money, I can give you the money."

"It's not money, Nikos. It's a job I didn't want. I'll handle it."

Nikos must have thought I was lying. "Is it drugs? I've got a place out west you can use if you need to get clean? I'll send you to one of those whatever they call them."

"Rehab? No, not drugs. I never used them."

"A woman then? You've gotten yourself mixed up with the wrong girl."

I took a swig of the sweet drink and let the carbonation scorch my throat.

"No, nothing like that. I said I'll handle it."

"The wrong woman can kill you, or get you killed. I was fortunate with Maria. I married the right woman, and that's what you need, Shane. A good woman. Your generation thinks it can find love in bars, and dance clubs and—"

"Nikos, it's none of that. I've got this. This is job-related. That's all, I promise."

"Wrong kind of job can kill you." Nikos said. His hand pulled in the cloth. "The stress."

"If you haven't noticed, Nikos." He looked at me. "Life kills."

I listened to Nikos's last sales pitch. He yammered on about retiring to Florida, about needing someone he could trust to look after his kingdom. That someone was me. When he said he thought of me as a son, I thought he had spread the schmaltz on thicker than a Capra film, but a thought came to me as I finished the Cola and suppressed the belch.

Nikos was a landlord, a millionaire several times over. He'd buy a place for a grand, fix it up, and now he owned a string of properties all over the South End. Nikos's reputation was solid, and people said nice things about him, how he'd give folks extra time with the rent, or he'd leave groceries at their door when the breadwinner had lost his job and pride. None of his buildings had ever gone up in flames, so I was curious.

"I have a question for you."

Nikos stood there, face placid as an undisturbed lake. "What kind of question?"

"Landlord stuff."

Nikos leaned forward, rested his elbows on the counter now, interested. "Shoot."

"Were you ever tempted to do a quick turnover, you know, with fire insurance?"

Nikos straightened up, as if he were offended. "Never."

"But suppose you wanted to…you'd know who to call, right?"

"Why do you ask me this question?"

"A case I'm working."

His eyes glanced to the street. "A case that involves dangerous men, like your friend?"

"He's all mouth and no teeth, once you get to know him."

"The point is you know him and he knows you. Are you working a case for him?"

"I'm working three cases, two of them involve dangerous men, that I know of."

"And the third case?"

"Cobwebs, real or imagined."

"I really hope you consider my offer," Nikos said. "Come, manage my properties, and allow me to move to Florida. I can get away from these winters and enjoy the sun before I die. You can live a life without looking over your shoulder every day. Find yourself a girl and have a family with her."

"And what?" I said with a smile. "Die of boredom."

Nikos waved me off, and walked the length of the counter, away from me. He pulled out a book from somewhere underneath and sat down. This was his way of sulking. A thousand times I'd seen him read a book. It reminded me of the professor. All the smart people in my life read. Piles of books from the Boston Public Library kept Nikos going after his wife died. I worried about him after Maria passed, worried the way you do about the oldest couple in the family. One of them died and the other spouse was dead within a year. Happened to my mother.

Gunshot City, Stab Central, and Overdose Depot were all aliases for City Hospital.

City was the centerpiece of pain and misery for Boston's poor, the place where the little people without insurance or sufficient scratch for the bill hope to leave without the toe tag. Home to surly nurses, lazy civil servants, overcrowded rooms, and gurneys in the hallways,

City had a series of underground tunnels and interconnected buildings. Everything from drug deals to pros turning tricks happened there. Patients knifed their own doctors in the ER. Only in City Hospital would the elevator man try and sell you stolen jewelry while you rode the lift.

Dick the writer mentioned situational irony. City Hospital was damn ironic.

Boston can't seem to help itself. In '73, not far from City, *Deep Throat* played at the Pilgrim and inspired an obscenity trial and a lot of couples—more so than that scene with butter in *Last Tango in Paris* had. Earlier that year, the judicial robes ruled on *Roe v. Wade*, which I bring up now because in late '73, a doctor was convicted of manslaughter for performing an abortion at City Hospital.

That doctor was black, the jury was all-white, and the verdict of GUILTY was swifter than Madge with Bounty paper towels, the "quicker picker upper."

JC asked me to meet him near the mouth of one of those tunnels. I could see the swarm of parked ambulances, or, as I like to call them, Death's Taxi Service.

JC or Jean-Claude Toussaint was a Haitian wunderkind. A doctor in his own country, he fled when "Baby Doc" Duvalier took over the Caribbean island. Smart, gifted, capable guy, JC failed his Boards by one point. He told me Uncle Sam imposed higher standards on doctors with foreign medical degrees. True or false, racist or not, I'd trust the man with my life. He started in a lab at City sharpening old needles for reuse. He worked his way up from there. Word got around that JC had medical know-how and he was sought out for difficult assessments. Word also got around he was a voodoo priest.

Tall as a drainpipe, black as charcoal and with a perpetual case of bloodshot eyes, JC strutted over to me in crisp white scrubs and not the wrinkled pajamas the other medical staff wore. The man took pride in his appearance, the way he presented himself to people. Add some meat on his bones, change out the hairstyle, and JC was as suave and silky as Sidney Poitier. When we shook hands, I palmed him two Jacksons and a Hamilton.

"What do you need?" JC asked.

"Not what, but where. I'd like to see a body in the morgue and get your opinion on the cause of death. Is that possible, or do I come back later?"

"No, we can do this now."

62

"Good. Oh, and I'll have a question for you when we're finished."

"This way, my friend."

The mouth of the tunnel was dark and cold. People read about the occasional homeless person found frozen stiff on Boston Common in the *Boston Globe*. Nobody learned about the popsicles found here, yards away from steel trays and slide drawers inside the City Morgue. JC said hospital basements were good for three things: a fall-out shelter in case the Commies dropped the big one, surgical theatres, and the mortuary.

JC asked me to stay at the end of the hall and out of sight. I hugged the wall and waited around the corner for his whistle. I watched JC whisper words into the attendant's ear and tucked my Hamilton into the man's shirt pocket. The man up and left for a prolonged cigarette break.

Death has an odor. I recognized it from the service. No amount of refrigeration muted it. There weren't enough disinfectants and aerosol sprays to mask it. Thousands of miles away and years later, I recalled the scent the way Proust remembered madeleines on Sunday mornings.

"Looking for a John Doe," I told JC.

"You need to be more specific."

"Burn victim. Symphony Road."

JC consulted a clipboard and ran a finger down the list. His finger had traveled long distance, long enough that I began to worry he'd turn up empty.

"Drawer 117," JC said. "John Doe, Symphony Road, like you said. BFD brought him in."

"Does it say whether an autopsy has been done?"

"Doesn't, but we'll know when we pull the drawer. Let's take a walk together."

The metal square, the number 117 reminded me of Nikos and his ice cream freezer, the curl of white vapor when he opened the flap for the kids.

"Burnt bodies aren't pretty," he said.

"Neither is seeing someone survive napalm."

JC pulled on the steel slide with some effort. A mortuary tray demanded strength, and not for death served up. Like the way a dead person never looked the same as they did when they were alive, a dead body was heavier than most people imagined. This wasn't Jack and Jill up and over the hill or the groom carrying his bride in her skimpiest lingerie into the bedroom.

I'd carried load in the army. I've humped a ruck half my body weight, I've hauled a wounded buddy over my shoulder over rough terrain. The adrenaline in my veins motivated me because somebody was yards behind us, trying to kill us. The things we carried, the memories we remember.

The body was inside a bag. Standard transport to a funeral home, or, after three months, when the body was shipped off to Fairview Cemetery where Boston's indigent and unidentified were buried. JC pulled the zipper.

"Tell me what you see," I said.

JC parted the thick plastic for a look at the pelvis and extremities. "Male, I'd say late teens to early twenties." He didn't touch the skull, but took a closer look at the charred remains. "Caucasian, and notice the indentation on his pinkie? He used to wear a ring on the finger." JC scrutinized both darkened hands and wrists. "I need to touch him." JC raised his chin. "Hand me a pair of gloves from behind you."

"This is starting to feel like an episode of *Quincy, M.E.* Am I supposed to say 'What is it, Sam'?"

I handed him latex gloves. JC didn't smile at my joke about the popular TV show and a recurring line of Dr. Quincy to his assistant. JC donned the gloves. I heard the snap. He hadn't been a coroner in Haiti, but putting on those gloves was a sacred act, a reminder of his sworn duty to do no harm and think science with compassion.

All that education and our country treated him like a janitor. Combat medics I knew at least had something to show for all the horrors they'd seen. Our government got wise to all their field experience and made them either nurse practitioners or physician assistants after a quick rinse in an education program.

"See how the arms are flexed at the elbows and wrists, here and here." JC pointed with a finger. "You were a boxer."

"Yeah, I was. You're saying he fought?"

"This type of flexion is called PA, Pugilist Attitude, and its consistent with heat-related injuries to the body. Extreme heat from the fire causes contractures, the arms and legs become flexed. There is one problem, though." JC lifted a crisp wrist. "See these indentations?"

"More jewelry?"

"These are ligature marks on the wrists. Our victim had been tied up at first."

"At first?"

"I don't see any residue. He broke free of the restraints. Let me look at one last thing," JC said.

I winced when JC stuck a gloved finger inside the corpse's mouth. The finger circled and probed inside the distorted orifice. I didn't know what to think until JC held up a darkened finger. "See that?" he said. "That's soot from the fire."

"Smoke inhalation. Anything else?"

"This young man did not 'go gentle into that good night.'"

JC zipped up the bag, pushed the drawer back in. When he pulled the gloves off, they made a vulgar sound, a loud thwack. "I haven't told you the worst part."

I looked at JC, incredulous. "What's worse than being tied up and suffocating to death?"

"This young man didn't just suffocate."

"What are you saying?"

"Your John Doe was roasted alive. Earlier, you said you had a second question."

I wondered how I'd break the news to Mr. B. He had hired me to find the kid. I found him. I had every reason to believe Mr. B would ask me to find the killer, which would then make me party to a disappearance at best, a murder at worst.

I pulled the photograph from my pocket and showed it to JC. The man must've seen a thousand dead faces in this icebox, so I supplied the sketch. "Her name was Luisa Ramírez, age thirty, Hispanic, as you can see for yourself. She died two years ago, over at Park Plaza." I named the Medical Examiner from the paperwork. "The ME first said accidental overdose, and then amended the COD to suicide."

"And you think the cause of death wasn't suicide?" I shrugged and pocketed the 4x6 when he handed it back to me. "Pretty woman," JC said. "I could ask around."

"I'd appreciate it. The doctor...think I can talk to him?"

"Good luck with that, my friend. He split."

"Let me guess, two years ago and before your time," I said.

"Correct. Good reputation, though. People say he did everything by the book."

"Split, as in retired?" I looked around the morgue for effect. "Or did he want a change of pace, like patients who left the office alive?"

In the long corridor to the outside world, he said hello to colleagues as we walked. The Medical Examiner was still an ME, he told me, but now he practiced his trade in Worcester, in central Massachusetts where people received twice the snow than the rest of the country. Connecticut, Maine, and Rhode Island got snow. Vermont and New Hampshire got snow, but Worcester was special. Worcester was New England's answer to Siberia.

Chapter Nine: Information, Please

I could hear it, the not-so feminine exchange between two women. I'd never forgotten the sounds of angry voices as a beat cop, the white heat of a conversation behind a door that could burn through the wood. Cops dreaded the walk-up, not knowing what was waiting for them on the other side. Domestic disputes were the worst. They never started small but they always ended big. I thought twice.

Whoever coined the idiotic phrase the gentler sex hasn't met daddy's little girl with a bloodied knife in her hand, lips slick with gloss, or entered a room to find big sister, gun in hand, sitting in a peacock chair, her boyfriend lifeless at her feet, while she smoked a cigarette down to the root.

One of the voices I knew. The other I'd not had the pleasure.

A surefire way to halt any conversation in a black home was to knock on the door like a cop. It's all in the knuckles for that rapid Rat-TAT-TAT, a sequence of Morse code white people never heard or understood.

Rat-TAT-TAT.

Silence. I saw a shadow under the door. I couldn't help but think of Serpico shot through the door. I heard floorboards creak, the lid to the peephole swivel. The lock scratched across the rail and the door opened up enough to pull the chain taut. If I looked up, I might see John; down, Sylvia. It was neither.

"Who are you?" she asked, polite but with suspicion in her voice. The absence of any local accent in her voice said she was from out of town. Her caramel eyes traveled sweetly and slowly over what she could see of me from her side of the door.

"You must be Vanessa," I said. "Please tell your aunt Shane is here."

"Let the man inside," I heard next. The aromas from Silvia's kitchen wafted around the edge of the door and my mouth watered. Sylvia's meals, her cooking, were home to me.

The chain fell. Door swung wide, Vanessa placed a hand on one hip and shifted all one hundred pounds to the other side, like a naughtier version of Donatello's David. I got the whole show of long legs in tight denim and the floral shirt with more colors than a rainbow, which included a cutout and exposed a navel. Then, I saw her face.

Governor Wallace in Alabama would've gone apoplectic at the blend of African and Caucasian features. Smooth, straight brown hair and a button nose proved miscegenation was alive and well in Canada. Her face would've ignited a hundred burning crosses on a hundred lawns.

"Don't stand outside when you can come in, Shane. I've heard a lot about you," Vanessa said. Her voice was soft and sweet as honey.

Sylvia punctured the mood. "It's Mr. Cleary to you."

I stepped into an embrace and a peck on the cheek from Sylvia. She ignored Vanessa and dithered on about bowls, table settings and who would sit where, and when dinner would be on the table. Sylvia flitted on like a moth in search of a light bulb.

I looked around the living room. Business had been good to both John and Sylvia. The shag rug and track lighting were new. The furniture and everything else consisted of African prints, tribal art, and earth tones. On the coffee table, I noticed a somewhat recent book that was outside of Sylvia and John's interest: *Helter Skelter*.

As I undid the buttons on my jacket, Vanessa stepped in front of me and her eyes looked up at me. She wore no make-up nor any lipstick, and she did more with the plain Jane look than most college grads did with a degree. "How old are you?" I asked.

She snatched my jacket and then smiled. "You know better than to ask a woman her age."

John strode in, a wide grin on his face, as Vanessa absconded with my jacket. We watched her turn tail into another room. Neither one of us mentioned that the hallway closet was next to the front door behind me.

"I see you've met my niece Vanessa."

"Not sure if met is the word for it. What's her story?"

"My sister in Montréal is in the middle of a rough divorce."

"Say no more. As a PI, I avoid divorce cases."

"My sister said Vanessa has been acting out."

"Is that what that was?"

John anchored his big hand on my shoulder. He squeezed it tight and whispered, "She and Sylvia don't see eye-to-eye, but act as if you don't notice. What are you working on these days?"

"More like, what am I not working," I said.

I mentioned the Symphony Road fire and a cold case. I asked after the professor. Lindsey lived in a room above Sylvia's restaurant rent-free and he helped her with occasional errands. Delano Lindsey played all the roles in central casting, from busboy to dishwasher, to maître d' and occasional waiter, which drew odd glances from her clientele. Sylvia served the best soul food in Dorchester. Black folks, unaccustomed to a white man serving them, came to love the professor because he worked hard, and never acted superior. When they learned that he was a professor, their respect doubled. They asked if he'd tutor their kids, which he did, and they paid him. Both John and Sylvia begged Lindsey to quit his 9-to-5 job with the paper, but he wouldn't hear a word of it.

John and I sat down in the living room. John owned a bar in Central Square and, like Lindsey, he played more roles than Lon Chaney. He was accountant, barkeep, floor sweep, janitor, and occasional bouncer. I met John while working the Braddock case last year. I was like Dr. Richard Kimble, a fugitive on the run for a murder I didn't commit, and John's bar became my church, and he became my priest of sorts, in that he gave me sanctuary.

Harvard Square and the famous university might've been blocks from John's business, but his Central Square was filled with cooks and crooks, communes, food co-ops, and lost hippies instead of students and scholars. And then there were the radicals, all the other Counterculture and Anti-

Establishment groups. You couldn't walk a block without a pamphlet from the Yippies. Central Square was home to more basement printing presses than all of Newspaper Row on Washington Street in the nineteenth and twentieth centuries, combined.

I heard every stump speech there. The environment was going to hell, they said, and would continue to do so, if we didn't do something now. And The Man was running the biggest con on the American people, from Vietnam to whatever passed for news on the idiot box.

Every block in Central Square had a committee and its share of characters. The cute blonde, who sold grass on the side, belonged to the feminist Cell 16 and taught martial arts classes in the Annex next door. Then there was the folksy musician who strummed his guitar and sang Joni Mitchell songs. An agricultural group called Massachusetts Tomorrow dug into cases of social injustice. A dozen other groups did sentry duty on the Commonwealth's ideas for a highway through their neighborhood and kept their eyes out for predators on local real estate. Central Square offered the kind of hothouse activism that kept Luisa Ramírez's blood hot.

With all that dissent, with all that passion, there was plenty of crime and drugs. Mostly drugs. John's bar was a stop on the pharmaceutical underground, one of the many places to arrange a score. Whatever pleased the Joneses, whether it was a joint, a tab, or a pill, Central Square had it, and John's place was a post office.

John might be black but he wasn't blind. He knew and understood commerce, but he allowed none of it on the premises. Meet and greet, customer and dealer, and negotiate the price and the amount of product there, yes, but off the two of you went, elsewhere for the exchange. Elsewhere was often across the street, a small peninsula of concrete and cobblestones, where the police kept a kiosk. Dealers dealt, users scored. Cops in blue looked the other way, with green in their pockets.

I asked John outright about Luisa Ramírez. I showed him the 4 x 6 print.

"Ever see her in your place?"

"No, I'd remember her face. Name sounds familiar, though. Case of yours?"

He handed me the photo back.

"A community activist," I said. "She OD'd in Park Plaza. My cold case."

"Park Plaza...isn't that in your part of town?"

He was right. Park Plaza was close to my South End. I was about to tell him I asked because I wondered whether Luisa frequented Central Square for a receptive audience, among all the rebellious types. The Revolutionary War after all was the most successful protest the people pulled off, and it began with passion, pamphlets, and pains in the asses like Luísa Ramirez.

I wanted to explore all the leads before I disturbed people with money. The people behind the Boston Renewal Effort were all kinds of green and connections. My case last year with Braddock proved to me cash and real estate got on well together, and it's a closed society. There was another reason.

I could've walked down to The 'Ham, where I talked to one of Tony's friends, the place where Connie Francis warbled in the background. The 'Ham was the all-white version of John's bar, except the clientele included people with extra vowels in their last names.

Ask around there about Luisa was an option but to do that, someone would tell someone about some guy who'd been nosing about with questions about some dead broad. The point is someone always talked to someone. The reason I didn't exercise the privilege was because Tony Two-Times and Mr. B would know I was working another case, which I don't think they would've minded, but they would've raised more than an eyebrow, if they discovered my client was the commissioner.

The 'Ham, as in Waltham Tavern on Shawmut Ave, was a cave with bad lighting and a ceiling so low the regulars developed scoliosis. A mobster ran the joint, and his merry hunchbacks doubled as bookmakers and leg-breakers, while he sipped espresso at a social club, up the street from them. And as the Tiber flows through Rome, a tribute went from him to Mr. B.

Like I said, Mr. B would know I was two-timing him, and then who with.

Tony Two-Times would visit me. He'd ask me why the boys, who reported to a boss who reported to his boss, said I was asking around about a dead Hispanic girl. I doubted they or Tony would use the word Hispanic when one syllable did the work of three. They question. I answer. I'd need bridgework.

"This girl's family hired you?" John asked.

"Family didn't hire me, though she does have a sister."

"Then start with her," John said.

"Address unknown."

"That shouldn't stop you," John said. "You're the detective. Find her."

Sylvia yelled from the kitchen that it was dinner time. John rose from the couch.

"All I have for a lead on the sister is a name on two-year old paperwork," I told John.

"The dead woman was at Park Plaza for a reason, right? I think you should be more cop than PI on this."

"Come again," I said.

"Get off your ass and knock on some doors."

On my way to my chair at the table, Sylvia came at me with a wooden spoon. I had to taste her latest creation of black-eyed pea, collard green, and sweet-potato stew. "Heaven in a mouthful," I told her.

"You're too kind," Sylvia said, all smiles until Vanessa reappeared.

"I'll sit next to Shane."

"Girl, didn't I tell you already, he's Mr. Cleary to you."

There was a sound at the door, the scrape of a key and the turn of the deadbolt. I excused myself. Vanessa turned sideways as I brushed by her with an "Excuse me" on my way to the professor. I hated the idea of ambushing the man, like some 50's housewife, but I was anxious to hear some of his research on Symphony Road. I fired off a question as he struggled to escape his jacket.

"Can't this wait until after dinner? I'm famished."

"A teaser then, please."

"There's no peace in the Middle East."

I thought, The Syrian. "No peace in the Middle East" suggested there was nothing but sand for a lead. Had I misread Jimmy "Middle Eastern" at the police station? It seemed like I would have to wait until after dinner to hear the professor's findings.

I hoped Lindsey had something on the landlord whose property was destroyed in the fire. The cops said he was in Key West. I pictured him as a smug little Buddha with his nose covered in zinc, a tropical drink in one hand, a hooker in the other, the Hawaiian lei around his neck, while they both shimmied to the latest funk in a nightclub, or read from Hemingway.

We ate in silence. Vanessa didn't play footsies, but she pressed her thigh against mine. When I looked her way, my mind consulted statutes and jail time for...

"Mr. Cleary used to be a cop," Sylvia announced.

"Really," Vanessa about purred. "That sounds so dangerous."

I gulped cold water, undeterred by Vanessa's interest in law and order, though I recalled seeing the copy of *Helter Skelter* earlier. Sylvia's voice was cold as the skillet in the sink. "He can tell you what they do here to young girls caught boosting."

"You shoplifted?" I asked.

Vanessa face turned red.

"I won't mention the store, but thank God I know the manager there. This one here," Silvia said and pointed at Vanessa, "shoved bras and panties into her purse. Security held onto her until I came downtown to settle the matter. She's one lucky girl."

"Must you embarrass me, Auntie Syl?"

Vanessa pushed her chair back, for a dramatic departure. Sylvia's knife and fork stopped, then came the glare and Vanessa sat back down.

"Ain't nobody leaving or done until everybody's done," Sylvia said. "You embarrassed yourself. Imagine my horror when my manager friend showed me them undergarments. All the silk and lace you'd expect in a whorehouse."

"Must you?" Vanessa asked.

"There are two times to be quiet, during a thunderstorm or when grownups are talking."

And they were off.

The men around the table ignored the next set of volleys. John tucked his chin and the professor fixated on how much stew he could scoop with his spoon. I shoveled to the bottom of my bowl.

The dinnerware was new, a floral theme. When I reached bedrock, I counted the number of petals in the Fiesta flowers there. Then came the lull, the eerie silence.

"Have you ever shot anyone, Mr. Cleary?" Vanessa asked.

I coughed when her hand squeezed my thigh.

"Nessa, what a horrible question," Sylvia said.

"It's okay," I said.

"It most certainly is not."

Nobody thought about dessert. The conversation around the table decayed into small talk and then no talk at all. Sylvia was the first to push her chair back. The professor offered to help with the dishes. "No, Professor. You and Shane retire to the next room," Sylvia said. "I can tell he's been itching to talk to you ever since you came in the door. Go on, get, and you best join them, John."

"What about me?" Vanessa asked her aunt.

"Palmolive soap in the kitchen will soften those thieving hands of yours."

John and Lindsey exited the kitchen like schoolboys on the last day of school. I thought the two of them would collide on the sprint through the doorframe. Sylvia, her back to us, turned the faucet on. Vanessa lingered, until Sylvia said, "Gather up the dishes. They ain't got legs to walk themselves to the sink."

John and I resumed our spot on the sofa. Lindsey said he'd fetch his notes from his valise. John and I sat somewhat dazed, like we'd eaten too much Thanksgiving turkey. John asked me what papers Lindsey was off to find in his briefcase. I told him that I had asked the professor to research the fire on Symphony Road. I mentioned Jimmy C was on the hook for arson and homicide. I circled back to John and the home front. "Is it always like this?" I asked John.

"With Syl and Nessa?" he said. "Hell, they were tame tonight."

Lindsey returned. "I dug around," he said, "and I have been able to confirm

74

that the landlord in Florida owned the building."

"Landlord coulda hired someone before he flew the friendly skies," John said.

"Thought that myself, until I made a few phone calls."

Whether it was mood rings, divinations from the Magic 8-Ball or Ouija board, or that the professor was a Virgo, the chief editor at the newspaper sensed tenacity and hired him for it. Lindsey was a barnacle of an investigative journalist disguised as a copyeditor.

The professor reached down to his attaché case, which he brought with him. Lindsey popped the brass clips to open his carryall. The professor removed a yellow legal pad and liberated a Cross pen from a leather loop. I glanced at John, whose fingers were interlaced behind his head while we watched Lindsey.

"You asked for these." The professor handed me copies of photos he had found of Luisa Ramírez in the Archives.

"Thanks," I said, and thumbed through them fast. All action-shots of Luisa, as if she were laying down ordinance for Toastmasters International. All of the pictures depicted her as a woman on fire. Lindsey cleared his throat, in a way that told me that he wanted my undivided attention. I set aside the photostats.

"Shane seems convinced The Syrian was involved, so I pressed my sources in Deeds and Registry," Lindsey said. He turned over one more canary page and tapped the pad with his finger. "The Syrian's MO is unimaginative but effective. Multiple complaints."

"Which is why he's called a scumlord." The word I plagiarized from Dick Case without attribution broke the spell.

Lindsey looked up, confused. "What?"

"Ignore him, Professor," John said. "Shane thinks he's being clever."

"As I was saying, several complaints. Tenants have claimed he'll notify them of dates and times for repairs, but maintenance never shows up. When they do, it's on a different day and time, and they'll make a racket loud enough for them to want to abandon the property."

"Passive-aggressive tactic," I said. "But then he has on the book for breaking their lease, for past rent with interest, and he'll sic a lawyer on them to garnish their wages. He makes money, even when he loses money."

John sort of laughed and I asked him what was funny. He said, "The things people with money do when they have the law on their side."

"I called someone I know in Housing," the professor said. "There were hundreds of grievances against him from tenants, past and present; the reports on him from city agencies were atrocious. Name a violation and he has his name next to it. Bedbugs, exposed wiring, rats, roaches, toilets that don't flush and—"

"Excuse me, Professor," I said. "All this is interesting, but irrelevant. We already know he's a slumlord. If there's no connection to the torched building then ergo, no case."

"Indeed, but that's not to say he wasn't interested in it."

John asked and leaned forward, curious. "Interested how?"

"Six weeks ago—and mind you, this is in confidence from my contact in deeds—the landlord, before he flew to Florida, complained about The Syrian."

"Complained about what?" I asked.

"Harassment. The Syrian had hounded the landlord with an offer to buy the property. If the landlord in Key West had filed an official complaint, then we'd have something in writing on the slumlord. Without that complaint, there's no paper trial. We're back to square one and nowhere on arson."

John said, "Even if we had the complaint, the slumlord's lawyer would argue Mr. Florida hired someone to do the job for the insurance money. I'm assuming Mr. Florida has no history of arson."

"He does not." The professor tapped a line on his canary page. "The Syrian, according to my source, offered to pay Mr. Florida in cash."

John rested his forearms on his thighs. He looked like Rodin's *Thinker* if the philosophical man were a lineman for the Pittsburgh Steelers. "Guy wants the property bad enough to offer cold, hard cash, but why was he so hell-bound on it? I mean, the guy owns a ton of properties. Greed?"

"I have a theory," the professor said. John and I said nothing. John leaned back to contemplate his ceiling. I stared ahead, thinking another angle.

Irritated that neither of us had spat out an answer, the professor sighed. "Can't you see it?"

"See what?" John asked.

"The clue?"

"What clue?" I asked Lindsey.

"He owns other properties on Symphony Road," Lindsey said.

"So," I said. "John said the man owns a ton of properties."

"Hence, my point," Lindsey said. "Symphony Road is a game of Monopoly to him."

"The board game?" John said. "I don't follow."

A teacher to the end, Lindsey stared at me as if to give me, his prize student, permission to blurt out the answer. I caught the hint.

"Monopoly, as in the building that burned down was the last property on the street. Mr. Key West owned the last holdout, and The Syrian wanted it," I said.

The professor threw down pad and pen.

"Exactly," he said. "The Syrian owns properties in Allston, Brighton, and Cambridge. He has holdings all over Boston." Lindsey counted them off on his fingers. "Single-family and multiple-family units on Huntington Avenue, on Belvedere Street, Burbank and Hennessey Streets, but Symphony Road was the one place in Boston where he'd own every single building on the street, except for one. This last property was the final jewel in the crown."

"But burn it to the ground?" John asked.

I smelled coffee and my brain woke up. "He made Florida an offer and when that didn't work out, he scared him enough to fly south early for winter. The house goes up in smoke."

"Which means Jimmy isn't out of the woods," John said. "The insurance company could argue Florida hired Jimmy before he boarded the plane."

"They'd look into his financials and look at every transaction and I'm certain that'll find nothing between him and Jimmy," I said. "We need a stronger connection between The Syrian and the fire on Symphony Road. Let's not forget, nobody has been able to tie him to any of the fires on Symphony Road or elsewhere for years."

"Proves he's smart," John said.

"Proves he puts distance between himself and whoever lit the match for him. Professor? Did you say Burbank Street?" I asked.

Sylvia entered the room with a tray of coffee mugs. Vanessa followed her carrying a platter of pastries. She sat next to me. I selected a pastry and she placed a cocktail napkin on my leg. Sylvia noticed. I noticed.

NBC, the television channel, filmed its shows in Burbank, California. A west coast name in a New England city stood out like the one bad brick in the sidewalk. I inhaled the pastry, downed the hot coffee, and asked to use the phone in the kitchen. I dialed the number.

"Bill, this is Shane."

"Who loves ya, baby?"

"Cut it out, Kojak. I need a favor. Kiernan. Know the name?"

"Unfortunately."

"Has he filed any incident reports on Burbank Street in the last six months."

"I'll look into it. Why do you ask?"

"It's a long story."

"Suit yourself," Bill said. "Anything else?"

"Yeah, Symphony Road. Any reports from Kiernan there?"

"No idea, but I'll add it to your bill," he said and hung up the phone.

A client on Burbank Street hired me. The case was the stuff of Arthurian legend, if Arthur was a drug addict and beat on Guinevere because he was paranoid there was a Lancelot. There wasn't. While working that case, I discovered a subplot between Arthur and Boston's worst landlord. The sound of fury and filth came back to me.

So did the name: Sharif Faisal. Lord of the Sties. The Syrian.

Chapter Ten: Knock and Talk

I had a feeling there was a connection between Burbank Street and Symphony Road, a hunch Kiernan and his partner O'Mara were somehow involved with The Syrian. Bill's paper expedition might bear fruit, or not. Coincidences belonged to movies.

John's advice to do the tried-and-true police procedural of Knock and Talk was solid as hickory. Park Plaza was near me, in my neighborhood. He was right about that, too. I needed a good night's sleep. John dropped me off at Union Park in his new car.

I cursed the narrow steps up to my place and praised the handrail. Mrs. F's corgi barked as I passed her door. Rock Hudson's voice blared on the other side of the wood. Sunday night, the Lord's Day, and the landlady's canine yapped at me instead of enjoying *McMillan & Wife* with the missus. My mother adored Rock in the film *Giant* and said the critics underappreciated him in *Written on the Wind*. I was too tired to argue with the memory of her.

Delilah greeted me at the door and I appeased her with a plate of food and her favorite treats sprinkled on top. I undressed and reached for the pillow and said goodnight and hoped for a better day tomorrow.

Monday. Day two of the week and day one at Park Plaza.

Overcast skies and the weather was indecisive as Hamlet. I committed to not carrying an umbrella. I'd rather dodge the spitting rain. I covered the few block before it stopped. The sun remained hidden to mock me while a breeze chilled me. The lack of trees in the area created a valley of steady gusts and cranky pedestrians.

The corner of Stuart Street reminded me of my childhood. A large 5 and 7 on the side of a building once greeted pedestrians and cars here. My father and I visited the 57 Restaurant because it served the best roast beef sandwich in Boston.

My best memories of my old man included this place, Friday nights of *Fight of the Week* on our Zenith, and the show *Car 54, Where Are You?* The last fight we watched together was Paul Pender against Terry Downes at the Garden in '62. It was Boston against the British all over again, the fireman from Brookline against the Paddington Express; more like Pender ripped the stuffing out of Paddington Bear. The frustrated Downes resorted to head butts and dirty heels in the corners.

A Howard Johnson's Motor Lodge replaced the 57 Restaurant. No more roast beef with fries. All I have to do is hear the song "Oh, What A Night" and the line "Late December back in '63" and a riptide of memories drowned me. Sixty-three was the year *Car 57* was garaged for good. Sixty-three was when Kennedy visited Dallas, and sixty-three was the year my father killed himself.

Our sofa. Our living room. Our television set. His revolver.

Park Plaza stank of wet cement. Lindsey taught me a curious fact. Concrete cures, it doesn't dry, and the more it gets wet, the stronger the smell becomes. The same could be said of corruption and Boston. The more the mayor and his legion of committee advisors and real estate developers and experts on the environment stirred the idea of Revitalization and Renewal, the more the people of Boston slapped them down on the Park Plaza Project. People like Luisa Ramírez.

Mayor White and his coterie of specialists wanted to redraw and redefine the neighborhoods of Back Bay, Beacon Hill, and Boston Common, which meant the destruction of low-income housing, which included buildings in Park Plaza. The poor, the elderly, and the disabled would be evicted. Where they went was their problem.

The city's elites, the Brahmins, believed in their City on the Hill, and that a man without money or a job was proof he lacked moral character and a compass. Our social betters reminded everyone they were the first people, the ruling class. It was all bred in the bone, they'd tell you, because they possessed the right blood. These were the people whose ancestors drove a line of wooden stakes into the snow as a dividing line, to separate them from the Indians. These were the people whose forefathers hung Catholics and Quakers and heretics. Blacks, Irish, Italian, Jews, and other unwashed and uneducated immigrants were their servants. It was the natural order, the social compact, and the way God intended it, or so they claimed.

I've been inside their homes. I was reminded to know my place when I was a student at St. Wystan's. The Boston Brahmin chattered like a chipmunk inside his brownstone, while the help circulated canapés and champagne. He lived to inherit his great-great-grandad's money and the seat on the Board. If he parted his hair the wrong way, he learned to live off of his trust fund.

He wore Brooks Brothers suits with the foulard tie in the fall and winter; seersucker suits with a straw hat, and maybe spectator shoes during the summer. His mate was a woman from the tennis set, or a distant cousin on the family tree. The Brahmin woman obeyed her man, and she lived the Trinity of hair up, hem down, and sex in the missionary position.

They said what they believed and talked poison with a posh accent. Public housing and other forms of assistance were "Populist nostrums that should've died with FDR, and LBJ had hobbled the future of the Republic with his Great Society." A helpful hand, they said, discouraged motivation and stifled ambition.

Luisa Ramírez and others tried to stop all that, even if it meant the adult bookshops, strip joints and topless bars in the Combat Zone stayed.

I stood in front of the building where she died. The glass in the front door was yellow from nicotine. A vestibule led to three steps up to a larger area. An overhead light flickered like the heartbeat of a dying man. A wall of mailboxes, a crypt with names, some faded and others absent faced me. The elevator ahead looked disused since the mid-century. A fat cockroach scurried across the dingy linoleum, up and over my shoe. I chose the stairs and walked up to the fourth floor.

My hand quit the bannister because it wobbled. Luisa had died in a studio apartment, number 420. There was no name on the mailbox or a number where I expected one. Hotels disliked the number because of its association with potheads. A group of kids in California called The Waldos would meet in front of a statue of Louis Pasteur at 4:20 p.m. and smoke joints.

I pulled the picture of Luisa from my pocket. I looked down the hallway and counted twenty squares, ten doors on each side, not unlike a cell block. John said to knock on some doors and find answers. It was a traditional approach, a time consuming one. Cops canvassed crime scenes for the slightest crumb of a clue, or hoped to find a witness and record a statement. There was no way this Knock and Talk would move as fast as an inmate processed at Walpole.

I knocked on the two doors, soft, like a civilian. The doors opened enough for a pair of eyes. I held up the picture and said the name Luisa Ramírez. The door slammed shut. I proceeded with patience and resolve. Five doors later, I understood rejection like a Jehovah's Witnesses, a Mormon, and that kid who sold magazines and memberships to Columbia House.

I tried again. This time, a young man in dirty jeans and a dirtier sleeveless shirt answered. Too hip to ask me what I wanted, he stood there, a cigarette clamped between his lips. He held an ashtray in his hand. I showed him the picture and said nothing. He closed the door.

A weak rap on the next door, and it flung open with the speed of someone mad at the maid who'd forgotten the Do Not Disturb sign on the doorknob. A Hispanic woman, a child on her hip, stared at me, choice of profanity not far behind. She seemed on the early side of twentyish and the kid, a Terrible Two, glowered. I lifted up the picture.

"Luisa Ramírez. You're looking for her. I heard you in the hallway," she said.

"She lived on this floor. I wondered if—"

"You wondered wrong. Lou is dead, so stop asking questions."

"I know she's dead, but if I could—"

Each time I started a sentence, she'd bounce the kid faster on her hip. His face crinkled and threated to cry and holler. She sensed it and tried to hush and shush him.

"You a cop?" she asked, as if it were an insult.

"Used to be. I'm a PI now. I could show you identification."

"A badge means shit around here." She continued to jostle the kid. "Nobody cared the day she died. The cops took her out of here, like she was trash."

"The cops moved her body?"

"What does it matter to you?"

"Cops don't move bodies, miss."

"You telling me what I saw?" She scowled as if I had questioned her intelligence.

"I believe you. Really, I do, and anything you saw is important to me, miss. I'm sorry I didn't catch your name. My name is Shane Cleary."

"My name is on the mailbox downstairs, like it's always been."

I leaned back and looked at the numbers on the doors on her side of the hall. Apartment 418. The numbers were decrepit but readable, despite the paint chips and the cracked wood.

"She died next door to you. Were you home with your son?"

"He's not my kid. I'm babysitting."

"My mistake."

The kid had calmed down. She realized she had committed to more than a hello. I wanted to reassure her. "All I want to know is what you saw or heard. A conversation? Catch a name in the air?" She cold-eyed me. "Anything you can give me would be helpful."

"I doubt it."

"Let me decide that."

"You don't understand. It's not safe here."

She gripped the door, and I worried. If she backpedaled into her apartment, I'd lose her. If I barged in, a coerced statement wasn't worth the paper it was typed on.

"Okay," I said. "Okay. One question, a yes or no. Is it not safe because of the cops?"

She didn't answer at first. She nodded.

"Listen to me carefully. I don't want to talk about this in the hallway."

"Say what you got to say there, and say it fast."

"Luisa's death was no accident," I said. "And she wasn't trash. She was a lady who wanted to help others." I said it because I believed it. I said it because she nodded, and her eyes glistened when I first mentioned the dead woman's name. She may have not shared a cup of coffee with Luisa, but she'd seen the body, and it had affected her. She cared.

"I can't help you," she said.

"Is there anybody else in this building who could?"

"Try the second floor," she said and shut the door.

I slid my card under her door, in case she changed her mind. I was conflicted. I had another floor, and a dilemma. If I stayed, I might get answers and find this person on the second floor. If the cops this woman was afraid of showed up soon, there was no way they'd let me leave. I didn't belong to the scenery here and they'd know it. They'd start asking question until they found the young woman, who had shut her door now. Nobody would ever know a thing about what had happened to me or Luisa Ramírez if I stayed.

If I left and returned to question people on the second floor, there's a good chance that gossip would've ruined any chance of anyone talking to me, and the cops might be onto me. Bad cops and snitches inside public housing were like the wet cement I hated. Their smell was unmistakable, persistent, and it never went away.

If, however, I returned knowing the names of the cops who walked the beat here, and if I disappeared, or someone else died or was harmed here, somebody would know it.

Bill would know. I'd make sure of it. He'd get me the roster of cops who toured Park Plaza. It'd be a long list of suspects, but if I were to end up in several Hefty bags, Bill was my insurance policy that someone would know about my visit here.

I walked downstairs to the mailboxes. I wrote the name and apartment number of the helpful tenant into my small notebook. I copied the names of all the tenants on the second floor.

I would call Bill from the Howard Johnson's coffee shop, explain the situation to him, and put the research on my tab.

Chapter Eleven: Shadow Allowance

Arlington Street provided the straight arrow to the Public Garden for my meeting with Pinto. "Near the ducks. 5pm, Monday" like Dot's message instructed me.

It was five, the day done, and the sidewalk was a stampede for the commute home. Hot weather, cold weather, or indifferent weather, the crowd negotiated the pavement the way Bobby Orr advanced the puck against the St. Louis Blues for the Stanley Cup-winning goal in overtime. A foot here, an elbow and a turn of the hip there, they'll go full horizontal, briefcase or purse raised high, into any one the subway stations for the escape from the office.

Street traffic was no better. New York City had nothing on Boston drivers. Sure, both sets jockeyed several thousand pounds of metal and rage. There was a difference, though. If the light blinked green and nobody moved fast enough for him, the New Yorker lowered his window, and spent his vocabulary all in one place, his language running bluer than a longshoreman's. He might even open the door and threaten to beat you to death with a manhole cover or with a convenient tire iron in his hand. Mr. Bostonian seethed instead with centuries of repression. The nicer he was to you face to face, the more he hated you. He'd wait for you in your driveway, in the dead of night and lit the match for the cigarette with his thumbnail after he was done with you.

The Public Garden was across the street from me, at the corner of Arlington and Boylston. I waited near the crosswalk. Cars sped pass me in a blur, a horn blared when another leadfoot changed lanes. The light changed and I gave myself a few seconds before I crossed the street to avoid the inevitable renegade who ran the red light.

Luisa Ramírez advocated for those without a voice. Bostonians never forgot what had happened to Scollay Square, nor did they forgive the politicians and Brahmins behind the forced evictions. Overnight, thousands of Jewish, Italian, and working-class families were handed a pittance and given the choice to either relocate or have their heads cracked with nightsticks. In my South End in the Fifties, the residents of New York Street were forced out, their houses razed to create commercial real estate.

The park had its own activists against the Park Plaza Urban Renewal Plan. Friends of the Public Garden railed against the construction of any buildings that would overshadow their beloved park and ruin it for all the citizens of the Commonwealth of Massachusetts. Shadow allowance was the term architects used for permissible height, in compliance with city ordinances. Anything higher than the restriction required an appeal for variance.

A breeze swept in, the treetops of the elms in front of me shivered as I entered the park. The place needed more greenery, the planted kind and not the money kind that was dropped into pocket squares at the State House. Armed with spray cans, vandals had defaced several statues and monuments. Cheap Romeos stole tulips and other colorful flowers. The foot bridge could use a pair of supports to straddle the pond that was drained every year before the weather turned too hot and the water became fragrant as an open sewer.

I walked a gauntlet of trees and evergreen bushes. I saw plenty of ducks. I searched the walkways for a man alone, and scanned the water's edge for Pinto. As I was coming out of the curve in my path, I saw him.

No wave, no nothing. The cigarette between his lips pulsed red and black, as if it were a beacon in the dying sunlight. His hand reached into a white plastic bag I recognized as Wonder Bread from the red, blue, and yellow dots on it. Like something out of a gothic novel, he was standing beneath a weeping tree whose bough arched over the water. Instead of bits and pieces of bread, he threw a whole slice of bread and watched the ducks descend on it and tear it to pieces.

The closer I approached, the more I saw how short Pinto was. The average

American male was five-foot-nine. I met the man in a car, so I had no idea about his height and weight. I look at him now, and think a damn good tailor had created the illusion of some heft and broad shoulders to Pinto. I wouldn't put it past him if he had had the steering wheel and dashboard in his jalopy lowered.

A lot of men in history were short. Napoleon was five-six, Picasso, five-four, and Beethoven, was five-three. Pinto weighed about a buck twenty-five and stood five feet in his brogues, if that. Meyer Lansky was also five-foot, and he was better at making money than Carnegie and U.S. Steel.

Another slice thrown, Pinto watched the ducks work themselves into a frenzy over the bread.

"You enjoy seeing them fight, don't you?" I said.

"Why should I make it easier for them?" He dusted his hands of crumbs.

"Darwin would've loved you," I said.

"I'd like a status report, and not a biology lecture, Mr. Cleary."

"Let's back up for one second," I said. "When I accepted this case, you asked me to shine a light on whatever I discovered on Ramírez. Your exact words. How about a little give and take here, a little push and pull? Can you tell why the Commissioner thought there was more to her death than an overdose?"

"I don't know why the commissioner thinks the way he does, Mr. Cleary."

"No, you wouldn't. You do whatever he says, like the dwarf in your book."

"I was honest when I said I don't know. What's with the question?"

"Because I think you're holding out on me. You put me on this case, you tell me you how you've been my guardian angel, but you don't say squat about leads, or how you saved my life. Then you sweeten the deal to come work for you by offering me my pension."

"Again, I was honest. The pension remains on the table, and I do have people looking after you, Mr. Cleary. You'll have to trust me on that."

Pinto spoke in a voice calm enough to beat a polygraph.

"Trust?" I said. "Someone tried to brain me at my office. Guess my guardian angel must've gotten his wings clipped, or your friends, the ones looking out for me, aren't so motivated to keep me alive. Did you know I was attacked in Park Plaza last year? Cops. Bill saved me that night, thanks to a shotgun he kept in the trunk of his car."

"Can we focus on the Ramírez case, please?"

"How does the Commissioner feel about dirty cops?"

"You think they're involved."

"Does a plant need sunlight?"

Pinto stood there, twisting and tying off the end to his Wonder bread.

"Last year. The case with Braddock and his wife. Remember it?"

Pinto asked questions like a lawyer. He knew the answers before he asked them.

"A rhetorical question. Asked and answered," I said.

"Your friend Bill asked you to look into a disappearance. You went to Bay Village to follow up on a lead, and you had an altercation. Correct?"

"Ambushed is a better word."

"A cop attacked you then, right?" He flicked his cheek, as if a bug had landed there. "A cop with a scar on his cheek."

"Same cop I saw at the station with Jimmy," I said. "Sonofabitch looked right through me, as if he had diplomatic immunity. So, you're saying the Commissioner knows about him?"

He waved a finger. "I didn't say that."

"Oh, then I must've missed something somewhere between *attacked* and *scar*, because I thought we were talking about bad police. What are you saying then?"

He faced me and, for a guy a foot shorter than me, his eyes met mine somehow.

"Ask yourself this, Mr. Cleary? You're ambushed, your word for the altercation, and yet you managed to survive. Ask yourself, how was that possible?"

"Easy. Jimmy showed up."

"With his cleaver."

"How did you know that?" I asked.

Pinto snapped his fingers. "Like that, Jimmy showed up at Bay Village in time to save you."

"So you're saying that you—"

"What can you tell me about Ms. Ramírez?"

"Park Plaza is infested with drugs, the people there aren't afraid of the pushers or their thugs."

"Dirty cops then?" Pinto asked.

"I need more time to prove it."

"I'll give you seventy-two hours, and we meet here."

Chapter Twelve: Bucket of Blood

It hurt to knock on this door and not because of the sore shoulder, the sore arm, sore everything. I had been jumped a block from my apartment.

It happened to the best of us at. Guy breathed in one too many drinks at the Rainbow Lounge, on the corner of Tremont and West Springfield streets, and he should expect a reward for his indulgence. Loosen the tongue, say the wrong thing to the wrong lady in any one of the bars, cafés, grilles, or lounges in the South End and the penalty was bruises, a fat lip and a black eye. That wasn't me, though.

I lost some blood, my .357, and my hat.

I rested against the doorframe. The volume on the television on the other side of the wood was loud and obnoxious with canned laughter. I winced and lifted my arm. Slim chance my weakened knock could compete against Bea Arthur as *Maude* on television. With a lame fist, I hammered the wood.

The lock turned and I pushed the door open. Nikos pulled me in. The sight of Nikos in his white Hanes t-shirt, matching boxers and his black socks would've cracked me up, but my ribs ached too much. Nikos whistled, said something in Greek before he guided me to his armchair. He moved the TV tray aside and let me collapse into a ratty wing chair that even Archie Bunker would've hated.

"I'll get you some ice."

Through the good eye I watched his dark feet scamper to the kitchen. My head lolled and then the kaleidoscope of images, such as the chain on the door, fluorescent coils on the ceiling, and the *TV Guide* and the remote control on the night table next to me.

On the far wall, a Felix the Cat clock blinked crazy eyes and swooshed his tail to count the seconds to the minute, to the next hour. Marie loved that fixture, and the creepy clock reminded me to feed Delilah.

Nikos instructed to hold the small bag of ice against my eye. He pushed his chair back and propped my feet up on the footrest. He was my doctor, my interrogator, and I was his patient and victim. "Bunch of punks rolled you?"

"No," I said and shifted away from the spring digging in my back.

"We ought to call the cops."

"I could do without the mutual admiration society." I must've sounded foggy because Nikos asked me to repeat myself. I did better. I told him the truth. "It was the cops."

"Are you sure?"

I relayed what I could remember. There were two of them. At first, I thought they were delinquents behind me, hungry for some fast cash. I knew I was wrong when I listened to their footsteps. Cops walk with a certain cadence, the way their shoes touched the ground. Next thing I experienced was a hood over my head. The black-bag treatment.

Not terribly original, but effective. Nobody talked so there's no way for me to identify voices. One pair of anonymous hands pinned my arms back and another worked my ribs and stomach. One shot to the face explained my eye. A round in boxing lasted three minutes. This didn't; they didn't. One of them treated me to a nightcap, a blackjack to the head. I woke up on the ground.

"You're lucky they didn't kill you," Nikos said.

"It was a message to get lost, stay lost, or else."

"Your latest case, I presume."

"One of them," I said. "Got any aspirin and some water?"

"Which case, or should I not ask?"

I didn't want to sink Nikos into the tar pit that was my life. I offered him the stenographer's version and I didn't want Nikos to know about Luisa and Park Plaza, so I said, "Arson. A slumlord named Faisal."

"The Syrian?"

"I'd rather not continue this conversation, if you don't mind."

Nikos padded his way to the kitchen. The freezer door made that sucking sound and slapped shut. Ice cubes dropped and rattled against glass. He handed me the water and told me to wait. A trip to the bathroom, another sound, the medicine cabinet this time, and I heard him shake the bottle to dispense pills.

"Bayer's is all I've got," he said in front of me, pills in his hand.

"Take it for pain. Take it for life."

Nikos looked at me weird.

"Slogan. Aspirin commercial."

"Shut up and take them. We need a drink."

After I'd swallowed aspirin and water, I tilted my head back and checked the landscape with hands. My nose was fine. All the cartilage was sound and intact. I moved my eyes up, down, and around. No floaters. My tongue counted teeth.

Nikos returned with two glasses, two ouzos over ice, the Greek answer to Italian sambuca, in one hand; another cold compress in the other. I accepted my glass and bag of ice. Nikos looked as if he wanted to say a few words before we made a toast.

"Some case, some message. Why not kill you?" he asked.

"A lot of reasons. Maybe the desk sergeant likes me, or nobody wants bad publicity."

Nikos studied me. His lips tightened and his dark eyes repeated the nurse's appraisal. He hadn't said a word about how bad I looked. I figured he'd let me discover that joy in the morning when I looked in the mirror. "Bad press for whom?" he asked. "The cops or The Syrian?"

"Take your pick."

"Think these two work for Faisal?"

"I have eyes on one cop in particular."

"You said two cops attacked you."

"I know what I said. My ribs can count, Nikos. Toast?"

Nikos held his glass out. I extended mine. We clinked. He toasted to our health in Greek. The ouzo went down fast. I wanted some sleep. "I need a favor."

"What?" Nikos asked.

"Delilah, my cat."

"I'll take care of her. Anything else?"

"Yeah, there is. When we talked, you said you'd know who to call if you needed matches for one of your buildings. I need names."

Nikos told me to get some sleep. He pointed to a bedroom.

The sounds of something sizzling, and the seductive scents of bacon and coffee lured me out of my sleep. I rubbed my temples and remembered everything. The alley. The beat-down. Nikos. Aspirin and the ouzo. There was the odd sensation of something next to me.

My eyes closed, a tail slapped my face. Delilah stepped onto my chest and issued a pathetic reprimand, along with cat breath. I apologized and rubbed a favorite spot behind her ear. She took to my chest like a baker did to dough. Knead. Need. Knead. Every claw performed the curl-and-release method of her penance and my flesh.

I turned my head and saw the bedside table. Nikos had left me two presents: my .38 and a note. I reached for the note and was reading it when Nikos entered the bedroom.

He handed me a cup of coffee. He pointed to my .38. "I thought you'd need it. Hope you don't mind I brought her here. She looked lonely."

"She always looks that way."

"Come out to the living room for eggs with toast."

I noticed the change of clothes he'd thrown over a nearby chair. All I needed was a close shave, and I'd look human again. I threw my legs over the side of the bed, so I could join Nikos for some breakfast in the other room. I took the cup of coffee.

Sunshine filtered through the window and hurt my eyes. Nikos handed me a piece of paper. He then kicked off his shoes, leaned back in his armchair, and put his feet up on the rest. Same black socks. "You asked for names, if I was ever tempted by insurance money. Remember? That list will keep you busy."

"Yeah, I remember," I said. "Thanks for this."

"You'd make a terrible parent, you know that?"

Delilah slinked into the room and meowed in agreement. I looked at her and her eyes narrowed. I sipped coffee. Nikos used a special coffee pot with a narrow neck. Boiled, stirred once, his coffee was strong enough to wake the dead. I started in on the eggs and saved the toast until I'd broken the yolks.

"Any of these names dangerous?" I asked.

"They're not what I would call voluble."

Nikos read a lot, which explained the vocabulary, the expensive substitute for talkative. Delilah walked over to the armchair. She looked up to find a landing so she could petition Nikos for affection. I had abandoned her. My ear rub was forgotten like a bad one-night stand. Nikos buried his fingers in fur and said, "You didn't tell me there was a body involved."

"Okay, there's a body involved."

"Read it in newspaper. One hell of a case you caught. Arson, potential insurance fraud, and maybe a murder."

I angled my buttered toast at an egg yolk when someone pounded on the door. Delilah jumped and bolted to somewhere unknown. "Expecting someone?" I asked and Nikos shook his head. "Were you followed?"

"How should I know? I'm not James Bond. I own a greasy spoon."

I told him to wait until I returned with my .38.

The thump on the door was louder on the second round. I suggested Nikos answer as I placed myself on the blind side of the doorframe, gun ready. He asked who it was. No answer. He looked over at me. I nodded. He turned the bolt but kept the chain on.

Nikos held the door ajar. "Yes?"

His profile paled. I heard sounds. Click. Click. I lowered the gun.

"Tony?"

"Morning, Cleary. I smell coffee. May I come in, or what?"

"How'd you find me here?" I asked.

Tony pointed to Nikos. "I followed this one from your apartment. Hard to miss with a cat carrier."

"You were sitting on my house?" I said.

"What's it to you? The boss asked me to keep an eye on you. Now, you going to let me in, or what?"

"Let him in," I said to Nikos. Tony stepped inside, cigarette unlit.

Tony Two-Times eyeballed the room, but it wasn't to admire the décor. Men like him were soldiers about windows, drawn curtains or blinds, entrances and exits. I could relate to the habit. Tony may not have seen a day of secondary school, but he calculated all the angles and the area of the apartment faster than any math teacher in the Commonwealth. He pocketed his lighter.

"Got anything for me?" he said.

"I might. Take a seat and we'll talk."

Tony didn't need a lighthouse to find the table and chair, but he chose to stand instead of sit. He peeled off his jacket and hung it over his arm. He had no shame about exposing the cannon he kept in a sling under his arm. Delilah slinked out, acting as if she wasn't scared. "Nice cat."

"Nicer piece there," I said. "Wouldn't have pegged you for a semi-automatic kind of guy. They're known to jam."

Nikos came and went to his kitchen. He handed us fresh coffee. The lack of sugar and cream was his subtle hint about not wanting us to linger in his home. Tony saw the note from Nikos. He picked it up and read it. His eyes avoided mine.

"Know any of those names?" I asked him.

"Matter of fact, I do."

"Has your boss ever used them?"

"Yeah, sure, but I can tell you right off this first name isn't good for the recent campfire." I wasn't about to ask why. I'd let Tony fill in the blank. "Guy is doing a stretch in Walpole."

"Off the list then. Second name?"

Tony's hand raised his cup of coffee. "Good coffee. This name here I've heard, but if I'm not mistaken the guy's got a leg in a cast on account of a skiing accident at Killington. I'll need to verify that for you."

"Do that, please. And the last name?"

"Boss would never use him. Guy is sloppy, and the Boss doesn't like sloppy."

I put out my hand for the paper. Tony gave it to me. I double-checked the last name while I sampled caffeine. Tony Two-Times watched me as I moved around him. "There's the sofa, Tony, you'll need to sit down for this."

The request threw the big man off. Nikos was doing the slow sip with his coffee. Delilah guarded the doorway to the kitchen. Tony got comfortable on the sofa, leaned back and said, "Have you got something for me or what?"

"Depends."

"Depends on what?"

"Can you tell me anything special about the don's kid?"

"Special, like what? You've got the description and last whereabouts. What else do you need...birthmark, freckles?"

"Tell me a little about this kid, like what his personality was like?"

Tony looked at me as if I had asked him to defend a doctoral thesis. He was not a man accustomed to baring his innermost thoughts. In his world and in that of most men on either side of the law these days, men went to work, provided for their families, and the family dog was their therapist.

They believed childhood belonged to mothers and that the home was a sanctuary. Every night ended in a gossamer haze of bedtime stories. Summers were full of sunshine and the sound of the Good Humor truck heard approaching from down the street. As long as their kids didn't go without and they had clothes on their backs and change in their pockets, they had done their jobs.

"What do you want me to say?" Tony asked. "He's family."

"Enough with the Sicilian vow of silence. It's not like I'm asking you if he violated the Mann Act. What was he like?"

"It goes like this," Tony said in slow, deliberate words. "I picked him up once at school, and he was ashamed that a kid on the playground had picked on him."

"A bully, so what?" I said. "Everyone's had one of them in their life."

"You don't understand. That don't fly in our world. We teach our kids that when someone does something to you, then you come at them three

96

times as hard so they think twice about messing with you again."

"And who taught him that?" I asked.

"Everybody, on account of his father. He disappeared."

"He ran off?"

Tony's face darkened. "I didn't say that. I said he disappeared. Anyhow, I tried and the don tried, but nothing stuck because the kid got beat on, and then he'd start doing to kids what'd been done to him. He'd been kinda of sweet until he started doing that."

"Doing what?" I asked.

"You dense or something? Bullying 'em, like he had something to prove."

I could have said something about the kid's desire to gain their respect, be thought of as a man, but I didn't push it because what Tony admitted to me had been hard work for him, and not even the most sadistic shrink or guards at Bridgewater State Hospital would've gotten as much out of him. Now that I had this information, the toughest question came next.

I hated asking personal details. The less I knew, the better. Distance helped form objectivity. This case, I didn't ask for it, but nobody refused the don. Phillip Marlowe disliked cases involving adultery or bad marriages, but I took them when it paid the rent. Burbank Street was a good example. It was fast, dirty as in unpleasant, and she paid me well for my time and the extra effort. I don't care for cases involving kids, either. Unless you're a rattlesnake, there's enough heartbreak all around as a PI.

"Jewelry," I said. "Did the kid wear a ring?"

The tough guy's face wrinkled in confusion, as if he'd sniffed propane gas.

"Specifically, did this kid wear a ring on his pinky?"

"Yeah. A crucifix ring, like Mr. B used to wear, you know, on his pinky before…"

"He lost it," I said.

That small detail about the kid's ring would not have been in the papers. Elbows on his thighs now, Tony did the math and put his cup of coffee down. His hands moved to the sides of his head next and his fingers did small circles against his scalp, as if a bad headache was coming.

"This is bad. This is really bad," he said. Tony sighed long and hard. "I don't want to be the one to have tell the old man. Why the hell was the kid in that building?"

I tipped back some coffee. I wanted to relish this rare advantage over the gangster.

"I'll tell Mr. B, but I need a favor from you first."

Big, meaty hands and palms up, and all I could picture were those paws taped up, gloves on, and my head pounded into mush if this backfired on me. Tony Two-Times did favors for Italians, with Italians, and everyone else went into the spit bucket.

"Meet me at Foley's Café tomorrow night?"

"Which one? Downtown or your neck of the woods?"

"My neighborhood. East Berkeley Street. Say curbside, around eight?"

"Not for nothing, Cleary, but don't you think a wop like me walking into a place like that will stand out?"

"I'm counting on it. We've got ourselves a deal, then?"

"Yeah, we do," Tony said and rose from the sofa. We didn't have to shake on it. We both understood what was at stake. "Hope you know what you're doing. I can't hold him off much longer. He wants answers."

"Just to be clear, Tony," I said, "the don gets the bad news from me. I'll see you at Foley's tomorrow. Understood?"

"Whaddya think, I'm an idiot or something? That's not why they call me Two-Times. I'll see you eight sharp."

Our eyes met. I'd play the messenger, and if this played out wrong we'd both need pallbearers. The promise to meet Tony at Foley's ate into my seventy-two hours Pinto had given me.

Chapter Thirteen: Vaseline Alley

I made the bed, showered and shaved, and started the day later than I'd expected. I used the phone in the bedroom and sat down on the bed. I dialed the number and leaned back against the headboard.

"Mercury Answering Service. This is Dot."

I said my name and she let out a little sigh, the kind your mother made when she was disappointed with you. Dorothy was single and without children, but she leveled disappointment with expertise.

"Something wrong, Dorothy?"

"I know you're a private investigator and all, but I don't understand how you stay in business when your clients don't bother to leave a name and a number."

"The message, please."

"First, it was the man and the ducks. I've wondered whether you're in the spy business, Mr. Cleary, because your clientele leave the most cryptic messages."

"Another man, another mysterious voice, I gather?"

"The opposite, I'm afraid. This time a woman called. Enigmatic, just the same."

"What did Miss Grey on Vague say?"

"Room 420."

I tried to speak but my voice was caught in my throat.

"Are you alright, Mr. Cleary?"

Hearing the apartment number jolted me.

"Fine," I said and rubbed the back of my skull. "It's okay, if there's no number. I know who it is."

"Of course, you do. You're the PI."

"Please tell me how she said it?"

"Excuse me? She simply said four-twenty."

"She did, yes, but how? Did she sound scared? Was her voice shaky?"

"Well, now that you mention it. She did sound upset, but the call was so brief."

"You done good," I said. "When did she leave the message? The time and date."

Dot told me and I clenched my eyes shut. Somehow someone knew I'd been around Park Plaza asking questions, and they moved in fast on Apartment 418. She called and left a message, which was a good sign. She was alive.

"One last thing, Dot, and try very hard to remember. When she left the message, did you hear anything in the background?"

"No, nothing at all."

I wasn't sure whether that was a good or bad thing. What it meant, though, was there was no screaming child in the room. She'd balanced that kid on her hip and consoled him when I, a stranger, knocked on the door. If something terrible happened to his babysitter, the kid would've been a four-alarm fire in a two-year-old body.

Or he could be with his mom.

I hung up the phone. I banged the back of my head against the headboard. I deserved it. Whatever happened at Park Plaza occurred in a small window of time, and I was responsible. I traced the sequence of events.

I had left my card under her door. I met with Pinto within the hour. Something happened in the interim. She called me, talked with Dot, and left her message. A lead will sometimes call to say they had forgotten something I might find useful. Not her. Not this time.

I was ambushed later that night. Coincidence or not, whoever rattled her had eyes on us. They'd have a car sitting on the building.

Which meant I couldn't just walk through the front door.

I thought about what to do next. Dorothy had proven herself as observant as Spade's secretary Effie Perrine, more than just a number-taker and a parrot for messages. I had to feed her questions, sure, but she had enough recall to help me and the resident whose name I gleaned from a mailbox for Apartment 418.

Isabella Rivera.

I contemplated the room while I holstered my snub-nose revolver. The bedroom was dark as a hangover. The décor was asexual and ecclesiastical. A Shaker would've had no objection to the bureau and its five drawers. There was an Orthodox triptych on the dresser. The somber faces in each panel would've discouraged any impure thoughts. The cross above the highboy pinned a brittle palm frond to the wall

The clock on the nightstand, hands frozen at three o'clock, was a Westclox with Art Deco numbers. There was a chair and a door to a closet. There were two windows, one where a tree obscured a view to the street, the other a peeper's delight with a lace curtain panel.

Across the street I could see another window, and half of a naked woman with long brown hair inside the frame. I watched her lean over and disappear, and then snap back into view, the hair in motion like a wave, which her hand grabbed, twisted into a ponytail and tied off with a rubber band.

My heart won't forget the things it should. I thought of Cat Braddock and my fling with Gloria, the waitress from the diner. I realized two things. First, I had a sex life but no love. Second, Nikos had given me his room. I'd forgotten the older generation slept in separate beds, like Lucy and Ricky Ricardo.

I called John in Central Square and asked to borrow his car. I wanted to visit Apartment 418, and assess the situation, and do it fast. Like a good friend, he could tell from my voice that I wouldn't be asking if it weren't serious. He told me to swing by the bar for the keys.

Which I did.

John used to drive a gold Cutlass, but he traded it in for a blue Chrysler New Yorker with a vinyl top, sunroof, Corinthian leather interior, and 8-track stereo. John tinkered with the engine on weekends, so the car had muscle and swagger. In addition to speed, I choose the car for a reason. Park that land yacht in Park Plaza and it'd blend in with whatever the pushers and pimps used.

He looked good with the car. It wasn't what I would've picked if I owned a car myself. I couldn't be bothered with driving in the winter, watching a vehicle depreciate in value as the salt on the road ate the underbody of the car to nothing but gristle, and I didn't have the biceps like John did to maintain the roof with regular sessions of Armor All.

When I skirted the perimeter of the plaza, I noticed an ordinary Plymouth, and two ordinary guys inside, as in ordinary for thugs from South Boston, except two things didn't jibe with their presentation. These guys dressed the part, like Bobbsey Twins, in their matching leather jackets, turtlenecks, and gold chains around said turtlenecks. The haircut, however, was regulation BPD. The cherry on top was when I looked at the plates. These mooks were either undercover, or these two from Southie purchased the car at a police auction. That the car was the latest and greatest model said, highly unlikely.

I parked behind Isabella Rivera's building in Vaseline Alley.

Every city has at least one Vaseline Alley. Boston has several. This was the place for quick sex, up against the wall, out of sight and away from the harsh winter wind. I suppose it could be fun, once, if it weren't for the other forms of night life that liked to use the alley for drugs and drink. Vaseline Alley was where you found the discarded bottles of boozehounds, syringes shared by addicts, spent rubbers, and rats.

Like Jimmy, I hated rats.

The back door took a little work, but I managed to pry it open, and walked up the four flights to Isabella's apartment. The hallway was quiet. Too quiet. I knocked on her door and said my name softly through the wood. She opened it, chain in place, and then closed it again to undo it and let me in.

Inside, I saw the kid in a high chair, SpaghettiOs smeared all over his face, and a can of Chef Boyardee on the counter. I said hello to Isabella. We had matching shiners. She'd been worked over, and there was no foundation or makeup tricks from any of the Hollywood studios or experts at *Cosmopolitan* magazine that could hide it.

"I didn't tell them anything," she said.

"Them?" I said. "How many were there?"

She held up two fingers.

"If it took two guys to give you a shiner, I'd love to see what you did to them."

She sort of smiled at my wisecrack, my attempt to lighten the mood, but my smirk dropped when she put a hand to her face. The back of her hand looked as if it had dated rough concrete. I lifted my chin, and asked without asking.

"Cheese grater from the kitchen. I didn't say one word about you."

"Cops?" I asked, and she nodded.

She was tough, and I'd hesitate to step into the ring with her. The kid, who was quiet, recognized me. He waved. I waved. He resumed eating and creating Abstract Art with his food.

"Follow me," I said and she did. We visited the window. I pulled the curtain aside.

"Those two down there?" Another nod. "The one in the driver's seat attacked me."

"What's the scene here?"

"They're protection for the local dealer."

"For a cut of the action, they look the other way, I get it."

I released the curtain and let it drift when the car door opened. Passenger exited first and then the driver. Words were exchanged. The uneven walk, the lump under his left arm said the driver was packing. He glanced up to our window. I was certain he didn't see us but I wasn't taking any chances.

"You and the kid, road trip. Now."

"Huh?"

She hadn't moved so I grabbed her by the arm and walked her back to the kitchen.

I lifted the kid up, and placed him in her arms. I told her to wash his face and to get a jacket on him. We were going out the backdoor. I took a kitchen chair and angled it on its rear legs and jammed the top rail under the doorknob of the front door. It wouldn't stop them but it'd buy us time.

She baby-talked the kid, and coaxed him into his coat. She moved fast, but the kid was a kid, and moved like there was all the time in the world. Women and mothers have patience, men don't. We were leaving now.

"What will his mother think when she comes home from work, and finds us missing?"

"We can worry about her later." I pointed to the kid. "They'll harm him this time."

She didn't answer, instead she grabbed her purse on the counter. I figured she needed her keys, wallet, and whatever else women kept inside their handbags.

We hotfooted our way out the door to the end of the hallway, towards the stairwell for our exit, to the street below and John's car.

The kid was compliant and quiet. He probably thought of this as some grand adventure, or a rerun of *Batman*, with me as Batman, babysitter Isabella as Catwoman, and him as Robin. Down and around the stairwell we went.

Fourth floor.

Third floor.

I stopped because I heard footsteps.

It could be a building resident.

It could be someone coming inside for a drink, for a shot, or to rob a tenant.

I leaned over the railing, careful not to expose myself.

I saw a hand, the barrel of a revolver. I squinted because I couldn't believe it. Same length, 4-inches, and same blue-steel. A .357 magnum.

I put my finger to my lips to signal silence and I motioned to her that she and the kid should go back up the stairs and wait behind the door to the third floor there. She mouthed, "What about you?" I gave her the okay sign. Women and children, first. She pivoted and, to her credit, moved fast without a sound, and opened and closed the door like a cat burglar.

I kept an eye on my friend below and didn't move until I had to. I moved fast and joined her and the kid. We waited behind the door, my .38 drawn.

I listened, and waited. I guessed the number of steps he'd have to take until he passed our door. I prayed I'd gotten the count right. I eased the door and came up behind him. He sensed my presence, but I was faster, and came down hard on the back of his head with the butt of my revolver.

He wasn't out cold, but dazed and confused. I kicked the gun away from him and picked it up. I examined the .357. Either we shared the same taste, the same dislike for the original walnut grip, or I won the jackpot of coincidences.

Same heft. Same Eagle grips, checkered coke bottle with S&W medallions. Same .357 I had lost when I was jumped on the way home.

Chapter Fourteen: Evasive Maneuvers

The doors clapped shut and I turned the engine over and used the hood ornament as a rifle sight and aimed for the end of the alley. The metal door to the building flung open and banged hard against the concrete. The cop ran for the car, a radio in his hand. I stepped on the gas. I had been so concerned with the gun, I had never thought to frisk him, and now he was communicating our position to his partner on the other side of the building.

Whatever work John had done on the engine saved us. The Chrysler New Yorker sang over the asphalt. The motor growled and then purred and accelerated down the lane until suddenly, another car came into view.

The blue Plymouth, our other cop.

I cut the wheel to the left so he wouldn't T-bone us. I clipped his fender and, for a second, our cars were locked in a deadly tango, cheek to cheek. I could see him and he could see us. I turned the wheel to the right to push him off us. There was the screech of metal on metal as I scraped a layer of paint off the left side of his car, and drove him to the sidewalk across the street. It didn't work. He stepped on the brake and put himself behind us for a game of Steve McQueen on the streets.

I looked to the passenger side. She was okay, the kid was alright, and my stolen gun was tucked under the armrest, asleep. I checked the rearview mirror. The Plymouth stood idle in the middle in the street. The driver's partner hopped in. The street was empty, and the light ahead was green and would turn amber soon. I accelerated to leave him with a red light.

I wanted the company of other drivers on the road, the safety of the herd, if these two planned to chase us. I looked up into the mirror. They'd made it through the light before it turned red, too.

I decided I'd do one big loop around the Common, including the Garden, and blend in with the other cars until I came up with a better idea. Returning to Nikos's with cops on our tail was out of the question and it would jeopardize his safety. Those cops would lay the hurt on Nikos and add his real estate to their drug trade.

I thought of the movie *Jaws*. Bruce the shark ate and swam and swam and ate. He had to move or he'd die. So did I. So did we.

The ebb and flow of pedestrians, the green light to red light to green light, kept them off me. I counted on the mesmerized tourists to the Public Garden and the Common, the lost and confused map readers in search of the Granary Burying Ground to frustrate them. I relied on the flocks of shoppers walking uphill, away from Downtown Crossing, bags in hand from Filene's and Jordan Marsh to act as a barrier between us and the rogue cops.

I kept on moving and they followed. He tried once to come up on my side, but I blocked him with a lane change. I decided I'd do one last loop. I let the gravity of Beacon Street give the car additional speed until I could cut a sharp turn onto Arlington Street, another hard left onto Boylston, sprint up Charles Street and back to Beacon, where I'd fake him out into thinking I'd do another round of the Garden.

I wouldn't. I didn't. As he sped up, I darted for Storrow Drive.

With the Charles River and MIT on our immediate right, Storrow Drive was New England's answer to NASCAR, except there were no rules. Road signs meant nothing. Every year, the news channels reported the same type of accident, the kind where a bridge acted as a can opener and peeled the top off of a truck because the driver thought his rig could clear the height of the overpass. Lane changes on Storrow Drive come out of nowhere for the untried, and the sudden EXIT ONLY confused everyone but the seasoned Bostonian driver.

I breathed a steady rhythm, hands and fingers tight on the wheel. I put eyes on the rearview mirror, then the sideview mirror for the car behind me. We were in the far-right lane. There was a truck in the middle lane with another car behind it. All the exits on Storrow Drive were on the left side of the highway. We were two miles away from Park Plaza, but in Massachusetts, on the road or on the T, those two miles were forever far and away. I wanted these two cops to think I'd ride the right lane all the way to Cambridge.

They took the bait and goosed the gas to overtake the truck. They planned to ride up behind me and force me off the road. I had a different idea.

I cut the wheel left, crossed the lane in front of the truck, and into the lane for the exit for Fenway Park. The trucker didn't have time to hit the brakes. He maintained his course, and our dirt bag friends had no choice but to stay on Storrow Drive. I coasted through the exit, smooth as a pinball rounded the curve and scored points.

"I can't believe it. We lost them." She reached over and hugged me and kissed me on the cheek. "Now what?" she asked.

It was a great question and reminded me of a multiple-choice pop quiz that included the dreaded essay. I couldn't take them to my office or my place in Union Park, because that was unwise. Anybody who wanted me could find me there. I could ask Nikos but now was not the best time. I looked around, familiar with the area because of Bill, and decided on my course of action. The place I had in mind was the least likely place to find a woman and child. I was then left with a more serious headache. I needed a plastic surgeon for John's Chrysler. I glanced over at the kid, who seemed drowsy, ready to nod off.

"You're going to be okay," I told her. "I've got an idea."

I don't think she believed me. I slowed the car down on Charlesgate and stayed to the right so the street changed to Boylston Street. She leaned forward and turned the dial for the radio. She didn't search for a favorite station. She accepted whatever was playing. The first few bars to a Four Seasons song played, and I shut it off. She shot me a surprised look. I had acted impulsive, rude, and I was embarrassed. "Sorry," I said. "Bad memories."

"Girlfriend?"

"Worse."

She noticed I had angled the car to the curb.

"Hope you're open-minded," I said.

She read the address aloud. "Twelve Seventy. What is this place?"

The answer to her question was the couple leaving the building. Arm in arm. Adam was in black boots, Levi jeans encased in leather chaps, and a white t-shirt, while Steve wore construction boots, tube socks, short shorts, and a half-shirt that exposed Chippendale abs. Adam sported dark hair and a thick moustache while Steve was blonde as a Malibu bunny with feathered hair.

"Afraid to ask, but how do you know this place?"

"My friend Bill is gay and a cop."

I didn't have time to explain my history with Bill. The car attracted attention. There was the dented headlight, the damaged fender and a side that looked as if Delilah had dragged her nails down the length of the car. If I'm lucky on payday, Mr. B and Jimmy will help me settle the bill for the facelift and bodywork this car needed. I might break even, since I had to settle my accounts with Bill for research and with JC for whatever he might've found on that Medical Examiner in Worcester. I unlocked the doors and took the keys out of the ignition. She said the kid was asleep and offered to carry him inside.

The 1270 was four floors of decadence, with a roof deck. We were on the ground floor. The first floor swung both ways, tame enough that straights wandered in to enjoy the jazz pianist and his ensemble. If a drag queen served them martinis, they thought it was cute and something to scandalize their in-laws with over Sunday brunch.

The remaining floors were full of mantraps, the stuff of Tiberius and Caligula, and if all of that weren't enough, the rowdier crowd traveled back and forth between the club and the leather bar down the street. Bill called the 1270's second floor Orgy Town, and left out the details. The third and fourth floors, Bill said, were more of the same, but the music changed with the party drugs and theme. The music varied from the nihilistic rage of punk to funk, to disco grooves and pop rock. The roof deck was for fresh air.

I came here once with Bill. People glittered, people swayed and the music pulsed. Some revelers took poppers while they danced, others mellowed out in the corners with disco-biscuits, or what the suburbanites called Quaaludes. Fashion styles ran high and the boys were competitive about boas and bellbottoms and ruffles. Nobody dressed the same twice, and everybody came for a slice of couture and the cat walk.

Cops knew about the Twelve Seventy and other gay clubs. Club owners paid cops for protection. The Boston PD didn't care so long as the adventurous and curious didn't hurt anyone, and they seldom did. Everyone lived out their secrets and desires and cash washed away the morality.

We walked over to the bar. A blond rocker behind the counter was cleaning glasses, his shirt splayed open and his mane of hair was shaggier than Robert Plant's. The drinking age in Massachusetts was eighteen, and I'd put him at a precocious sixteen.

"You the bartender?"

"Who's asking?"

"Not a trick question," I said, and pointed to Isabella. "She'll have a club soda with a twist, and give the kid a Shirley Temple if he wakes up."

"Hey," Isabella said to me. "I can order for myself, thank you very much." She turned to the kid, "I'll have a JD, double, and my friend the chauvinist here is paying."

"Yes, ma'am."

"Don't call me ma'am."

I left a bill on the counter. "Is Dan in?"

His eyes lifted and indicated the far side of the room after he snatched the Lincoln on the wood. I checked the mirrored wall behind him. Dan the owner had emerged from his office, but didn't see me yet. His office was small as a roach trap, complete with a desk, a phone, and a filing cabinet he parked onto a dolly. I inquired once about the rigged set-up. He said if he was ever raided he could wheel all of his accounting down the hallway and into the alleyway. I asked him, "What happens if you don't have enough time?" He held up a book of matches, and pulled open one of the drawers. I peeked inside and understood.

Flash paper. Bookies used it.

He'd drop a lit match and his records went poof. No evidence.

Dan was the oddball of the Twelve Seventy. He was straight.

I watched Dan work the room, greeting patrons and pretend he was listening to their latest news. Then he looked up. Dan saw Isabella and the kid. He crossed the room in double-time. "What the hell, Cleary?"

"Relax, but I need your help."

Dan didn't hear a word of what I'd said. "This is no place for a kid."

"Says the man who has a minor behind the bar," I said.

The gears in Dan's brain grinded down to a halt. "Need my help with what?"

"A place for them to stay for the night. It's temporary, I promise."

"Do I look like a Holiday Inn to you?"

Dan and I both knew he kept a flop room. He was older than his revelers and he confessed to me that he'd sometimes sneak a cat nap. I assumed the room he kept was clean and PG-rated. Perfect for one night, or until I can get Bill to collect them, whichever came first. All I needed from Dan was his hospitality.

"I need these two here, maybe one other person, where nobody will look for them."

"One night becomes two, and now you're asking me to shoehorn another person?"

"Maybe," I said.

"Nobody can't say you don't have balls."

"C'mon, Dan. I'm in a jam. What do you say?"

The table nearest us looked up from their game of canasta. Two couples played against another couple, the two decks of cards spread out on the table. I had not known canasta could be played that way. The clear stuff in their highballs was water, or gin or vodka. They played and listened to every word.

"I'll have Bill take them off your hands as soon as possible, I promise."

Dan pointed to the kid and his sigh of exasperation was legit. "But a kid?"

"In a jam, like I said."

Sweat beaded on Dan's forehead, and he fidgeted as if he'd snorted his fourth cup of coffee. Like I said, Dan wasn't gay but he could mimic Paul Lynde. "If you haven't noticed, this isn't *Mister Rogers' Neighborhood.*"

I put my hand on Dan's shoulder and turned him away from the bar and tried a different approach. "The girl, her name is Isabella. She's the kid's babysitter. You've got a room full of grandfathers here, and they'll occupy her and the kid. You don't have to do a thing. Buy them dinner, find a television set, and give the gal the key for trips to the bathroom. C'mon, Dan. Consider this a favor, man, and I'll put in a good word with our mutual friend."

His face and mood changed at the thought I'd speak to Mr. B for him.

"A favor?" Dan said.

"A favor."

"Because I've got a problem with the bar down the street. People are talking, you know."

"Losing money to them, is that it?" I asked.

"As if," Dan said. He curled a finger and invited me closer. "You might want to advise Tony Two-Times to reconsider where he keeps his storage."

"Storage?" I said. "What the hell are you talking about, Dan?"

"You didn't hear it from me, understand?"

"Let's hear it," I said.

"Storage, as in bodies in the basement."

Chapter Fifteen: Not for Nothing

Tuesday was young and I had time to talk with Isabella before the crowd filtered in. She told me where the kid's mother worked, and I told Bill where to find her. I fed him the name Toni Ruiz and told him that I was with Isabella and the kid. He remembered their last names, Ruiz and Rivera, from the tags on the mailboxes on the second floor. The description Isabella gave of the tyke's mother was easy enough to convey to him. Toni Ruiz was the youngest waitress there. Bill, however, balked when I insisted he wear his uniform.

Bill worked Vice, sometimes Narcotics. He loved it, and the brass appreciated his collars because he made them look good on paper and at meetings. Bill moved between the two departments, like an interlibrary loan. Bill undercover was a cross between the Marlboro Man without the horse and a leather boy with his motorcycle. I pushed hard to make the sale.

"She'll see a cop in beat blues, Bill. What's not to trust?"

"Excuse me, but didn't you just tell me the people in Park Plaza were scared of cops?"

"Cops on the take, yes. Cops who work with pushers, yes, but do you think those cops were wearing uniforms? No. The answer is no, Bill. Wear your blues so she trusts you. How else are you going to convince the woman to come with you?"

"Simple. I tell her I know where her kid is."

"And you dressed undercover, like you're on a sting as a hustler, would end the conversation before it began. She'll think you kidnapped her son, which is why I say wear the uniform, which brings me to my next request."

"You do know how to pile it on. What is it?"

"Bring her to the Twelve-Seventy."

"You're killing me, Shane Cleary. A cop dressed as a cop walking into a gay club."

"Hey, not my fault you're in the closet. Tell your friends it's Family Night."

"Address where this Toni Ruiz works?"

"Between Harvard and Porter Square. Sixteen-eighty-eight Mass Ave."

"Cambridge. Got a name for the place?"

"Nick's Beef and Beer House, but there's something you should know."

"Always something with you, Shane. Does she work there, or not?"

"She does. You won't miss her."

"Because she's the youngest gal there. What's this something I should know?"

"Look for the sign instead of the street number."

I couldn't lie. It was true. Everyone in Massachusetts used landmarks.

"Got it. I'll look for the sign," Bill said. "What else?"

"The sign doesn't say Nick's Beef and Beer."

"What then?"

"Eef and Bee Ho," I said.

"Let me guess, Nick fell off, and the missing letters give the place character?"

"Oh, the place has character."

"My turn to torment you," Bill said. "Remember the list of names from the second floor Park Plaza you gave me? I've got something for you."

"Those names were for safekeeping, in case something happened to me. I didn't ask you to do research."

"I didn't. This is more of a comment, in case you had asked me to do research. I hate to break it to you but those names on your list, especially Ruiz and Rivera, are common Hispanic last names, like our Smith and Jones. And that educational moment, my friend, was brought to you by WGBH Boston, the power of public information."

"I had that coming to me, thanks," I said.

"I'll pick up the waitress and take her to the Twelve-Seventy. Then what?"

"She'll stay the night with the babysitter and kid. I talked to Dan."

"Then what?"

"I need to find them a safe house."

"It's always an unexpected pleasure with you, Shane Cleary," Bill said and hung up.

Without knowing it, Bill had given me an unexpected lead with his tidbit about Hispanic last names.

Where Nick's Beef and Beer House was short on letters in their sign, it stretched the dollar. There were few places where you could find a monstrous double cheeseburger with fries for under three bucks, and beer that tasted like beer and didn't make you feel like the middle man between the bar and the bathroom.

Graduate students on stipends, the university's idea of minimum wage, went there for the generous food portions and construction workers and the wayward businessman slummed there for a liquid lunch. The crowd flowed in and out of the place, buttons unbuttoned or belts loosened for a glutton's feast, and everyone said, to hell with cholesterol today and say hello to the cardiac ward at Mass General tomorrow.

Nick's was known for waitresses with an attitude. The old girls there, who controlled the floor had stories to tell about how tough women had it before, during, and after the war. You didn't know half of the time whether it was World War One, Two, or the Civil War, but nobody challenged them, not even the macho construction workers who whistled at anything in a skirt. If one of these dames sat at your table while you were eating, cigarette between her lips so she could add up the bill, you'd let her and liked it.

People came for the cheap food and because they made you feel like family. They'd give advice if you asked for it. They'd give you a hug if you needed it. They worked hard, these women. They carried more pitchers of beers on any given day than Brigitte did during Oktoberfest. When one of them died, people came to their funeral and the tears were sincere.

Toni Ruiz worked there for two reasons, according to Isabella. One was to pay her for babysitting her kid. The second was to save enough coin to get her and her child out of Park Plaza. I suspected another reason why she wanted to flee the sewer.

Bill had unintentionally dropped a clue on me, but I couldn't confirm my theory until we met. Not for nothing, there's a lot to a name, even the most common one.

Chapter Sixteen: Strike A Match

When Tony Two-Times followed Nikos home and we talked over coffee, Tony had reduced the list of arsonists from Nikos to one name.

I traced the name to a small side street off Harvard Ave in Allston. For a man in his thirties, he rented out a small cell inside a beehive of students. Named after an American painter, famous for its stockyards, Allston was famous for students too poor to afford housing at Boston University or Harvard, and for having the easiest zip code to remember in the Commonwealth, 02134.

This brother of the flame would've blended in with all the undergraduates and post-docs if it weren't for his fashion sense long past the expiration date, with scuffed Buster Brown shoes and frayed laces, a dingy white dress shirt, and a faded tie around his neck. I watched and waited, hoping he'd show up or leave his apartment when I spotted him.

I stepped out of John's banged up New Yorker and shut the door quietly. Someone else, yards away from me and up the street, didn't. He slammed his car door closed louder than Cap'n Crunch cereal. I watched the big lug lumber down the uneven sidewalk toward me. Tony Two-Times.

"What the hell are you doing here?" I asked him.

"I could ask you the same."

"Following up on a lead, which you kindly gave me, and you?"

"I figured as much, so I shadowed you."

"Since Park Plaza?" I asked and he nodded. I shook my head in disbelief. "I could've used backup."

"If it were related to Mr. B's case, I would have." Tony pointed to the apartment complex. "This, however, is relevant."

"Thanks."

"Nice car, by the way," Tony said. "Good luck getting it fixed."

"You're going to help me get it fixed."

"In your dreams, Cleary."

"At least tell me why were you tailing me?"

Tony Two-Times was not only fast on his feet for a man of his size, but he had surveillance down better than Hoover's best men. I'd never seen him at Park Plaza and I doubted his victims did either. "I've been seeing a lot of you lately," I told him.

"Life ain't so good on the homestead with Mr. B. The old man loved the kid and he's making everyone miserable."

We came up on Larry Getz, who was as oblivious as Fredo Corleone was of the two guys crossing Mott Street to whack his father at the fruit stand. Hand inside his pocket, Getz searched for his keys. It came up shaking; the keys jingled as he tried to get the key inside the lock.

"You must be something with matches," I said. He turned, surprised. His keys clattered to the floor. "Better pick those up, Larry."

He did. "Who are you and what do you want?"

"Name is Shane Cleary. This is my friend. We need to talk. Inside would be nice."

He opened the door and then tried something stupid. He attempted to bolt into the lobby and slam the door in my face. I grabbed a hold of his cheap tie and didn't let go. I muscled my way inside and Tony shut the door behind us. Leash in hand, I walked Getz to his apartment and told him to unlock the door, which he did, and Tony shoved him inside. We made a good team.

"Are you a cop?" he asked.

"I was."

A fast scan of the place revealed an American Tourister blue suitcase on the bed, open like a clam. Socks and underwear formed a fort around shirts and slacks in the center. "Going somewhere?" I asked.

"None of your business."

"Don't be like that, Larry. A defensive attitude helps no one." I saw a men's magazine on the edge of the bed. "Let me guess, you read it for the articles?"

"As a matter of fact, I do, you judgmental prick."

Tony smacked Larry on the side of the head. "Be nice."

"What did you do that for?" Larry said, rubbing his head. "I wasn't lying. There's a great short story from Stephen King in there. The man is a master of the horror genre."

I did the quick flip of pages and found King. There was fright on the left, Miss Bottomless, on the right. Heebie-jeebies and smut do go together. Modern publishing had learned something from Freud. I threw the magazine on the bed. "Let's talk horror, Larry, because your life is about to become a nightmare."

I took hold of his tie again, reeled him in, grabbed him by the throat and squeezed. His eyes bulged and his face turned red. I shoved him. He landed on the bed; the springs creaked. He coughed and sputtered.

"You and I are going to have a talk," I said.

I pulled up a chair. He put his back to the wall, arms crossed and legs splayed. A well-placed heel would've put an end to his bravado. I noticed a square matchbox nearby and picked it up.

"Like matches, Larry?" I pushed the tray and chose a match from the box. I showed it to him. "These are good and reliable for lighting the stove's pilot light."

I scraped the match across the coarse surface on the side of the box. We watched it together. Once the spark disappeared, the flame changed from a light blue to red and then orange.

"Beautiful, isn't it? This flame," I said to Larry, who sat there mesmerized. I handed him the live match. "Here, hold it."

He held the matchstick until the fire ate up the rest of the wood. He blew it out, and you'd think his puppy had died. Larry sat there, forlorn and glassy-eyed. I inhaled deeply and exhaled. "I love that scent, don't you?"

Larry nodded and licked his lips.

"Nothing like the smell of a wood-burning fireplace on a cold winter night."

Larry closed his eyes and breathed in deep. I could tell he was fantasizing. I allowed the man his moment of ecstasy. I waited until he opened his eyes so he could see I had an unlit match between my fingertips for him. "You want to light one, don't you?"

"May I?"

I lit his match and extinguished it. It was cruel of me, a real tease, but all part of the game and much better than Interrogation 101 the cops used on suspects.

"Why did you do that?" he asked.

"Because I'm disappointed in you, Larry."

His face drooped. Confront a man with his addiction, his obsession, and he'll do whatever you want in order to appease the demon in his blood. The problem was that same addict will tell you whatever you want to hear.

"Disappointed in me, how?" Larry asked, a touch of the tongue to wet his lips again.

"Tell me how you do it, Larry."

"Do what?" he said, confused like I wanted him.

My eyes did a panoramic sweep of the apartment. "You live in this dump, surrounded by college students, in a buildings owned by Boston's worst landlord."

"It's cheap."

"Here's a curious question for you," I said to him as I placed the head of the next match against the red strip.

Larry's eyes widened. "What's your question?"

"Did you know there was a body in the building?"

"Body?" His voice and mood darkened. "I don't know what you're talking about."

"Yeah, you do." I shot upright when he stood up. "You read it in the paper and you panicked, didn't you?" I pointed to the luggage. "That's why you're ready to bolt out of Dodge." He moved, and I grabbed and squeezed his flabby arm. "Didn't you look around to see whether the place was empty, Larry? Did you even look?"

120

He pulled his arm away. I let him pace, I let his feet work the floorboards, I let him calm down. Cops think they have to hammer a suspect. They don't. They'll badger and confuse, mock and mislead a suspect. They'll get a confession, but not the truth. The legal system was more about Daylight Saving Time than it was about justice. Save time. Save paper. Cops were taught to make life easier for the DA. You told the suspect if he doesn't confess, if he doesn't take the deal, the DA will come down twice as hard on him for not accepting his offer. Larry returned to his bed and sat down.

"I read about it in the *Globe*," he said. His eyes were wet and bloodshot now. "I didn't know, I swear. The job was to torch the building, and only that. I was told it was empty."

"And you believed him?" I said.

"You didn't think to check?" Tony asked.

"Why wouldn't I believe him?" he said. "There was no body. I swear. You believe me, don't you?"

I shook my head. Something didn't add up. Larry wasn't a good liar.

"I want to, Larry," I said. "I really do, but there was a body. Tell me more about the job."

I could see where this was headed. He was distracted, about to panic. Larry slapped his forehead. "I am so stupid. Idiot. How did I get myself into this mess?"

"Focus, Larry. Tell me about the job."

"I was told it was a standard insurance gig."

"By whom, The Syrian?"

"Yeah."

"Sharif Faisal hired you?"

"Yeah, him. Why? Other than the body, is there another problem?"

"Yes, Larry, there is. It wasn't his building so this wasn't an insurance job. Give me something I can use, Larry."

I had repeated his name twice to show empathy and concern. I feigned exasperation. I raised my hands and let them collapse against my legs for a loud slap, and laid into Larry.

"Seems to me, he set you up. The man is a weasel, you and I know it. You're in deep—"

"I know. Shit. I'm such an idiot. Shit."

"Your problem isn't the district attorney, it isn't prison time."

Larry's eyes narrowed. "What the hell are you talking about?"

"The person who died in the building was a young kid, Larry. He wasn't dead and placed there after the fact either, Larry. The kid had been hog-tied and at some point, he woke up, Larry, and he realized what was happening to him, and he struggled. He struggled and died a horrible death."

Each time I said his name, I wanted to him to hear the hammer and the sounds of his coffin being nailed shut. It worked because Larry Getz was blubbering.

"Oh, Jesus. Oh, sweet Jesus. Poor kid."

Larry sobbed, his face wet from tears. He was ready for the knockout punch.

"The person who died in that building wasn't just any young kid, Larry."

He looked up. "What are you saying?"

"The dead kid was the nephew of a mafia don."

Larry arched his head back and addressed the ceiling. "Oh, Jesus, Mary and Joseph."

"Mafia, Larry. We both know their justice doesn't come with a blindfold. I can think of a dozen ways they'll kill you, and none of them are quick. If you're lucky, they'll stick you inside an empty oil drum. How long you last will depend on how fast you breathe and how much room you take up. If they want to be merciful, which I doubt, they'll kill you, like this one guy I knew. They stuck his head inside a vise."

Larry looked at me, the panic of a condemned man in his eyes, as he wiped away snot with his shirtsleeve. "And crushing my skull is supposed to be kind?"

"Oh, they didn't do that to the guy, Larry. Too obvious."

"What then?"

"They slit his throat." I placed the matchbox on the bed near him. I waited for the heaves to subside and waited for the defeated voice. "You're here to kill me, aren't you?" he asked me.

I parted my jacket so he could see the dark stock of the .38. The sight of it instigated pleas to spare his life; a lot of pathetic groveling and offers of money; promises to God and the saints that he'd quit the torch business, and that on his mother's grave he would disappear for good. I let the show run until I was ready.

"I'm not here to kill you, Larry. The don hired me to find his nephew—and I did, but that doesn't get you off the hook."

He was eager to listen to me. I didn't have to beat him with anything, or shine a light in his face, or tie him to a chair and deprive him of a glass of water, or have him soil himself.

"I can help you, but you've got to tell me how you started this fire."

"The roof," he said.

Larry explained in simple English. The rooftops to most buildings have smokestacks and they acted as the airway. All you had to do, he said, was leave an opened can of gasoline inside the stack. A match can spark the fire, but squalor guaranteed success because the hallways were filled with debris and cluttered with newspapers and other combustibles. Hardly sophisticated. Hardly how Jimmy would do it.

"And you always start the fire from the rooftop?" I asked.

"Yeah."

"And you checked the building for people?" Tony asked.

"I told you I did."

"Including the basement?" I asked.

"I couldn't. It was locked, I swear."

Tony pulled up a chair, turned it around and straddled it. "Know who I am?"

"No, but I can guess you don't work in an office," Larry said.

"Here's the deal," Tony said. "You come with us and we'll do the best we can to keep you alive." Tony glanced to the suitcase. "Run and you're a dead man." Larry went to say something but Tony held up his hand. "I know what you're thinking; you believe you're responsible and you are, but there's a difference."

"There is?"

123

"You didn't tie up the kid. Someone did and that someone used you. It's thin as a razor but sharp enough of a nuance that it may just save your life."

"It can?" Larry said wide-eyed. "You mean I could still—"

Tony stood up, moved the chair and said, "Not for me to decide. You have a decision to make."

Chapter Seventeen: Burbank Street

L arry sat in the backseat with his suitcase clutched to his chest. I parked John's wounded car and hoped for the best from a conversation with Nikos. Tony opened the door for Larry and we entered the luncheonette together. I asked Larry to park it at the counter. Nikos looked up. I could tell he recognized Tony. I ordered a grilled cheese sandwich for Larry. Tony asked for a vanilla shake. We sat a few feet away from Larry at the counter. Nikos walked over.

"Nikos. This is Tony Two-Times." Nikos stared. "I'm in jam," I said and pointed to Larry. "Any chance he can stay at your place, or at one of your apartments?"

"Hiding from the police?"

I shook my head. "The mob."

Nikos looked at me weird and then glanced at Tony. "But I thought, he—"

"I am," Tony said. "And I'd consider this a favor, if you don't mind."

"Not like I have a choice, do I?" Nikos focused on me. "Anything else?"

"Any of your apartments come with parking, a garage?"

"Yes, why?"

"I need to hide a car."

Nikos turned away to start on Larry's sandwich and Tony's drink.

"I assume that's a yes," Tony said, as he reached into his pocket and placed some loose change on the counter.

"I'm paying," I said.

"I know you are." He looked down at the spoils. He used two fingers to push dimes to me, and then pulled two dimes toward himself.

"What's with the change?" I asked Tony.

"I need one of my boys to collect my car in Allston, and to send over a ride. If you need wheels, I suggest you join us. The dimes in front of you are for the call, if you need to tell your friend his car isn't coming home tonight."

While Larry ate his grilled cheese sandwich, Tony slurped vanilla shake through a straw. I dialed John's number in Central Square. He answered. Like most men, John didn't appreciate foreplay so I was straight to the point. I told him I still needed the car. He accepted the fact. I expected him to complain about how he was getting home. He didn't because he wouldn't. All he said was that he expected a full tank of gas and his car washed and detailed. I said that I would and hung up, knowing his car needed a whole lot more than soap, suds, and the interior vacuumed. A whole lot more.

When Tony's ride arrived, it was a dark Cadillac, like I expected, with a young kid behind the wheel, which I had not expected. Tony Two-Times assumed the passenger seat, while I sat in the back.

The more I thought about it, the more I liked the idea of Tony Two-Times as my backup. Tony asked, "Where to?" and I said, "Burbank Street." Another reason I liked working with Tony. He didn't ask too many questions and neither did this kid. At some point, the silence ate at me.

"Does the driver have a name?" I asked.

"Sal, Mr. Cleary."

"Nice to meet you, Sal, but please call me Shane."

After a green light and a turn onto Mass Ave, Sal oriented the boat towards Burbank Street. Lots of sandstone and red brick, façades with ovals and square windows, and every building had its own heavy glass door. Syrian territory.

While Sal stalked for a parking spot for the Cadillac, I filled Tony in on the wife-beater in residence, and how I knew he was The Syrian's go-to for shady jobs. I learned all about him from the creep's ex-wife, a former client, who relocated to Florida.

"This low-life got a name?" Tony asked.

"Jerry, but for our purposes it's Jeremiah."

126

Tony's eyebrows lifted. I offered a simple reason without more backstory. "He hates being called Jeremiah."

Jerry started out as a third-rate burglar. The man stole anything and everything to maintain his drug habit. Instead of supporting his wife, any and all of his money went into his veins. She paid the bills. I didn't understand what Marilyn saw in the loser until I realized she was one of those women who believed she could change a man.

Jerry was bad luck—a real rabbit's foot with an ingrown toenail. His wife tried and tried until he exhausted her patience. Marilyn called me one night. I remembered the conversation and the desperation in her voice. She'd named a hotel on Soldiers Field Road. We met there. She told me she had filed the papers for divorce with a lawyer who had recommended me to her, if she needed more dirt on her loser of a husband. My guess was that he had heard about me through the fog around Bray and Cat Braddock.

She was low on cash and I felt bad for her. After I gathered enough evidence on her douchebag of a husband, I bought her the ticket Florida. The case introduced me to The Syrian, and I included the name Faisal several times in my notes to her lawyer. Marilyn paid me back, with ferocious and unforgettable grudge-sex on her last night in Boston. I recovered afterwards at the nearby IHOP.

Sal craned his head to verify the number on Burbank Street. "This is it," he said.

The Syrian latched onto Jerry as his eyes and ears within the building, then promoted him to do his dirtier work, according to Marilyn. The Syrian had needed a rat and Jerry needed money for his habit, and so their relationship was born.

Tony instructed Sal to stay in the car. Tony and I evaluated the building before we walked in. Tony Two-Times huffed and puffed his way up several flights of stairs, holding the bannister for support, and hating Sharif Faisal with every step. Tony soldiered on, panting. I waited for him on the landing to Jerry's apartment. When the railing on the third floor almost gave way, Tony shook his head in disbelief. "This falafel is some piece of work."

"You want that cigarette now?"

127

Tony gave me the evil eye. A man with no sense of humor is a dangerous man, and Tony Two-Times was as deadly as they came. In his back pocket, he kept an ice pick with a cork on the working end. I knew because he took it out before he sat down at the lunch counter. I saw his choice of sidearm, too. Under his coat, he carried cold metal, as in an untraceable but reliable revolver this time. Automatics eject brass, and Tony wasn't the kind of guy who'd spend his time picking up casings off the ground.

I did the policeman's knock on Jerry's door. Since he had The Syrian for a protector and cops paid off, I knew he'd fling the door wide with the attitude dialed up between inconvenience and faux outrage. The minute the door cracked I kicked it in and jammed my hand into his throat until I had Jerry pressed against the wall, and about an inch off the hardwood floor. It wasn't a remarkable show of strength. Junkies weren't known for their weight.

"Hello again, Jeremiah. Remember me?"

He choked and foamed spit while Tony closed the door. Jerry's eyes welled with tears of panic when he heard the door's soft click. I lowered him.

"It's time we had a talk, Jeremiah."

Jerry checked his throat with an anemic hand. "What the hell do you want?"

"Answers, for starters," Tony said, hands folded in front of him.

"Who's this?" Jerry asked as he rubbed the back of his head.

"The last face you'll ever see, if you don't talk to us," I said after I smacked the side of his head. "The Syrian isn't going to protect you now, Jeremiah." Another slap, this time, hard across the face. "Time to talk, Jeremiah."

"Stop it, and don't call me that."

"I'll call you whatever I want." I grabbed a handful of shirt and cocked my fist back. I needed Jerry to focus. Tony stood there and did his soulless stare. He could do this all night long and not blink once.

"Into the living room for a conversation," I said.

"I've got nothing to say."

"Sure you do," Tony said. "Move or be moved."

Jerry ushered us into the other room. Even Tony did a double take at the mess. His Italian respect for home and hearth took umbrage at the sight.

Bums in Manhattan's Bowery kept their small square of concrete cleaner than Jerry did.

"Will you look at this sty," Tony said, and turned to Jerry. "What is wrong with you?"

Newspapers were stuck to the floor. Swanson TV dinners, some crumpled, others whole, were scattered about, covered with things that moved. I kicked away what looked like the remains of Salisbury steak with mashed potatoes. Nudie magazines were splayed open to the month's special. A roach the size of a grasshopper scurried across the room. There was a threadbare La-Z-Boy and God knows what living inside it. The one item in the entire menagerie that appeared clean and respectable was the television set. Fresh aluminum foil was wrapped around the rabbit ears.

"So this is life after Marilyn?" I asked.

"Get to why you're here."

I didn't answer because an object on a nearby shelf had caught my attention. I approached it with true reverence. My hat. This unwashed barbarian had my fedora, a gift from Jimmy. I removed it from the shelf and checked the brim, crown, the lining, and band. Mine.

"Where did you get this, Jerry?"

"Friend gave it to me," he said with a catch in his voice. I got in Jerry's face and Tony crowded him from the rear. We bookended him.

"I'll ask again, and I want an answer. Where did you get this hat?"

"Some guy."

I punched him in the gut. "Wrong answer, Jeremiah."

Tony reached down for a fistful of hair and yanked Jerry to standing and whispered into Jerry's ear. "The man asked you a question. Here's a little advice. Your answer should include a noun, as in person, place, or thing. You've got a head start. The hat is a thing." Tony twisted a knot of hair. "Tick-tock, tick—"

"All right, all right. It was a guy." Jerry's hands shot up in front of his face, thinking I'd punch or slap him again. "I don't know his name, I swear. It wasn't supposed to be like that."

"Like what, Jerry?" I asked.

129

"Pay him after the job. He came by after and that's when I gave him his money."

"What job, Jerry?"

"I don't know and I don't ask."

I moved within an inch of the man's face. Tony tightened his grip. I liked the way Tony worked. He didn't need any prompting. Jerry's face contorted in fear. I've seen that same look in abused dogs.

"You don't know the guy's name. Is that right?" Jerry nodded. "And you know nada about any job?" Jerry bobbed his head. "How about you answer this question then? Where did the money come from?" Tony squeezed hard. I thought Jerry would lose some scalp. Jerry whimpered instead of talking. I disliked interrogations, but enjoyed this one.

"Okay, Jerry. I'll make this easier for you. I'll give you a multiple-choice question. Sound good to you?" Jerry blinked. "I thought so. Did this money come from A, your fairy godmother; B, a cop named Kiernan; C, Kiernan and another cop named O'Mara; or D, your boss, Sharif Faisal. What'll it be, Jerry?"

Tony cocked Jerry's head back. The bulging eyes this time reminded me of a Chihuahua. "Answer the man," Tony said through clenched teeth.

"E," Jerry said.

Tony and I looked at each other. Jerry wasn't Mensa material but he knew the alphabet.

"I don't follow," I said somewhat patiently.

"Kiernan, like you said. He showed up with the money and the hat. No O'Mara, although there was another guy."

"This guy have a name?" I asked.

"No, but he had a scar on his face."

"On his cheek?"

"Yeah, how did you know?"

"I ask the questions here, Jeremiah," I said. "And the money?"

"The guy with the scar carried the cash. I don't know why, but I'm sure the money was from Faisal. Had to be, with that kind of scratch." Tony relaxed his grip.

"And Kiernan carried the hat," I said. "Go on."

"Kiernan said some guy would stop by later to pick up the dough. That guy showed up. I gave it to him. No questions asked. I know nothing about the job the guy was hired for. Honest."

I held up my fedora. "And the hat?"

"Kiernan said he found it and called it a souvenir."

"The fire on Symphony Road," I said.

"What about it?"

"Tell me what you know about it."

"I know nothing about that, I swear."

I didn't believe him. Jerry had slathered on too much emphasis. I looked at Tony. He understood. He reclaimed Jerry's hair. I wasn't sure what Tony would do, but I learned then and there gangsters improvised.

Tony dragged Jerry across the room, through all the horrid mess on the floor, to the steam radiator. The schlep Jerry hadn't put two and two together until Tony worked the black gauge. Jerry looked nervous as a kid in an itchy brown sweater. Tony turned the dial one last time. The cast iron fixture hissed after someone in hell had picked up a hammer. We heard a series of clangs and a perverse gurgle, then spits and crackles.

Tony looked over his shoulder to me. "Which is his best side?" Tony twisted Jerry's head, left and then right. "I like to leave something for his mother."

"You choose. He's all ugly to me," I answered.

Tony bent Jerry over within an inch of heated steel. Jerry was crying. Should a tear drop, Jerry would see it sizzle like a cracked egg in a skillet.

"Symphony Road, Jerry. What can you tell us?"

"Nothing. I know nothing."

"I don't believe you, Jerry."

Jerry's arms flailed. He screamed. I gave Tony permission with a nod. He let Jerry's face touch the hot surface for a second. Jerry didn't like it. Jerry screamed some more. "Okay. Okay. I'll talk," he said through the tears.

Tony yanked Jerry's head up. "I don't believe this piece of crap." About to return Jerry to the griddle for a repeat, Jerry relented. "All right. All right.

I'll tell you what I know."

"We're listening."

"He did it." Tony pulled on some hair.

"Who did what?" I asked. "I want specifics, Jerry."

Tony bent Jerry over, the man's head a millimeter down.

"I said I'll tell you."

"You said that more than once, Jeremiah," Tony said.

"Faisal doesn't own the building, the one that burned down."

"Tell me something I don't know," I said.

"He made the guy an offer."

"Which guy?" I asked, remembering Key West, Florida.

"Faisal made an offer to a pro to burn it down, but the guy turned him down. Faisal got angry, so he hired this other guy."

Tony loosened his hold a little. "This guy, who turned him down, have a name?" I asked.

"All I know about him was that he was high-end and he didn't like Faisal."

"Enough for Faisal to want to even the score?"

"What?" My question surprised Jerry. Tony's polished dress shoe pressed down on Jerry's foot. Hard. Jerry panted, "Could be. How the hell do I know if he wanted to even the score?"

"And this other guy he hired. What can you tell me about him?"

Tony said, "A name would be nice."

"Some hack Faisal found on the cheap. Never met him in my life until payday. I swear to God. Guy introduced himself to me as Larry, but I don't know whether that's his real name or not. I try not to ask too many questions."

"How much did Faisal pay this Larry?" I asked.

"Five large."

"Five-thousand dollars? Cheap bastard, your boss."

"What can I say? That's Faisal for you. Now, can you ease off?"

Tony released Jerry. I put on my hat. Tony threw some bills on the floor and encouraged Jerry to hire a maid and clean the place up. He threatened to return and verify that his money was spent on housework and not junk.

The trip down the stairs was easier on Tony's pulmonary system. We waited on the sidewalk for our ride. I noted Tony fiddling with a cigarette.

"To smoke or not to smoke. That is the question," I said.

"Time to reconsider my habits."

"Violence to others or unto yourself with the cigarettes?" I asked.

"I want to quit smoking," he said.

"You may not want to quit just yet. I have bad news for your boss."

Chapter Eighteen: Yes Man

I went to Nikos's apartment and called it a night. My Tuesday proved long, in tooth and claw. Larry ruined any chance for relaxation, for me to hear my own thoughts. Back and forth like a hamster inside a cage, he went on and on about what might happen to him, what will happen to him, and whether Faisal or THEY would show up at his door. Nikos was in the kitchen talking to himself in Greek. I found another room for privacy, dialed Bill at the station and asked him my question. "When we last talked, I forgot to ask if you had anything on Kiernan and Burbank Street for me?"

"You're like a rash that won't stop itching." I heard papers shuffle. "A recurring domestic beef, real frequent flyers. Romeo and Juliet are still together, still at it, apparently. I've read all the incident reports and I noticed a pattern. Kiernan and his partner visit every month, like clockwork."

"He's doing maintenance," I told Bill.

"Maintenance?"

"The professor researched properties Sharif Faisal owns."

"And?"

"And our slumlord owns buildings on Burbank Street, including the one in which our hand-happy husband lives in. My guess is Kiernan and his partner are receiving payoffs or instructions at Burbank, or both, and the husband is The Syrian's bagman."

"That's a hefty accusation." I heard the springs in Bill's chair creak. "Got anything to back it up?"

"Yeah, I do, but first ask yourself this, Why is Kiernan filing reports on a domestic disturbances when the wife has been out of the wedding picture

134

for months?"

"She left him?"

"I drove her to Logan myself and watched her board a plane for the Sunshine State."

"And plenty of arson fires since then," Bill said, then pivoted to play devil's advocate, like I knew he would. "Maybe she returned without you knowing it, and reconciled with the creep."

"Doubt it. I still get postcards from the Sunshine State. Talk soon."

I hung up, forgetting to ask him about his trip to Cambridge for me.

The DA needed to arraign Jimmy soon or spring him loose. District attorneys don't push cases they know they can't win, and the Second Coming would happen before Jimmy accepted a plea deal. I thought about the possibility that Marilyn may have left my card behind. Kiernan could've picked up my business card God knows when, or the easier answer is that he saw me at the station and one plus one adds up to Mr. Mysterious trying to pick the lock to my office. I rethought the situation and concluded that Pinto had no stake in the B&E into my office. The needle on the immoral compass pointed at Kiernan. I returned to the other room. Larry had calmed down some.

Nikos reappeared with a bottle and a glass for his guest. He poured ouzo into a taller glass and offered it to our arsonist. Nikos held the neck of bottle for immediate refills. Nikos preferred to lubricate the man into submission rather than listen to him prattle on about his life expectancy.

Nikos said Larry would stay with him until the cleaning service was finished with an apartment he had for my "friend." Nikos said he'd stock the place with food and made sure that the lights and stove in the place worked. If he felt generous, he might find Larry a television set. I said that I appreciated it. I appreciated it a lot and said good night.

Larry took the couch, and I called Dan the manager of the gay club where I had stashed Isabella and the kid. I told Dan that the Madonna and child would stay one more night. I claimed a development had come up. Dan had not mentioned Toni the waitress from Nick's Beef and Beer House, so

I assumed Bill couldn't break away from the station house for the trip to Cambridge.

Tony and I had a date at Foley's Café. I needed the rest and I took it. When I woke up, both Larry and Nikos were gone. I presumed Nikos had tucked Larry into new digs, like someone in the Witness Protection Program, and he was tending to his grill and counter at the luncheonette.

I explored the medicine cabinet in Nikos's bathroom. I fetched gauze and wrapped up my hands. Not quite sixteen ounces, the weight of gloves a middleweight like myself would use, but I could put mitts over the wraps. Late March temps at night have been nuttier than the Mad Hatter, and the dip into the forties provided the excuse to wear them.

Eight o'clock. Foley's. I planned to make Officer Kiernan my Yes Man.

I took to walking to the Café like a Theravada Buddhist. Those monks I'd seen in Laos walked everywhere, and did it as a form of meditation, which they called bhavana. Everything to them was bhavana: sitting, standing, or walking. Every activity, they said, could be transformed into opportunities to cultivate concentration. I reflected while I walked. I meditated on the here and now. I maintained an awareness of movement, on the path in front of me and not the destination, although the sensation of being followed dogged me, from the moment I left Nikos's apartment building. I looked once and then twice. Nothing. I returned to my thoughts.

The choice for the meet with Tony was either the bar near my apartment, Foley's Café, or Doyle's in JP—as in Jamaica Plain, another section of the city. I couldn't show up at Doyle's without a cop thinking of making an omelet of my face. I stood a better chance at Foley's because the place drew a better crowd from the rank and file. Here, among all the dark wood and mirrored glass, the Boston Police Strike of 1919 was organized and hatched.

The Police Union and the Patrolmen's Association was the phoenix born from the ashes of the strike. Irish cops experienced another blight, when the WASP Governor Calvin Coolidge turned public sentiment against them. The brass sided with the politicians. Coolidge quashed the strike with State Guards, and declared that he was for law and order and that unions were un-American. Coolidge rode his slogan on the train into the White House.

136

Good cops, cops who remembered their history and those who railed against abuse and corruption came to Foley's. I stood a better chance there of breathing with both lungs, and I had the added benefit that I was on familiar turf, my South End.

While I waited outside for Tony, I drifted into thinking why both Foley's and Doyle's called themselves cafés and not a bar or a pub. Both places served beer and food. Then again, I never understood why shops closed late on Thursday in Boston.

Quarter to eight and I saw a different Cadillac, same kid driver and Tony Two-Times pull up. Put Tony in any car and it'd still look like a hearse. Tony lowered the window and I ducked down to say hello and to get a look at the chauffeur. Sal, no more than eighteen, was behind the wheel in a tailored dark suit, light shirt, and a tie with dots. I spotted a crucifix ring on the smallest finger of the hand he had on the wheel. Tony said, "You remember Sal. Kid is a solid wheelman if we need to make a break for it."

Tony opened the door and buttoned his topcoat after he'd stepped out. He said something to the kid in Italian. The Cadillac floated away. I cracked some joke that the Cadillac was a French car. Tony ignored me.

Luca Brasi in *The Godfather* and Tony could've been separated at birth. Tony exuded sinister for a six-foot radius around him. He survived his trade long enough that gray hair dusted the hairline above his ears. He adjusted a thin scarf around his neck and his breath ghosted in the raw air. "Believe this weather? Anyway, this is your show, Cleary."

"Before we go inside, Tony, I've got to tell you something. Listen and don't react, and don't ask questions, like how I know what I know."

"Jesus, Cleary, you sure you're not one of us?"

"What...why?"

"Cause you're talking like a wiseguy."

"The Twelve-Seventy, you know it?"

"Yeah, the fag bar." He raised his hand. "Pardon my French. My wife says I should be more sensitive. The homo bar."

"Joke all you want, Tony, but there's a bar down the street with a basement."

He looked at me as if I'd stepped on his shoe and ruined the shine.

"What about the basement?" he asked.

"I think you should reconsider where you do your storage before it becomes a problem."

Like Luca, he stood there and stared at me. Unlike Brasi, Tony was not at a loss for words. "Consider it done. Now, let's go inside while you still have the Luck of the Irish."

I opened the door to Foley's and let Tony in first. I walked behind him into the noise. Heads turned. The Foley boys were behind the bar in their white shirts and jackets, in uniform like their granddad when he started the place in 1909. Regulars were perched on their barstools. The off-duty cops were not subtle about the way they sized up Tony and me.

Kiernan and his partner O'Mara were there. They'd seen me in the large frameless mirror behind the bar. The looking glass behind the counter dated back to frontier days and served the same democratic purpose to lawman and criminal alike. A man could see someone coming up behind him. Didn't work out so well for John Wesley Hardin in an El Paso saloon but, if it had, Bob Dylan wouldn't have a song about the outlaw.

There was no music playing, only chatter. The place could use a piano player, or some tight ensemble trading fours and eights over a backbeat. I did the Gary Cooper and stood my ground. I dry-washed my gloved hands. Tape and gauze were ready to unloosen bone and blood. Tony stood behind me.

O'Mara whispered into his partner's ear. Kiernan's eyes checked the mirror. He let out a disgusted sigh. He took a healthy gulp from his pint of Guinness. He turned and faced me, placing both elbows on the bar rail behind him, chest exposed.

"You hadda ruin my night, didn't you?"

"Came to thank you, Kiernan."

"With Magilla the Gorilla behind you?"

O'Mara choked on beer. He thought his partner's line was funny. Nobody laughed. He tried again. "Thank me for what?"

I took a few steps forward. Every pair of eyes on me.

"You and your partner did me a huge favor, and to all the honest cops here."

"No idea what you're talking about."

"You and your partner over there signed your death certificates."

"You're talking out of your ass, Cleary. Forget you're the one with the target on your back?"

I looked over my shoulder at Tony and then at Kiernan.

"You know, if he's a cartoon character, then what does that make you? Quick Draw McGraw with his sidekick? What was his name?" I snapped my fingers. "Oh, yeah. Baba Looey, the donkey."

O'Mara glass smacked the wood when he set it down. I didn't stop there.

"Funny thing, Kiernan, because I had you pegged for Snuffles. Remember him? He's the cartoon dog who wouldn't work unless he received a biscuit. I think Snuffles is apt, since you don't do a damn thing unless a dollar bill jumps into your pocket."

That got some sand into O'Mara's crotch. He approached and I swung with a right hook. Down O'Mara went. Kiernan stepped up and we were eye-to-eye.

"Why are you here, Cleary?"

"Nice of you to back up your partner while he's tasting the floor."

"I asked you a question. Why are you here?"

"Three reasons." I held up fingers, as if were announcing the round in a prize fight. I raised my thumb. "First, I lost my gun, so there's witnesses here should my piece suddenly be matched to a homicide." Pointer finger up. "Second, I lost a nice hat, and I'm sentimental about that hat because it was a gift."

"Fuck you and your hat. I'm not the hatcheck girl. And number three?"

"That one is a real doozy, Kiernan. Remember the fire on Symphony Road?"

"Yeah, what of it?"

"There was a kid's body inside that building." I raised my middle finger.

He stared at the middle finger. Kiernan smiled, like I expected he would. I wished for a piano, so I could close the cover on his neck. He continued to beam that Colgate smile of his. I could count all the white teeth. He said what I'd expected him to say: "Last I heard, your fag friend Jimmy is going down for that."

"That's if the DA can make a case, and the clock is ticking."

His beer breath was in my face now. "What's that clock got to do with me, Cleary?"

"Burbank Street."

"Is that supposed to mean something to me?"

"It's where your boss, the slumlord, pays you and Officer Looey there."

My eyes looked down at O'Mara, who came to his knees and then to his feet. He rubbed his jaw. Kiernan bumped his chest against mine. I wasn't moving. Kiernan's blue eyes sharpened, and I could count his pulse from the throbbing vein in his forehead.

"Are you implying something?" he asked.

"Good to hear you deny being on the payroll in front of all these people, but I'll get to the point."

"Do that, Cleary."

"The dead kid was connected." I whispered into Kiernan's ear, "And here's the best part: you know before the don does."

I hit him hard in the stomach and steered him into the bar. He bounced off the wood as if they were ropes. He walked into a jab, hook, and uppercut combination. When he hit the floor, his head did a light bounce in the dust and shelled peanuts. I used my foot to flip him over on his back. O'Mara sat this round out. "A word of advice to you, O'Mara."

"What advice can a rat like you give me?"

"The legal kind, as in you two oughta make sure you've named your beneficiaries."

I backed off and backpedaled. "Sorry for the interruption, folks."

A stoical Foley worked a glass with a dry cloth, as if he expected a genie to materialize and grant him a wish.

We headed outside, Tony and I. The wind blew the door shut and the elevated train rumbled over East Berkeley Street. The exterior to the subway's walkway over the street reminded me of an indecisive penny, as

140

in whether it wanted to be blue or pale green after so many years of being exposed to the elements.

Tony nudged my shoulder. "What the hell was that in there?"

"Playing a hand."

"Lot of balls to do that, in a room of cops, and what's this I hear, about a missing gun?"

"It's not missing anymore, Tony, and neither is my hat, but I wanted to see how they'd react and they didn't."

"Which proves what? Enlighten me."

"Proves they didn't take my gun when I was attacked, though I'm sure they're a part of Park Plaza?"

"What the hell is it with Park Plaza?" Tony asked. "I see you in a car chase but you never explained a word of it to me."

"You said it didn't concern you because it was unrelated to the case Mr. B hired me for. Your words, Tony. If those two," I pointed to the bar behind us, "were in on it, they would've known I was reunited with my gun."

"Still haven't an idea what the hell you're babbling on about, Cleary."

"Best you don't, Tony. Better you stick to your storage problem."

"You know something, I agree with those two micks in there."

"About what?"

"Screw you and your hat, which I do know you have because I was there for that."

I tapped the side of Tony's arm. He glared at my hand. I told him we had a bigger problem. "What problem is that?" he asked.

"She's walking toward us."

"Good looking girl, but ain't she a bit young for you, Cleary?"

"I had a feeling I was being followed when I left Nikos's."

Vanessa, wearing a short coat and a top underneath that guaranteed an earlier than usual bedtime, was locked on us, like a kamikaze. She'd shadowed me somehow. She was either as good as Tony Two-Times, or I was losing my edge. Vanessa batted eyelashes and introduced herself to Tony.

The Cadillac stopped in the middle of the street. "Get in the backseat," I

141

told her.

"This is exciting," she said. "Will you be joining me?"

I opened the door and pulled the seat forward for her. I slid in after her and pulled the seat back so Tony could sit in front. The door closed. Tony turned sideways in his seat. "Where to, Cleary?"

Vanessa said my apartment. Her instruction to Sal the driver included a hand on my thigh. She let her fingers travel due north. "We can have a nightcap."

"And your aunt or uncle will each take one of my kneecaps."

I brushed her hand aside and changed the venue, giving Sal a new fare, Dorchester, after he dropped me off at Nikos's. I said that I wanted to be alone and I told Tony to expect another call from me. Soon. Vanessa huffed and crossed her arms.

Nightlights, traffic lights, and the South End's nightlife played against the glass. I could see Tony's profile in his window. A hand covered a smile as he wheezed through a laugh.

Chapter Nineteen: Watch Your Six

I pitched my proposal to Nikos and he responded.

"Shane, I will put this to you, as nice as possible. Listen to me carefully. I do not run a halfway house, a hostel, a hotel, or a bed and breakfast. I'm not in the tourist trade, the skin trade, or any other shady exchange. What I do run is a business, a respectable one with paying tenants, decent hard-working salt of the earth type of people, but…"

The critical pause. The if, but, the maybe.

I thought of Apollo 11, and all those engineers and technicians huddled around the console, who held their breaths and died a thousand deaths, anxious to hear an astronaut's voice. I was one of them now.

"However, I will do this under one condition," he said.

I maintained silence.

"If I do this, you will manage my properties, all of them, and you will collect the rents for me. You will be my property manager. You will be compensated well. You will be responsible for the upkeep and maintenance as if it were your own home and your cat Delilah lived there. You will do all of this, so I can retire to Florida. Do you understand me?"

Problem solved. Sort of.

I had to get to the Twelve-Seventy and bring the two women and one child here.

I'd do this the old-fashioned way. I took public transportation and, like the kid in high school without a car, relied on my friend Bill for the ride back to the South End.

I walked into the Twelve-Seventy while a jazz quartet dished out soft notes from a piano, delicate brushwork over cymbals, and a double bass thumped a beat as the saxophone moaned. None of this music would upset the geriatric set who nursed drinks straight from the blender, a Piña Colada and a Pink Squirrel here, and a Grasshopper and Velvet Hammer over there. There was a virile couple drinking a Harvey Wallbanger and a Gold Cadillac.

This crowd might be old and taking in their sustenance through a straw but they weren't dead yet. They bobbed and they swayed in their seats. I spotted the apex predator near a potted palm tree, a Noël Coward in a tux, the cigarette holder not quite as a long as Audrey Hepburn's in *Breakfast at Tiffany's*, but it threatened life outside of the six-one-seven area code. Our eyes met and I wanted to take a shower. Dan's maître d' saved me.

"About time," he said.

"Where are they?"

"Out of sight and way in the back," he said and threaded his arm through mine for the long walk into darkness. As he escorted me, he inquired about Bill's availability. A man in uniform appealed to both sides of the rope barrier between the sexes.

Bill's taste in men was fluid and prolific. When we'd met one time at another club in Park Plaza to swap intel on the Braddock case, Bill had burned through accountants and cooled off his hot streak with a bad boy who had a thing for feet, and I'm not talking about a fetish. The guy thought of himself as an artiste, in the same vein as Kazuo Shiraga, the Bruce Lee of performance art who painted with his feet. The relationship ended when an enthusiastic Derek used Bill's apartment as his personal studio. He'd laid down canvas and shades of red paint all over Bill's hardwood floors, and left the place looking like a crime scene.

I played along with my escort and encouraged him to ask Bill himself. I reminded him I wasn't a matchmaker.

"I'm open-minded," he said. "Casual works, too."

Bill saw me, stood up and waved me over. I pried my guide's hand off my arm and said I'd put in a good word for him. "I promise," I told him.

The place was dark enough that Bill, wearing BPD blues, blended in with the shadows. Several empties sat on the table in front of the ladies. I was certain none of them was a virgin drink. I didn't rate a hello from Isabella. The kid was asleep, and simple math left me with Toni Ruiz. "You must be the lady of the hour," I said.

It was hard to see her, but I felt her eyes on me.

"What's it to you?"

I had brought out the waitress in her, the one who had to deal with the blotto undergraduate who thought he was suave and seductive and the next Burt Reynolds, when he should've stuck to a burger and fries.

"I apologize if we somehow started off on the wrong foot. I'm here to help."

"Did I ask for your help?"

"Toni," Isabella said, her hand on her friend's arm. "He's okay."

"Says who? You?" she said to Isabella. Toni turned her attention to me. "You show up, talk to her, asking questions about Lou's death and the next thing I know, some goon tenderized my friend's face."

"My mistake then," I said, then turned sideways and indicated the door with my hand. "I'll return you to Park Plaza forthwith."

"So I can watch those cops kick your ass?"

"I can take care of myself, Ms. Ruiz. I managed to get your friend out of the Plaza, didn't I?" I pointed at the kid. "I got your son out, safe and sound. He's your kid, right?"

She sneered. "Some nerve you have asking about pedigree."

"Right," I said. "What will it be? Stay with me, or Officer Bill drives you home?"

She stood up. The kid stirred and nestled his face in her hair, wanting more sleep.

"Either way, you or *Adam-12* over there has me marked as rat bait."

"I'm offering you a choice."

She moved the kid, and rose out of her seat. She started stuffing things I couldn't see into her purse. The child yawned, recognized me and his fingers pumped up and down as a hello. I said hello.

"Don't you interact with my son," she said. "You've created enough trouble, and you dragged us into this mess you made."

"Mess I made?" I said. "Let's get something straight here, sister. You were in this mess, long before I showed up, because of where you live. If it's not heredity, then it's environment."

"What did you say to me?" She came forward and Bill stepped in.

"Don't, Bill," I said.

Her head turned. "Yeah, don't, Bill." She came up close to my face. The scarce lighting revealed curly hair and dark eyes, the kind that melted into a soft brown in sunlight. "What did you say about heredity?"

She reached for the lapels on my leather coat, but I caught a wrist and pulled her in close, before she decided to knee me.

"Heredity," I said. "Quick question for you, Toni. Is the father a drug dealer?" She tried to free her wrist. I squeezed harder. "Not one of those cops, I hope." If she could've spit in my face, she would've. "A user then? Was the kid's father a user? You do live in a drug den after all."

"Was," she said. "He's dead. Now let go of my wrist."

"Was," I repeated. "Are you a user?"

"Was," she said. "I got help."

I released her. She rubbed her wrist. "Do we have some place to go or not?"

"We do," I said. "All three of you." I turned to Bill. "Parked outside?" He nodded.

They collected their things and arms worked their way into jacket sleeves. Isabella carried the kid, and as Toni brushed past me, I grabbed her bicep, gently this time. I saw the flash of surprise in her eyes. "We don't have time to be at each other's throats. I'm here to help and I mean it, okay?" She stared at me and then blinked. "Good," I said. "We'll continue this conversation later. Go, and I'll meet you outside."

"You're a real charmer, Shane," Bill said. "Now what?"

I told him about Nikos and his offer to put the girls and kid up. I told him I'd meet him outside, and he'd drive us. I found the bill on the table and said I'd pay it. Bill stepped away and I whistled. He turned. "What?"

"Watch your six with the maître d' on your way out. He wants your number."

Chapter Twenty: Auto Row

I t was late Wednesday night. While I was relieved Isabella and Toni and even Larry were safe with Nikos, I knew nothing was guaranteed. Mr. B wanted an update, possibly Larry for curbside justice. My seventy-two hours were about to expire with Pinto and he wanted something. The man wasn't Social Services and I couldn't palm three people off on him. Which meant Isabella, Toni, and I were due for an extended and unpleasant conversation about what happened to Luisa Ramírez at Park Plaza. Last but not least, John's car needed reconstructive surgery. Which is why I was prowling Auto Mile in the middle of the night for a solution. I had a solid idea.

Every hundred feet, the street lights pulsed a rhythmic beat. Nighttime was the best time to drive John's busted car down Commonwealth Ave. There was little traffic, less chance of cops seeing the Chrysler New Yorker or me behind the wheel.

I turned the dial and settled on some jazz. As the last strains of Fats Navarro's trumpet concluded "Lady Bird," the DJ threw out some trivia to listeners while he cued up the next record. Navarro had died at the age of 26 in 1950, from TB and heroin addiction, days after an appearance with Charlie Parker. The man was buried in an unmarked grave in New Jersey. "Grave marker 414, in the Rose Hill Cemetery in Linden, New Jersey," the man on the radio said.

I was two years old then, but the musician's young age and his problem with heroin made me think of Luisa Ramírez in Apartment 420, alone and dying in a tawdry room with a tourniquet around her left arm. She was gifted and successful, a bright light in community politics and then, like that, dead at thirty from an overdose. I couldn't recall where the paperwork from Pinto said she was buried.

"And this next song, folks, is 'You'd Be So Nice To Come Home To' from the album *Art Pepper Meets the Rhythm Section*. The year is 1957."

The fast keys of the pianist and faster notes from the alto saxophone floated up a memory of my father talking about what life was like for him when he was ten years old. Where I'd spent that same year gaping at holiday displays in the windows of Filene's and Jordan Marsh in downtown Boston, he'd come here to Automobile Row.

Number 808 Commonwealth Ave on my right was where he watched the latest Cadillac rotate on a platter, not unlike the one on the DJ's turntable. As a kid, gangsters and successful businessmen drove Cadillacs, the mid-level manager chose either a Chevrolet, an Oldsmobile, or a Packard. The working stiff short on a dollar, like my father, settled for a Ford because it was cheap and what he'd known growing up. Cars he'd seen as a kid weren't automobiles, they were called touring cars, and it wasn't streets they rode on but pleasure roads on Sundays after church. Everybody back then resorted to public transportation, either the bus or the trolley.

The 808 was the Fuller Building or Fuller's Folly and one of many of Albert Kahn's buildings on the avenue. He was the architect responsible for the Lincoln Memorial. I could point out every feature, crevice, style and secret on this street. The Shell logo, for example, used to live opposite the 808, but was moved across the river later. I could tell you that Ellis the Rim Man was where people first learned to tap tires with their foot to check the air pressure. I know all this because my father was an automobile geek and he'd wanted to be an architect.

Like the Art Pepper song, my father liked to come home to my mother and me and to his *Architectural Digest*. Instead of becoming an architect, he went to work to support his mother and his sisters, and into the service when his country needed him. He survived Guadalcanal and Korea, which he never discussed with me. No sooner had he returned home from war, he was out the door again to work, this time to support his own family as a foreman and union negotiator for a construction company. The day he died, a copy of his favorite magazine was in his lap, opened to an article about some Roman Palladian villa in California.

Most of the dealerships had vacated their palaces on Commonwealth Ave, migrated to the burbs and settled for a peck of land on a strip of highway that ran through Norwood or Dedham, leaving Boston University and realtors to swallow up most of the buildings Fuller had built on Auto Row.

Cars and crime. He discussed the connection.

My father explained how he had worked on a '28 Franklin roadster once and found a small oil tank installed above the carburetor, with a valve operated from the dashboard that let oil drip into the intake manifold. There was also an extra perforated pipe attached to the exhaust pipe that ran parallel to the back bumper. He said it was the first time he had seen a bootlegger's car, with a built-in smoke screen. Rumrunners would have their car's undercarriage rigged to haul more booze.

Cars and dealerships. I discovered that relationship on my own.

In addition to protection money from construction, gambling, bars and restaurants, fish and produce, and waste disposal, car dealerships were not only mobbed-up, they offered other perks. Need a car to disappear after a hit, visit the dealership. Need your vehicle tricked out to hide narcotics inside the door panels or wanted a stash of guns installed with the custom leather interior, ask the dealership. Capone established that tradition. Al had his Cadillac painted green and white to look like a cop car, and his set of wheels was said to have more armor plating than a Sherman tank.

I eased the bruised Chrysler down a side street not far from the 808. In the dead of night, when the real music played, a mechanic emerged from the garage. Like the white hat for the construction crew supervisor, this guy was wearing the white overalls of a manager. The look on his face was not friendly and the words out of his mouth were not the flight attendant's "How may I help you?"

"You blind or what? We're closed," he said and pointed to some sign with the smallest print possible. When I turned off the engine, I thought he'd pop a blood vessel, and when I opened the door and exited, that one of us would need an ambulance.

"You deaf? I said the shop is closed. Come back tomorrow."

One garage door was closed, the other one wasn't. There was light, there were men in overalls and there were noises: the dings and rings of the air compressor, and of the impact driver removing lug nuts that sounded like the M16 I carried in Vietnam, set to automatic.

"I'm here on a referral," I said and told him I was reaching into my jacket for my notebook. He didn't look like he carried anything harder than a wrench, but I preferred not to test my luck. Down this street, at this time of night, nobody would know I'd existed or disappeared. Another perk for the mob and associates.

I unhooked a pen from an inside pocket and clicked it. I wrote down the phone number to the Waltham Tavern. The way his eyes read the piece of paper, I knew he was familiar with it.

"Ask for Tony," I said.

"Tony Two-Times referred you?"

"Glad you could recognize the name from the number." My head turned toward the car. "Like I said, a referral. I assume Tony's a frequent customer."

"Yeah, he sends over cars all the time."

He said he needed to make a phone call first. He shook the piece of paper in his hand, somewhat annoyed as if I'd asked him to wake up his mother. I said I'd accompany him to the office because Tony probably would want to have a word with me. He led the way instead of walking behind me, which was a relief.

I followed him into an office with lights so bright they almost blinded me. I saw the floor shop and the repairmen in their natural habitat of dirt, oil, and grease through clear glass, while the Good Humor Man at the desk worked his fingers around the rotary dial.

He said the name and waited while someone on Shawmut Ave did the slow walk through the cavernous 'Ham to find Tony Two-Times. I studied the man's face for a reaction. The minute his expression changed, I knew the baritone voice of my favorite mobster had caressed his ear. He handed me the receiver. Tony asked me what this was about and that included one well-placed and timed profanity.

"I need a car repaired," I told him.

"Do I look like Triple A to you?"

"I'm in a jam, Tony, and could use the help."

"When does your problem become my concern. Wait a second," he paused. "This has to do with that car at Park Plaza, doesn't it?"

"You were there, weren't you? Look, I need this bumped to the top of the shop's list here. Don't be difficult, Tony. I gave you the heads up on that other thing that could become a real headache for you and our mutual friend. Storage, remember?"

"Storage, and you expect me to foot the bill?" he said.

"Storage, and your generosity is most appreciated."

"You're something, Cleary. Put the other guy on."

I handed the receiver back to Mr. Clean. Tony talked; he listened. I waited and looked around the rest of the office. There was a monstrous water cooler plugged into the outlet, and it hummed. Behind the counter and against a wall was an aquarium, filled with large scary-looking fish, and at an angle from the tank was the Men's Restroom, its door open to reveal a sanctuary as immaculate as the office I was standing in.

The toilet and the pedestal sink were American Standard, both white and made of porcelain. There was a waste basket and a hamper whose lid was weighed down with a stack of magazines, which I assumed were the American Standards of *Sports Illustrated* for amateur and recreational jocks; *Muscle & Fitness* for gym rats; and *Playboy* and *Penthouse* for those preoccupied with journalism.

I observed the fish while I waited. A massive one, gray with florescent orange scales, brooded and patrolled the length of the tank. This creature looked like a volcanic rock with fins. The other fishes were smaller and gray, spotted, or striped.

He hung up the phone and held out his hand for the keys. I surrendered them without saying a word. "Tomorrow, late afternoon is the best I can do," he said.

"Appreciate it, thanks." I peddled some soft talk. "Those fish behind you,"

I said. "I've never seen the likes of them. What are they?"

He glanced over his shoulder. "Oscars," he said. "They're South American, and related to piranhas."

"Domesticated piranhas?"

"Nothing tame about them," he said. "You see the largest one?"

"Can't miss him."

"We named him Tony, after your friend, and he comes in handy sometimes."

"Handy how?" I asked.

He didn't answer me, but he gave me a smile a dentist would've found uncomfortable.

"Oscars. Piranhas," I said. "Aggressive, like Tony."

"Aggressive, sure, but there's one difference between these fish and Tony." He turned sideways so I could view the tank. "The Tony inside the tank there likes flesh. They all do, really, but he's acquired a real fondness for it." He looked through me with the deadest pair of eyes. "You'd be surprised the things you find inside cars these days."

Chapter Twenty-One: The Things I've Learned

I slept the night dreaming about fishes with sharp teeth.

I was enjoying the shower until I sensed someone was watching me. I pulled the curtain aside and saw Delilah on the sink. I told her to chill and returned to the steam and spray. Nothing could beat a bathroom and the amenities after you've gone without in Uncle Sam's army. The things you miss when you're in the field.

There were a lot of things I had to relearn after I'd left the service. You didn't eat like a normal person in a mess hall and Tabasco went well with everything. You inhaled your food in the army because you had to be someplace soon, and you made sure you were there fifteen minutes early. You didn't point at someone or something; you kept your hand flat, four fingers and thumb locked, and you indicated the object or person in that direction as if your hand were a knife. You didn't fidget or express impatience in the line for the bank teller, the line to board a bus, or any other line. You stood silent. You didn't sleep, you napped in every conceivable position. And you didn't complain. Comfort was luxury and luxury encouraged complacency. Out in the world, you shined your shoes, ironed your clothes, and lined up your buttons to declare that you had character and integrity. You valued economy and simplicity.

In-country, in the bush, you were your rifle and your rifle was you.

My first year out was the hardest. Sudden noises rattled me. A car backfired and I'd seek cover. I walked into a place and my eyes scanned entrances and exits, who might be a threat, who might be carrying a weapon, and where I could find a seat with my back against the wall so I could watch the room. If I were to become physical with someone, I pulled back and restrained myself because my first instinct was to kill. I'd rather be savaged than kill again. And I have killed.

I killed for Uncle Sam for four years and six months as an infantryman, from '66 to '69. I separated from the service in early Seventy. I'd stayed longer than I should've because I had no purpose in life and nowhere else to go. My parents were dead. No relatives, alive or known.

I left when I realized killing and politics were stupid and senseless. I left when I became exhausted seeing more and more of my friends killed and maimed, and I didn't enjoy killing another human being who had no quarrel with me until I showed up in his backyard.

I returned from Vietnam like Huck Finn, and the American bed was the first thing that tried to civilize me. I was lost in a haze before I joined the Boston Police Department. That good idea lasted two years, about as long as a light bulb, and it ended when I'd testified against Douglas. I probably would've left sooner, but the trial made the decision for me.

I turned the dials until they squeaked and the pipes shuddered. I swept the curtain and pulled the towel towards me. Delilah walked around the rim of the sink and sat down and looked up at me. I petted the top of her head. Her eyes closed in bliss, opened and refocused.

"Sorry I've been out so much. You know you're still my girl, don't you?"

She meowed. I dried off and wrapped the towel around my waist. I wiped away the steam on the mirror with my hand, as if I could erase memories. I never forgot any of the faces of the people I'd killed. Shooting someone with an M4 or an M16 was easy, either from a distance or up close, but to use a Mark II knife or my bare hands was a different story. No priest would ever understand what I have to say through the confessional grate, and I've tried. I tried.

Another luxury I enjoyed was a shave. We seldom shaved in the field, but there was hell to pay if you'd let your hair grow long. I looked at myself in the mirror. I lathered up and swept the blade while Delilah voiced her complaints about the change of venue and personnel. She was not used to the new accommodations. She took to Nikos, liked to circle his legs. I suspected she had little use for Larry.

"I know you want to go home. Be patient a little bit longer, okay?"

She mewed, jumped off the sink and landed like a paratrooper who'd caught a breeze under his canopy. She swished her tail and dismissed herself without permission.

Today was JC's day off, and I knew where to find my Haitian friend.

Jean-Claude Toussaint frequented the Charles River Esplanade in good weather. He'd walk with a book until he found himself a bench he liked, often under a tree, and he'd read for a few hours.

The path along the Charles by day was a haven for joggers, picnics, or a game of frisbee or touch football. And by night, the trees provided shade and secrecy for men tired of the bars nearby and wanted thrills in a public place.

Cops knew the Esplanade was a cruiser's delight, all eighteen miles of it, though the hottest spots were between the Hatch Shell and the Mass Avenue Bridge. We also knew kids addled on testosterone drove down on the weekends from Lynn and Medford or wherever to enjoy a fag hunt. We busted a few of those hooligans.

If a homo was murdered, and many were, we'd often find his body in the reeds in the Fens. The Fens were harder to police and, every now and then, we'd have to lob tear gas into the reeds for a Clear and Catch.

I spotted JC and whistled. He turned his head, waved, and set his book down on his lap and waited. JC out of scrubs was dignified and dapper. It was too early in the year for linen, but his choice of hat said he believed warm weather was coming. JC was more accurate than the weatherman on TV about many things not the weather, possibly because of his skills in voodoo. I do believe he held some sway in the darker world because none of the geese came near him. As I approached him, I could see a small stack next to him.

"What's with the paperwork?" I asked.

"Copies you might find interesting."

"I have originals."

"You don't have these."

He handed me a file folder. I leafed through the contents. I saw more of the same as I went on, but stopped when I read the death certificate. I was certain it was a duplicate at first, but my eyes hurt from the double and triple take after I'd read the crucial line. "He thought she was murdered?"

"Says 'Homicide' on that piece of paper, don't it?"

"How did you get this?"

"Copied it when he wasn't looking."

"You went to Worcester?"

"Godawful place for a Caribbean boy. I tried calling him, but he hung up on me the moment I said Luisa Ramírez, so I paid the man a visit."

"And he talked to you?" I asked.

"He took one look at me and we talked, once he'd assessed the situation."

"What situation?"

"That I meant him no harm. He realized I wasn't sent to put the hurt on him. He figured out I wasn't police, number one; and I was after the truth, number two; and most important, though, he realized I was a doctor, too."

"How?"

"We have a secret handshake," he said and then laughed. "Mon, you're wound tight for a white boy. The man knew I was a doctor when I said I might've seen a body recently with Pugilist Attitude."

"Smart. Speak to a man in the language he understands, and you have a conversation."

"Live under the likes of Duvalier and son, like I have and you become resourceful. It's like how you know someone was an ex-cop or former military, or black over the telephone."

"Some might say that's racist, friend."

"Works both ways. I know a white person when I hear one. You know what you know, and don't be ashamed about it. Let's not lie to ourselves here."

"Back to Luisa Ramírez, please."

"Technically," he said, "she died of an overdose, but she'd been helped along."

"Helped how?" I asked.

"The tourniquet and the injection site."

JC and I stared out at the water as rowers sculled past us.

"You do know that you can determine handedness from a dead body, don't you?" JC said.

"Luisa wasn't right-handed?"

Joggers shuffled behind us. Talk about assumptions. The percentage of the population that was southpaw and the percentage that Kinsey claimed were gay was ten-percent. I don't believe the sex doctor's claim, but I do think straight and right were the majority.

"A right-handed heroin addict would've used his or her left arm," JC said.

"Someone injected her. The report didn't indicate a struggle."

I described the post-mortem photo to JC. The print was one Weegee himself could've snapped with his Speed Graphic camera. I mentioned how she was reclined on the sofa, head tilted back and the needle in her left arm.

JC listened and then spoke. "Your copy of the report doesn't mention a struggle. The original did. Someone clocked her in the back of the head."

"Daze her long enough for the hot shot," I said. "Did he say who forced his hand to change the documentation?"

"No names. He did say he was visited by two off-duty police officers, who drove all the way from Boston to convince him that it was in his best interest to redo the paperwork, which he did."

"How did he know they were cops from Boston?" I asked.

"He saw the plates on their car, and instinct filled in the rest. The positive, in all of this, was he knew there'd come a day when someone would ask questions, which is why he held onto documentation."

"Suicide," I said. "Perfect way to tarnish someone's legacy. Question now is why was she at Park Plaza."

"Any ideas?" JC asked.

"Working on it." I reached into my pocket for money. JC refused. "I can't and I won't." JC stood up, ran his fingers along his waistband. He adjust his

158

straw hat. "There are sinister forces at work here, my friend. Have you ever heard of Baron Samedi?"

I said I had not. JC pointed at the paperwork in my hands. "Somewhere in there, you'll find where she was buried."

"Okay, but what's that got to do with Baron What's-His-Name?"

"The baron don't like where's she buried, my friend. You see, where I'm from, he's the spirit who, despite all his decadent ways, is responsible for the dead crossing over. One of the ways he does that is he'll dig the grave himself and welcome the person."

JC put his hands in his pockets and stared at me with eyes I could swear had changed color. Perhaps it was the shade, or the angle of the sun and shadows.

"What are you telling me?" I asked.

"The baron didn't dig her grave, and nothing will be right between this world and the next until he does."

Chapter Twenty-Two: The Talk

I had asked Nikos to move Isabella, Toni and her kid to a safer place in one of his buildings. He honored the request by moving them into a two-bedroom apartment. Toni asked and received a few days off from work, citing a family emergency. Isabella was "between three jobs that never paid what one good job should," as she put it.

I told Toni over the phone I'd stop by at ten in the morning. We needed to talk. I insisted, and we'd have the conversation over strong coffee or something stronger, her choice. I arrived ten minutes early, knocked on their door. I could hear Channel 5's *Good Morning!* on the other side of the wood. Willis and Langhart, the two anchors for ABC, were gushing over each other like lovesick teens. I recognized Janet Langhart's voice for other reasons.

Janet was an attractive Black woman, a model before the studio hired her. She and her partner, John Willis, would exchange cutesy banter and work their chemistry into a froth while they covered local artists like Sidewalk Sam, events and regional news. The audience ate it up. Her only dark moment was when she'd blurted "Christ Almighty!" after a clip from the movie *French Connection* was played in front of a studio audience. All of New England, PTA moms and Christian groups sharpened their pitchforks overnight.

Then there was the memorable interview on live TV with a rising star of the runway. Since Janet had been a model in her past life, everyone expected a fluff piece, as if the two women were sisters who'd pledged the same sorority. The first few questions were as soft and airy as cotton candy. At one point,

Janet asked the long-legged beauty how she had become successful, how did she come to grace the covers of so many glossy magazines, and then land this lucrative contract with one of the top cosmetic companies in the world. Everyone assumed, as Janet and I had, that her guest would answer with a small dose of false humility, a dash of self-deprecation, before she gave the inevitable clichés about dedication, persistence and long hours in front of the camera.

Nope. The model's answer set the switchboards on fire.

"I fucked everyone."

Isabella answered the door and I stepped inside. Nikos told me the previous occupant of the apartment had died, and when I viewed the décor I understood why.

The place came furnished and I doubted the décor would rate a featured spread in *Home* magazine. The first thing I saw was my reflection from a mirrored wall in the dining room. The shag carpeting, the soft kind for the feet after a hard day's work, was wall-to-wall in the living room, and that alone indicated Nikos charged above-market rent. To my left, the entire length of the kitchen counter was butcher block, and the cabinets were light wood and finished with knobs that looked like the dial on a safe. The dishwasher and refrigerator were a couple, in their matching color of pale and sickly yellow. The kitchen carpet included every shade of brown, and a geometric pattern from a Freemason on an acid trip. I'd bet good money the floor came alive at night.

I dreaded a visit to the bathroom. I pictured tiles everywhere and the sole mirror in the room opposite the toilet. You could watch yourself watching yourself. I imagined other horrors, such as bedroom walls with flock wallpaper, the motif of life under the microscope magnified and velvet to the touch. If there was a den, I anticipated wood paneling, more earth tones, and a floor-to-ceiling fireplace. I might find a wicker chair in the corner for the kind of naughty fun you'd see on a loop in a stall with a sticky floor in the Combat Zone.

Isabella took my coat and hat. She mumbled something about Toni and

161

the kid, about putting him down for a nap, and that Toni would be out after a quick shower. I checked my watch. The office crowd took a fifteen-minute break for a coffee and cigarette around this time. The kid was in training for the nine to five hustle, long before he'd be able to tell time on the clock on the wall in the kitchen.

She said there was fresh coffee in the kitchen, and she'd tell Toni I was here. I ventured into the kitchen. The oven was a Hotpoint and in a shade of light green, somewhere between avocado and pea soup. The stove was electric and the coil used to boil water was dying a slow orange death. The wooden beads for eyes on the macramé owl tacked to the wall watched me as I sat down in the vinyl chair at the table.

All criticisms aside, the place was clean. There were no signs of neglect, and it was the Milky Way for distance from what these two ladies had for digs in Park Plaza. I paid particular attention to details because Nikos drafted me as his property manager for his sayonara to the Sunshine State. I wasn't convinced the color schemes and interior design were safer than any gig I took as a PI, but the job as Property Manager reeked of steady income and the promise of a crate of oranges from Florida every holiday.

While we waited for Toni, Isabella handed me a ceramic mug and a spoon and pointed to the cream and sugar on the table. Isabella seemed at home, relaxed because she was braless and wearing a t-shirt and shorts and walked around barefoot. I took my coffee black as battery acid. The Merry Mushroom design on the cup reminded me of hobbits and that alone undercut the jolt from my caffeine.

"We've got time," I said to Isabella. "Tell me a little about Lou. You were friends, right?"

"What's to tell?" she answered. "Oh, you mean, what was she like when she wasn't burning her bra and sticking it to the Man?" She sipped some of her coffee. "People thought she was some nasty type, a militant, but she wasn't. I mean, yeah, she had an acute sense of right and wrong, a real firebrand at the sight of injustice, but she was soft, in her own way."

"Soft, how?" I asked.

"She was the kind of gal who liked to wear an oversized t-shirt and baggy sweatpants, and watch old movies on weekends. *Mr. Smith Goes to Washington* made her cry."

"The filibuster scene?" I asked.

"Sobbed every time. I guess it wasn't that far of a cry from what she was doing in real life. But you want to know something I always remember about her?"

"What?"

"Popcorn," she said.

"Popcorn?"

"Jiffy Pop, the kind you put over the flame on the stove. She loved it, and she was scared of it. Oh my God, it was hysterical to watch her standing there at the stove. She worried the minute the aluminum foil started bulging. She watched and waited, always freaking out over how high the thing would rise. She worried it'd blow up in her face, and there would be popcorn everywhere."

Isabella started laughing, caught up in the memory of her friend. I could picture it. The slow increase of kernels popping, first one and then another, and then a stampede of pitter-patter, the foil distended like a pregnant belly, and the smell of popcorn in the air. The laughter I was hearing was deep and real, from some well that told me that Luisa Ramírez was not just an acquaintance. When Isabella told me that day that cops had moved the body, she hadn't said it with the detached voice of someone who had turned cynical from a life trapped in the projects; rather, she said it with the tremor of outrage beneath the skin, the feeling of being helpless.

Toni ambled into the kitchen in jeans and a blouse in a psychedelic print. The frilly scarf around her neck made no sense to me. She parked herself in the chrome chair with the hideous floral print. She spooned two large mountains of sugar and poured a river of cream into her cup of Juan Valdez. After the spoon completed two circles and tapped the rim, she spoke. "Izzy says you wanted to talk."

"Geez, Toni. Must you be so hostile? The guy saved my life, and yours probably. Have a little gratitude."

Toni's tone conveyed more than the usual townie attitude. She projected rough and tough, which like most crabs, hid a softness and vulnerability behind the hard exterior, somewhere. The problem was that I didn't have forever to find it, or coax her out of her shell.

"Well, here's to Shane Cleary then." Toni raised her cup. "Look, it's not like I'm ungrateful or nothing, but I only have so much time off from work, little money to my name, and a kid to feed."

"I'll ask Nikos to bring over some groceries," I said.

"And money? I'd like to make my own, instead of a handout," she said.

"You can't make any, if you're dead. It's important that both of you lay low. I could give you money, or ask Nikos to spot you, but don't leave this apartment."

"Why would the old Greek be so nice to us?" Toni asked. "Is he looking for something on the side?"

"You're unbelievable, Toni." Isabella shook her head, disgusted.

"Simple. He's a good man," I said.

"Thank you for that Hallmark moment, and what's your deal in all of this?"

"Why are you so defensive and suspicious?" I asked her.

"Distrust is what's kept me alive. Now, you wanted to talk so let's talk."

"Okay, let's discuss Park Plaza. The cops, in particular."

"Who put you on the box of Wheaties?" Toni said. "I mean, why do you care? You have a death wish, or something?"

"People say I should leave things as they are, except I don't like the way things are. Does that answer your question?"

"Sounds like a man. I didn't ask to be saved."

Toni was one tough nut, and it wasn't my job to crack her, only to make sure someone didn't bury her or her kid or her best friend, the babysitter.

"I started down this road," I said, "to find out what I could about a woman found dead from an overdose, a suicide everybody said, except it wasn't—"

"Wait," Isabella said. "You're saying Lou didn't kill herself?"

"She was, as a friend pointed out, assisted and helped along. Someone conked her on the head, enough to dim the lights and long enough to inject her and then stage everything to look like a suicide, like a junkie who had underestimated the high. Except for one small detail." I let myself breathe before I said it. "Whoever killed her made a mistake."

"I knew it." Isabella slapped the table. "I knew Lou would never kill herself. That girl was too strong to take the easy way out. She was a fighter."

I didn't want them to know her friend never stood a chance with her killer, once they coldcocked her. I didn't tell them there were no defensive wounds, no nothing. I stated what I believed was the killer's intent: "Suicide was meant to discredit her, and smear her legacy. But here's what I don't get."

I stopped there. In the time I was laying down the bricks for a case of the premeditated murder of Luisa Ramírez, and restored Isabella's faith in her dead friend, I watched Toni's reaction to everything I said. She looked away, distant and focused on some spot on the wall behind me, and scratched her left arm.

"What don't you get?" Isabella asked.

"That can wait a moment. I have a question for Toni here."

Toni focused glassy eyes on me. "What?"

I lifted my chin. "You're scratching your left arm?"

"It itches. So what."

"Again, with the attitude," I said. "I suppose it's a nervous tic. I looked at the photo—"

"What photo?" Toni asked.

She'd shifted in her chair. Her hand slowed down to form a claw.

"The photo of Luisa dead, a photo of how the cops wanted her to be remembered." I looked to Isabella. "You told me they moved the body. Correct?"

Isabella nodded, and Toni had her head in her hands.

"Cops don't move bodies," I said. "And cops don't conveniently show up to a scene with a camera either. And as for the mistake they made, these cops didn't know Luisa was left-handed. They assumed, like most people would've, that she was right-handed. Most lefties wear their watch on the opposite wrist. A left-handed junkie would've used the other arm. They had no reason to think otherwise. I didn't. The one picture I have of her alive, there was no watch on her right wrist."

Toni said, "Not everybody wears a watch."

"I thought that, too, so I searched for other pictures. A friend of mine works at the newspaper. He combed through the archives, old copies and microfiche."

"And?" Toni asked.

"Luisa was never photographed with a pen in her left hand. Pictures always depicted her standing giving a speech, or looking intense—"

"Stop this," Toni said. "Leave it alone. She's dead and nothing will bring her back."

Isabella reached out with a hand. Toni pushed it away and directed her anger at me. "How about you answer a question?"

"Alright. Ask me."

"How did you get a hold of that picture, the one of her dead?"

"In room four-twenty, at Park Plaza?"

"Answer the goddamn question," Toni said.

"The picture was given to me and, before you ask who gave it to me, you need to know I was given a file along with it, by people who were suspicious about the narrative around Luisa Ramírez's death."

"Narrative?" Toni said.

"The story of someone who was a threat to politicians and businessmen who stood to lose a lot of money because she was loud and proud to help the poor. Someone who had to be put down."

It was a hard choice of words. Luisa Ramírez was a person and not a pet. I had said "put down" to underscore the point. Powerful people don't see people; they see inconveniences and obstacles in their quest for more power or to maintain what power they have. In their eyes, Luisa Ramírez was a nuisance.

"Suicide or not, she's still a junkie in everyone's eyes," Toni said. "Nothing's changed that narrative."

"It changes if I have the original ME Report, the one that was suppressed."

Toni's mouth formed a small o, and she turned pale. I explained.

"The Medical Examiner was told to change the cause of death, threatened, and then exiled west. I have a copy of his report. The cause of death was initially listed as a homicide."

Toni moved from scratching her arm to biting her lip. "Okay. And?"

"I have an unanswered question. I don't have the name of the cops who leaned on the doctor, and I don't know why Luisa was at Park Plaza. All I have is the name of her next of kin."

"Did I miss the question?"

I held up my hand. "Hold that thought. I think Izzy can answer something for me."

"I can?" she asked and shot me a weird look because it was the first time I'd called her Izzy.

"The cops who attacked you, were they the same ones who chased us?"

"Yes. I pointed them out to you, from the window. Remember?"

"And they protect whoever runs drugs at Park Plaza, but what about other cops?"

I described Kiernan and O'Mara to her, and she said that she'd seen them at Park Plaza. Not all the time, but enough to convince me they were players in a scheme that involved narcotics. I asked her, on a complete lark, whether she'd seen a cop with a scar on his cheek. Her body answered before "Yes" left her mouth. She'd hugged herself.

"Now, for something that has been bothering me for some time, and it's something that has been in front of my face this whole time. Every time I've been around the two of you, you've both shortened each other's names and—"

Isabella answered, "We're friends and that's what friends do. So what?"

"Does that mean the both of you were friends with Luisa? Luisa may have died in Apartment 420, but she didn't live there, and yet the two of you have called her Lou. Friends perhaps?" I pointed my finger at Isabella. "Let's start with you."

"What...why?" Her hand played with a gold chain I hadn't noticed around her neck.

"It's Izzy for Isabella, so that must mean Toni is short for something. My guess is Antonia. Am I right?"

Toni looked at me wide-eyed and it wasn't from the Columbian coffee.

"You're Antonia R. Ruiz, aren't you?" Before she could answer, I put the puzzle pieces together. "It was right there in front of me the whole time. Ruiz and Ramírez are common last names. The name for the next of kin on the paperwork was listed as Antonia R. Ruiz. The middle initial R is for Ramírez, isn't it?"

Toni's eyes were wet. She wiped away a tear and sniffled. "Lou was my sister, and I used Ruiz, my mother's last name, and Luisa dropped Ruiz and took my father's last name, Ramírez. I wouldn't expect you to understand, but middle and last names are done differently in our culture. Excuse me for a sec."

I looked to Izzy and asked, "Middle and last names are different how?"

"Have you heard of the writer Gabriel García Márquez?"

"Sure," I said. *Hundred Years of Solitude*. Why?"

"García was his father's last name and Márquez, his mother's."

Toni visited the sink and tore a piece of paper towel from the roll near the kitchen sink, and blew her nose. She returned and sat down.

"In all this time, nobody knew you were her sister?" I asked.

"Lou suggested I use my mother's maiden name Ruiz so I wouldn't attract attention."

"And why was she there?"

"I was pregnant at the time. Lou would stop and check to see how I was doing, and she'd give me money. She was determined to get me out of Park Plaza. She said things were heating up around the redevelopment project, and she expected resistance. After she died, I kept my mouth shut and did my best to stay invisible."

"I had it all wrong," I said. "It wasn't the businessmen in the renewal project that had her killed. Luisa jeopardized the business arraignment between cops and drug dealers."

"One dealer," Toni said and named him.

I asked for pen and paper, which Isabella fetched from a drawer and handed to me. I instructed them both to write down everything they could remember about the cops they'd seen and what they knew about this dealer. I asked for descriptions. I wanted dates and times, as best as they could remember them, and any other names if they had them, and I wanted it all in writing.

"One last question before you start writing," I said. Toni looked up at me, her mascara ruined. "This file I read said your sister did have a drug problem, but the ME said other than the injection site on her left arm, he couldn't find any marks on her body that suggested drug use. Am I missing something?"

"Her thing was pills," Toni said. "Ludes, in particular. My sister always had a hard time sleeping. What started as a solution became a problem. She started abusing, but sought help back home in Puerto Rico. She was still using the name Ruiz at the time, which is why nobody knew her drug of choice." She looked at the blank piece of paper. "You know whatever I write here I'll have to repeat in court."

Toni didn't push the pen and paper away, but she was tired, the kind of tired from being scared all the time.

"Something tells me you won't have to testify."

"Meaning I'll end up dead, like my sister, and what about my kid?"

"Let me worry about that," I said.

"I'm sorry," she said and looked down. "I'm ashamed."

"Ashamed? You have nothing to be ashamed about. You did what you had to do."

"Not ashamed about that, Mr. Cleary," she said and looked up at me. "I'm ashamed because I didn't claim her body. I couldn't. I didn't give her the funeral she deserved. She was my sister."

Chapter Twenty-Three: Seventy-Two Hours

When I asked for more time on the Ramírez case, Pinto had given me seventy-two hours.

With copies from the ME in Worcester in my jacket, and what JC told me about the doctor in my head, I added the handwritten statements from two women, signed and dated, for the rendezvous with Pinto. I'd leave it to more capable hands to trace the money the dealer kicked backed to the cops for protection and muscle. I returned to the spot where Pinto fed the ducks.

Ahead of me, the little man was standing in front of an enormous elm, hands inside his pockets, chin up and admiring the canopy overhead. The shade from the great tree almost swallowed him up. I stopped for a second when a black squirrel darted in front of me. Pinto saw me and checked his watch.

"I was beginning to think you'd use the full seventy-two hours. Any news?"

He began to walk and I accompanied him.

"Overdose, but not a suicide."

"We were afraid of that. Proof?"

"Inside my pocket, close to my heart."

I placed my hand on my chest, like a kid reciting the Pledge of Allegiance.

"Am I to take it that you have concerns since you're not forthcoming with it?"

"Cops killed her and cops run drugs in the plaza."

He pointed to something in a tree. I couldn't see what, but I'd assumed it was another squirrel. Intelligent, sociable and aggressive, they were notorious for mugging the tourists for food. I noticed clusters of mushrooms around the base of the tree.

"You can't see them, but you can hear them," Pinto said.

I listened. I heard the breeze through the treetops, branches swaying, and the cacophonous thrum of birds.

"Starlings," Pinto said. "Shakespeare used one to repeat the king's name in *Henry IV, Part I*. At the turn of the century, an admirer of the Bard, some idiot in New York, released 60 starlings in Central Park, and then the following year, he released another 40. That's 100 starlings."

"With all due respect, I can add."

"I'm certainly not telling you this fact to test whether you can add, Mr. Cleary."

"A metaphor then?"

"More like cause and effect; problem and deterrent."

"I'm listening."

"From that initial release of 100 starlings, we now have 200 million of the birds in North America. In addition to the godawful sound they make, starlings interfere with planes and their droppings are a scourge and damage buildings. Starlings are also thieves because they refuse to build their own nests. They'll overtake another nest and kill the occupants if necessary. Not unlike corruption. You know how you stop them?"

"The cops or the birds?"

"You prune the branches, or you find yourself a hawk. Let's continue our walk, Mr. Cleary."

A jogger flitted past us. Jogging was the latest fitness craze, after aerobics and jazzercise, two programs military wives developed. An old man on a bench was tearing up a stale bagel to feed the pigeons.

"Talk to me about what else you found," Pinto said.

"I have a statements from two witness."

"He or she was there at the time of Ms. Ramírez's demise?"

"She was next door and saw two cops move the body," I said.

"The other one?"

"Like the first witness, she can speak to the drug trade around Park Plaza. She named the dealer, and she was very detailed about the police involved, and she can support the Medical Examiner's theory that Luisa Ramírez was murdered."

"Support how?"

"Luisa was left-handed and she can speak to the fact that Luisa didn't have a history with narcotics. I'd prefer these two women didn't testify against the drug dealer and the cops on his payroll. I already had a run-in with two of his colleagues."

"I see," Pinto said. "You said descriptions. Do you think your witnesses can identify the players?"

"If someone showed her departmental photos, then I'm confident the answer is yes," I said. "Ramírez was killed because she was bad for business. Sweat the bad guys in the box, and you might learn how far and wide their business runs in the rank and file. The trail starts blue at the bottom but I wouldn't be surprised if you found brass at the top."

"Anything else?"

"The Medical Examiner in Worcester. Cops spooked him. I think with the right protection and assurance, he can be persuaded to make a formal statement."

I put my hand on Pinto's arm to stop our walk. He looked at my hand and I pulled it back. His eyes glanced up and the twilight hour made them darker. Pinto's sense of fashion remained ruffled and rumpled as an old dollar bill, but the smooth skin, the absence of worry lines on his forehead or crow's feet around the eyes gave him an ageless quality that had me thinking of cigars and cognac, a lit fireplace and the portrait of Dorian Gray above the mantlepiece.

"Level with me," I said. "How do you see all this playing out?"

"I don't like to speculate, Mr. Cleary."

"Indulge me. You asked me to look into Ms. Ramírez's death, and I've more than delivered. Agree or disagree?"

"I agree, presuming you hand me the report next to your heart."

I eased the paperwork out of my breast pocket. I held it in front of him, as if I had second thoughts about surrendering it. He was the worst kind of fish because he wouldn't reach for the bait. Dark shark eyes, the kind that belonged to Michael Corleone, stared back at me.

"You'll see to it that the Commissioner reads this?" I asked.

"He'll read it, yes, and he'll do what he will with the information."

"In a perfect world, the bad guys are thrown in jail, and bent cops get bounced."

"We don't live in a perfect world, Mr. Cleary."

I handed him the thick envelope. He didn't bother to confirm the contents inside. Either he trusted me, or he had decided to wait until he was behind the wheel of his junker to satisfy his curiosity. We stood there for a long minute, the chattering of starlings overhead, loud, insistent, and annoying.

"Imperfect as this world is," I said, "the Commissioner can prune a rotted tree."

Pinto smiled. "True, but I can't speak for him or for his right hand."

"Oh, how could I forget Shadow and his squad," I said. "But if you were to offer them advice, they'd listen, right?"

"They'd take it under advisement, naturally."

"Naturally," I repeated. "Perchance you might tell me what that advice would be?"

"I might suggest to the Commissioner that he'd make an example of one or two of the men."

He stopped on purpose, a pause for effect.

"One or two of the men…what about the rest?" I asked.

"I could suggest we leave them to you, Mr. Cleary."

"Me?" He tapped the side of my arm. I glanced at my sleeve. "What?" I asked.

"The Commissioner and Shadow can prune trees. I'm the dwarf, who gets things done, remember? You on the other hand have the most enviable role."

"And what role is that?"

"You're the hawk."

173

Chapter Twenty-Four: Details

I couldn't put Mr. B off any longer. I owed the man an update. I called The 'Ham and left a message for Tony. He returned my call before the song on the radio finished. He said he'd send Sal over to pick me up for the drive to Mr. B's place. It would be me, Sal, and Tony in the car to Neverland, as in Newton, as in the suburb that was never for the poor of heart or of pocket.

Sal stopped the car in front of a wrought-iron gate. A guard emerged from a pillbox. He approached the Cadillac like he was Border Control. His partner stayed inside the box.

Sal said something in Italian, the guy turned to his comrade, and the gate creaked open with a metallic sound. As we passed the two guards, I noticed bullet holes in the guardhouse. Sal flashed the high beams to alert the help at the top of the hill. Seconds later, lights bright enough for Fenway stadium illuminated the driveway. Wealth can buy sunlight at night.

Victorian mansions reek of death. This citadel on this hill had been built around the time new money in America were sending their daughters abroad to marry old money in Europe. I imagined marble with varicose veins in the foyer and a grand staircase of oak after the front door closed behind me. The butler's face, grim and gray, didn't move as he took our coats. The butler disappeared, and then returned. I expected and received the funereal line "This way, please."

The two stories of stairs were steep enough to make a mountain goat asthmatic. No doubt Sal and Tony were familiar with the place, but they deferred to the butler as to where the don would receive us in the necropolis.

The man in his evening tux stopped. His left hand lifted to reveal the path. Not quite Versailles, nonetheless, framed artwork accompanied us on both sides of a boulevard for a hallway. The collection was organized by nationality and movements. Constable, Cozen, and Turner represented the British; Géricault, Gros, and Ingres stood in for the French, while the Americans from the Hudson School were the last hurrah before the don's door. There wasn't one Italian in the bunch. The butler instructed Sal and Tony to wait, while he escorted me inside.

He parted French doors. I entered a dark, masculine, and moody study. Logs crackled in the fireplace. A bookcase filled with leather-bound volumes stood on one side of the room. I was disappointed not to find dead things mounted on the other wall or a bear rug on the floor. The don himself occupied the armchair in front of the fireplace. I saw the pale hand, its mutated finger hooked on the armrest. On a small stand next to him, I saw an empty glass and a decanter, half-full with whiskey.

"Have a seat, please," he said.

There was an empty chair next to him. I sat down and looked over his way. The don seemed pale, shrunken and harmless. A man was supposed to look different in his home, comfortable and less guarded, aligned to his inner nature. The don appeared old and fragile as onionskin. Ancient or not, decrepit or healthy, I never forgot that this man was a killer. Then I saw his face and understood.

Sorrow. Grief. I recognized the distant look because my mother exhibited the same state of mind after my father's death. The eyes said it all, as if the intellect had raked and reviewed every clue, every instance of where a person thought he could have done something different to alter the outcome.

I waited, aware that he had wanted to unburden himself. The awful things he had done in life he would never confess to a cop or a priest, but this was different. He was an uncle who had lost a nephew, a family member. He talked and I listened.

The don had said that, contrary to what outsiders might think, men like him had wanted a different life for their kids. When they were growing up, there were prejudices, the don explained. Italians were considered no better than blacks. He said that if a girl back then dated an Italian, it was considered an interracial relationship. "Believe that?" he asked me. "This damn country has always been about the color of your skin, or your religion. Negroes have had it worse, because you can't change black."

I listened to a lecture that Strom Thurmond would've appreciated. He explained the unspoken agreements people had, back in the day. The Jews would stay in the West End, the Italians in the North End, and the Irish in Southie. Everybody, he said had their own neighborhood and everyone was happy. More like the Warsaw Ghetto with a curfew, I wanted to say but I kept my mouth shut. I remember as a kid that, if you wandered into the wrong territory after hours, the locals chased you out.

"You must understand how it was," the don said.

"Because I'm Irish?"

"Did you know that British officers in World War I used to bet the change in their pockets on who would live and die after they ordered the Irish into battle?"

I sat there, hoping I didn't have to endure too much more of this. I tried to distract him. I told him we had to talk, and it was important, a matter of importance, and time was of the essence, and all the other polite clichés. The don had gas and, like the old Esso commercial, he had a tiger in the tank.

"You want to talk to me about my nephew," he said. "I didn't want the life I lived for him. I encouraged him to be an engineer if medicine didn't interest him. I suggested politics, but only after he graduated from law school. Ever notice how all the politicians are lawyers? No, not this kid. He wanted respect, for people to take notice of him when he entered a room. He equated fear with respect. The problem is he didn't want to do the hard work that earned real respect, the kind you get when you know something with your mind, and not because you can use your fists." He sighed and looked at me. "It's bad news, isn't it?"

"Afraid so."

"Let's hear it."

"I have an ask after I'm done," I said.

Coal black eyes, venomous as a cobra's, considered me. The don closed them, and opened them again. His hand stirred the air to start the conversation. "Fine, but tell me everything," he said. "Don't censor yourself on account of my feelings, or worry how I may react. I want the unfettered truth, then we'll deal with your request. First, did you find my nephew?"

"I found him."

"Not alive, I presume."

"No, sir. Not alive."

"An accident?"

"No."

"Someone has to pay then, regardless of your request."

If the don owned a walking stick, now would've been the time he'd have placed both hands on it and listened to my theory of the crime. He hadn't and he didn't. Both hands, like talons, clutched the armrests.

The day my father ended his life, my mother sat in the kitchen while the police investigated the room where he had killed himself. Nobody likes being the messenger or the recipient of awful news. Details were details, painful but necessary. This was the part of the job I disliked most. I hated it as a soldier, as a cop, and as a civilian. "Sorry for your loss" never cut it. Bad news was as inevitable as death.

Most especially death.

"There was a body found inside the building in the fire on Symphony Road."

"So I read in the paper. You think it's my nephew's?"

"The remains match the description you gave me for height, weight, and age. The dental records aren't in, but I'm convinced they'll match. There's another reason why I believe the body is your nephew. A personal effect. Did your grandnephew wear a crucifix ring?"

"Yes, I'd given him one. The body they have in City Morgue has such a ring?"

"The habit of wearing it left an impression on his pinky finger. He wore the ring you gave him on that finger?"

He nodded and said, "On his left hand. The papers said there's a suspect in custody, somebody we both know. I assume therein is your request. I can't and will not grant clemency, Mr. Cleary."

No heat from a fireplace could warm the cold presence in the room.

"I understand, but I can tell you the man we both know did not start the fire."

"How can you be sure?"

"We both know his specialty, and we know he's a pro at what he does."

"Mistakes have been known to happen."

"Not with Jimmy," I said. "The arsonist responsible for Symphony Road was a hack."

"So you know who started the fire?"

"I do, but there's a wrinkle." I waited until Mr. B looked at me again. "He didn't know your nephew was in the building, and it's not because he was careless. There's no way he could've known. Like Jimmy, he isn't a killer."

"I'm supposed to take your word for it? Because he says he didn't know the kid was in the building?"

Every mystery show detective, whether it was Dave Toma or Jim Rockford, enjoyed the sound of cuffs around wrists or the jail's door sliding shut. I did, too, even though I knew this wouldn't play out that way.

"I have proof," I said. "The newspaper left out a detail, and it's something only the killer would've known. The guy I know, who set this fire, didn't know this detail."

"What are you saying?" Mr. B asked. "I have people at the newspapers, and I was told everything I needed to know about the fire."

"And yet you didn't know it was your nephew."

"Like I would tell them my nephew was missing? And as you said, dental records needed to be reviewed, which is what a responsible journalist would do before they print a name. What's this detail you claim exonerates the man?"

I laid it out bare and simple as I could. "Your nephew was tied up when he died."

"You're saying he struggled?"

"I am."

"Asphyxiation?"

"Yes."

The log in the fireplace cracked and broke in two. There was burst of red, a blast of heat, before they both died down in hues of orange and soft yellow.

"And you know who did this? I mean, the person who hired this hack arsonist."

"I do, and now for my ask."

"Let me guess, you want to know why the man ordered the building burnt down?"

"No, I know why. He wanted the place, made a bid, got turned down and figured that if he couldn't have it, nobody else could."

"The greatest mistake in business is to make it personal. Your request?" the don asked.

"I want to find out why your nephew was in that building."

"Why somebody tied up my nephew?"

"Yes," I said.

"Need anything from me?"

"Tony, for when I'm make my move," I said. "I'll visit the man responsible for the fire myself, and ask him why your nephew was tied up and inside the building."

"And if he refuses to answer?"

"There's Tony."

The fire spat and sputtered, the air near the screen popped.

"And when you get your answers?"

"There's Tony."

My answer pleased the don. Color returned to his face. He folded his hands in front of his chest, twirled his thumbs in deliberation before he summoned the ancient butler. The man appeared and the don said something in Italian. I heard the names Sal and Tony. The don spoke to me while we waited for the butler to complete the roundtrip.

"I like you, Mr. Cleary, despite how the Irish treated Italians in this town. But that was way before your time. I'd like for you to consider me a friend should you ever need something. Everyone needs a friend. As to your request, I have one stipulation."

I didn't like the smile. I didn't have a choice. "Sure," I said.

"Sal joins you and Tony."

Sal was the don's protégé, and I understood the family business wasn't humanitarian work, like the Peace Corps or the Red Cross, but I didn't like the idea.

"All due respect, Mr. B, but he's a kid."

"You mentioned a detail in the papers, not intended for public knowledge. I have a detail of my own." Another smile I didn't like. "Sal was the victim's brother."

Chapter Twenty-Five: Road Trip

The don asked for a word with Tony Two-Times before we left.

I sized Sal up in the Versailles hallway. The kid was big on personal space. He put two feet of marble between us. Quiet, in his suit and tie, dark hair parted to the side, Sal could pass for a model or an actor. He was the kind of young Italian-American man mothers encouraged their daughters to date. Wholesome as bread, ethnic in a good way, Sal could have his pick of Catholic girls, ready for nights of cheap cigarettes, mediocre beer, and humdrum sex in the backseats of cars, if it weren't for the piece inside his suit.

I could tell Sal carried. The shortened stride earlier and the clipped arm swing on the gun's side gave him away. Without turning away from the Turner on the wall, I asked him, "A six, or semi-auto?"

"Excuse me?"

"Like to know what I have for backup. Are you Mr. Reliable with a six-shooter, or Mr. Modern, who wants and needs firepower. Which is it?"

I covered the two feet between us. He did exactly what I'd expected him to do.

"You turned," I said and he gave me the confused look.

"I came at you and you turned."

"So what."

"Are you really up for this, Sally?"

"What the hell are you talking about?"

"A guy moves in the direction of the piece on him. He'll pivot away from the person coming to him so he can give himself time to draw his weapon.

It's instinct, a reflex."

"Is that a bad thing?"

"It is if you're up against a cop." I let that sit for a beat and answered him before he said or asked the next thing. "You do that with a cop and he'll drop you."

"Isn't he supposed to identify himself first?"

"Yeah, and the Sox will win the Series this year." I unbuttoned his jacket and parted it. I was right. Semi-auto. "Tell me about your friend here."

Sal pulled it out of his waistband for Show-and-Tell. "Smith & Wesson Model 59, fourteen rounds. Stagger-stack magazine and double-action. Shall I continue?"

"Nice," I said. "Get yourself a proper holster before you blow your nuts off."

"How else were you able to tell?"

"Some guys can't stop touching it while seated, and this one is subtle…the clothes they wear are roomier, likely out of season to accommodate the gun's size and weight. Your jacket is two sizes too big. This concludes today's lesson."

"My uncle said you're all right."

"For a mick, you mean."

"He respects you." Sal buttoned his jacket. "He says you're not hot-headed, and you're the most dangerous guy in the room." Now he did the pause so I didn't ask the question. "He says, you've got nothing to lose, and when you use your gun, you shoot to kill." I looked at him, the one confused now. His uncle had never seen me handle myself. The kid explained. "My uncle read your files, Army and BPD."

Tony knifed through the small divide between us. Something had crawled into the man's shoes and gave him hot feet. Tony moved like a train, with speed and a destination. We followed him, expecting him to head for the Caddy outside. He veered off course to another car. He barked out the order to a valet for keys.

"Cleary, you're in front. I'm driving. Sal, you're in back."

"Why do I sit in back?"

182

"Because I said so." Driver's door opened. The bolt on the passenger side popped but I hadn't moved. Tony saw my hesitation and said over the hood of the car, "What the hell are you waiting for, an engraved invitation?"

I got in and Tony turned the engine over and Sal sat back in the seat. All that hustle, like a pregnant girl on the way to church, and he wanted the engine to warm up first. His eyes focused straight ahead, his fingers gripped the wheel. Tony the thinker. My hand ventured for the dial to the radio. His eyes warned me to reconsider my foolish idea. I made my next mistake. I talked.

"Thought Sal was the wheelman."

"Not today."

I commented on the leather interior, how it was black and joked if it hid blood better. Tony didn't appear amused.

"You want the Pan Am experience, is that it?" Tony said. "Fine, I'll give it to you. Glove compartment and the armrest next to Sal are stocked." He shifted gears and eased the car forward. "Body of the car, the windshield and all the glass you see are bulletproof. Happy now? If you want, I can describe the engine."

We swam down the long driveway. Gate opened, the Hollywood studio behind us, we coasted into the night, into the New England darkness the Puritans feared the most. There was not a word spoken for a mile. I adjusted to the silence, to blindness, to the ambient mood.

Tony's knuckles held the wheel, white, tight, and steady.

"How long has it been?" I asked Tony.

"How long has what been?"

"Without a cigarette?"

"A few days, I don't know," he said. "Why?"

"I read somewhere giving up cigarettes is harder than quitting heroin."

"It's not the same thing," Tony said. "I'm no junkie."

I turned my attention to the road. Faisal lived in Brookline and we weren't on Beacon Street, or Boylston, or Commonwealth Ave. Massachusetts wasn't known for road signs. Ask for directions anywhere and it's always straight ahead, a left or a right of some donut shop, or some dive restaurant, or a tree with a distinctive scar. An out-of-towner has no idea how many coffee shops, or bars there are in any given neighborhood. City planners designed road signs to be invisible until the last possible second. They'd allow enough time for a curse word. The headlights flashed against a sign.

"Did that sign say I-90 East?" I asked, but Tony didn't answer. When he goosed the gas, the destination snapped into view. "We're going back to the South End, aren't we?"

"Brief excursion," he said.

"I didn't forget anything at my place."

"Sure about that?"

"Yeah, I'm sure. What gives?"

"The don wants us to bring the arsonist along."

I imagined how Larry would react to the idea of a midnight ride.

"What makes you think I'm going to hand him over to you?" I put a little indignation behind my voice. "I told the don the guy didn't know about the body. Are you telling me Mr. B doesn't believe me? Is that what you're saying?"

I tried to act offended but I was nervous. I had asked the don to spare Larry. I revisited the conversation in my head. I should've mentioned the basement was locked. I should have described Larry's reaction to news of a corpse. Guys who lie well start with fibbing to their mothers. A great liar could convince the Pope Moses had dropped a third tablet in the desert and it was worth the Vatican's money to find it. Larry wasn't that. Larry was a bargain-rate firefly.

"Nothing will happen to the guy, okay. The don promised," Tony said.

"What if I don't know where the guy is?"

"Nice try," Tony said. "You know where he is." He concentrated on the road. "I know it. You know it. And the don knows it."

More silence. More white lines and asphalt.

"The don gives you his word this guy is safe, if his story checks out."

And there it was: the exception, the loophole, the Big If.

"It checks out," I said.

"I hope so for his sake. Now where do I go?"

I gave him the address to Nikos's place. I couldn't help but feel like Judas walking into the garden with the Romans. Nikos had helped me and given Larry sanctuary. At this rate, I'll be sending Nikos a fruit basket for several holidays, Catholic and Orthodox.

"You got keys for handcuffs on you?" Tony asked.

"Thought we'd never discuss your sex life."

"You're hilarious. I've got handcuffs, but no keys."

He knew there was a universal key to cuffs. I waited for his explanation.

"I'm used to putting them on guys, not taking them off. Have them, or not?"

"Yeah, I've got keys at my place."

Tony parked the car, the doors opened, and we reconvened on the sidewalk. The wind had kicked up. A wet moon hung in the sky, the smell of rain was in the air. I was first in line up the stairs, a traitor with no thirty pieces of silver, and two Romans behind me.

After a brief explanation, Nikos fetched his set of keys for Larry's apartment. If he were Pontius Pilate, he wouldn't have washed his hands for whatever happened to me. He held the keyring up for me to see and said, "Promise me I'm going to Florida when this is over."

I promised.

We walked downstairs to Larry's place. I knocked on the door before I used the key. Larry was in the kitchen. He saw us. He saw me, he saw Tony, and he saw Sal. It was like the scene when the guys came for Tessio in *The Godfather*. The cards were all played, the bets made, and now it was time to pay the house.

There's a fear that lives inside every man, a sensation he can't kill. The heart pounds, the blood pressure rises, and the mind races. It's a fear confidence can't overcome. Larry had that look in his eyes. A sense of failure was what you'll see in the faces of most men, and horror in younger ones, like the kids I saw in Vietnam. Sal was young—stupid young—like so many boys I met in the service. Youth afforded Sal the luxury to be cocky and confident

185

whereas Larry was on the other side of it all, afraid but resigned to his fate.

Nikos was another one who could understand what I was thinking. Florida was his sunset on the horizon and there he'd enjoy the review of a completed life, one that included a long and loving marriage, some material success, and the brief moment he enjoyed as a father. I'm confident he'd confront death with dignity.

Tony, on the other hand, has a fifty-fifty chance about his last moments. There will be no subtitles, no frantic moments, or signs of disagreement. Death will come for him in the form of a friend at the door, someone he's known all his life, and sent there to put a bullet in the back of his head. The other scenario was that Tony would be lured to a meeting, and he'll know it's his time. Acceptance.

I watched them in the kitchen. Tony turned his head when he heard the meow. I looked at Nikos, as if he'd betrayed me.

"What?" Nikos said. "The guy was lonely, all alone in this apartment, so I let him borrow the cat. I didn't think you'd mind."

Delilah sat on a rug facing me, Tony, and Sal. Her feline mind, if I could claim to know it, wondered who these creatures were in her new kingdom. She had conquered Nikos and Larry, but now two visitors warranted her appraisal. Her tail thumped the carpet.

She meowed again. Tony looked over at her. After the third meow, Delilah blocked Tony and Sal from leaving with Larry. Tony tried to shoo her away with a foot. Delilah hissed.

"Cleary, I always figured you for a dog person. You ready, or what?"

"For what?"

"For you to get that other thing."

"What thing?" Larry asked.

Mob guys and their code. Flour in a pizza parlor, for instance, could mean flour or it could mean heroin. Tony must've not wanted to spook Larry with the handcuffs yet. Tony moved and Delilah countered. He shot me a look. "Call off the little lion you've got here, please."

I called Delilah and gave her some affectionate strokes. I carried her over to the Barcalounger. My jacket must've have puckered and Tony saw my .38.

"What do you need that for?" he asked.

"I feel naked without it. Any objections?"

"None."

"What thing is he talking about?" Larry asked again.

"Time for a road trip," Tony said.

A short ride later, and we were in front of my building. I was given three minutes to find keys for Tony's handcuffs, so I sprinted up those steep stairs. A lot can happen inside of three minutes. A boxer survives or finishes off his opponent. In three minutes, I've sloshed through water, crabbed through mud, and moved through haze while mortar kicked up dirt and body parts.

I passed the landlady's fat dog barking. I reached my door with some air left in my lungs. I turned the lock and then the knob, opened the door, slid in and closed it behind me.

The room was dark. I crossed it without the light because I knew the place. Those keys Tony wanted were inside the desk by the window, which gave me a view to Tony's car. The streetlamp's light played soft on the car's hard green body. I saw another car snake its way down the street, its headlights dirty and yellow.

I hated running down stairs like I disliked running downhill. I slid into my seat. Tony turned the wheel and pulled away. Tony wiggled his fat fingers in front of my face. The keys, he wanted them now. I dug into my pocket, handed them over, and his hand closed like a clam and disappeared. I looked through the rearview mirror and saw headlights.

We drove through Brookline, a little hamlet the Algonquians called Muddy River. It's home to trees, the Green Line, and Boston's Jewish community. Tony was Dudley Do-Right at the wheel. He braked before the white line and stopped at red lights. He stayed in his lane. He checked the mirror with careful eyes for the safety of his passengers and others on the road.

All up and down most Brookline streets there are long and there were broad entrances and massive doors with clean glass, unlike South Boston, where residents were two steps from their front door to the curb.

A cop on a loud motorcycle came up on the right side of the car. He turned his white helmet our way for a look-see. The light changed and the bike roared ahead and cut Tony off. Tony Two-Times didn't honk, curse, or slap the steering wheel in frustration.

We crept up on where Sharif Faisal lived. Trees lined both sides of the street, their branches uplifted in prayer, and cars slept in driveways. It was too peaceful for me. I didn't like it. I didn't like it one bit. Tony looked left and then right while we prowled the street. Like me, he was looking for blind spots, plotting an entrance and an escape.

"You and Sal get out and wait," Tony said.

Tony threw the bolt. Larry reached for the handle. "Not you, my friend," Tony said.

I got out first and Sal followed and shut the door. Tony and Larry enjoyed an animated conversation behind glass. For a non-Italian Larry did his share of talking with his hands, until he couldn't because of the handcuffs.

"What do you thinking they're talking about?" Sal asked, hands inside his jacket.

"How should I know?"

"You're the one who went to the Sam Spade Detective School."

"I prefer Marlowe, and get your hands out of your pockets. People will think you've got something to hide."

"But I do have something to hide."

Sal pulled one side of his jacket to the side and revealed the Smith &Wesson.

"You're pissing me off, kid."

"What did I do?"

"It's what you didn't do," I said and pulled his hands out of his coat. "You don't want people to notice one single thing about you. Nothing. See, the houses here? Where there are lights, there are people, and nosy neighbors look outside their windows."

"Thanks, but you still haven't answered my question."

We both turned our attention to the discussion behind bulletproof glass.

"What do you think Tony is telling him?"

"He's probably stipulating terms," I said.

"What terms?" Sal asked.

"Whatever your uncle wanted that will keep Larry alive."

We watched for a few more seconds. The show ended with Larry handcuffed to the steering wheel. Tony emerged from the car. "God Almighty, that guy can sure jabber."

I didn't answer. I noticed a car turn the corner and park down the street. The headlights turned off and I wanted to see who would get out of the car, but Tony said we should go inside the building for Faisal.

The front door was locked. A callbox was on the wall, the names of tenants on narrow slips of paper next to black buttons. I doubted our notorious landlord listed himself on the directory. The man at the desk, the concierge, was our first point of contact. He looked like the nervous type, the kind who drank too much coffee, and ate cigarettes instead of a decent meal. He unlocked the door and stuck his head through the opening.

"You gentlemen can't park here. This is private property," he said.

Tony answered. "My friend here was a boxer."

"What?"

Tony pushed in the door. I decked the man and caught him before he hit the floor. We housed him in a nearby supply closet. I unclipped the ridiculous key ring from his belt before I let Sal truss the man up tighter than a holiday turkey. Tony stoppered the man's mouth with a rag.

"Sure he can breathe?" Sal asked.

"What?" Tony reconsidered his handiwork. "He has two nostrils."

When we returned to the front desk, I checked the directory and I was happy to discover I had been half-wrong. SF wasn't listed, but there was a blank piece of paper in a slot next to a number, on the top floor. Penthouse suite.

Chapter Twenty-Six: Borrowed Time

Tony reached inside his suit jacket and eased the Colt out of the stable, a six-inch barrel .357 Trooper Mark III. He looked at me and said, "What?"

"You're Irish, after all. A real Jimmy Files."

"Who is Jimmy Files?" Sal asked.

"Detroit cop and the real Dirty Harry. Overcompensate much, Tony?"

"Shut up, Cleary."

James Bond preferred Vesper martinis, a PPK Walther with a Brausch silencer as his pistol of choice, and here was Tony with a howitzer. The bell rang, the elevator doors parted.

Tony pointed at me to take the other wall. His instructions to Sal were limited to pointing at the ground and saying words in Italian, words which might've meant "Stay here" or "Wait."

The doors to the elevator tried to close, but Sal's hand stopped them. Tony's noiseless heel-to-toe maneuver on the thin carpeting suggested military experience. He glanced over at me. My .38 was out.

Faisal's chateau was a step up from his other properties. Locked front door and call box were the best his other tenants could hope for in the way of security.

A kick, a cough, the frustrated chime, the elevator doors bumped open and closed with Sal as the wedge between them to give us our way out. Tony and I proceeded. I've done this hundreds of times as a cop, and I didn't need to know how many times he'd done it as a mob enforcer. Tony moved well for a man in a tailored suit and homemade wing-tips.

I used hand-signs from my patrol days and sure enough Tony understood them. Our plan was I would go in first. I raised an opened hand. Tony shook his head and his finger pointed me and them him, as in "Me and You. Together." I was against the idea.

/ I would breach the door first and he was my backup.

Kick. Cough. Ding. Elevator doors.

Fortunate for us, none of Faisal's neighbors had excellent hearing. No sooner had I thought that a lady in hair-rollers opened her door. She saw us. We saw her and she shut her door. Tony looked worried about a witness. He hesitated. My hand hovered up and down in the air, telling him to relax. He had a right to worry about a positive ID, but I'd bet that there was no great love for the landlord. I looked at the floor under her door. No sign of a shadow. She wasn't there, with a curious eye through the keyhole. I placed my ear to her door in case she was dialing the police or a neighbor, like the nosy Gladys Kravitz from *Bewitched*. Nothing.

We continued until we came to Faisal's door.

Standard Operating Procedure was the first man kicked in the door after a knock and identification. That wouldn't be us. Like a no-knock warrant, there would be no rap on wood or declaration tonight. I was the first man through the door and the second guy secured the room. That would be Tony.

There was one problem. Like a cliché from a horror film, the door was unlocked and ajar.

Sharif Faisal expected company. If Tony cast his shadow across that wedge of light from the room inside, Faisal could answer any number of ways, and my guess, none of them healthy for Tony.

Kick. Cough. Ding. Faisal had to have heard the elevators.

I holstered my weapon. "What are you doing?" Tony asked.

I knocked on the door. Not soft, not hard, but I knocked and the door creaked open. I wanted Faisal and whoever else might be on the other side of wood to think I was alone. If someone drilled a nice little hole in me, or a shotgun blast splattered most of me onto the wall, Tony would storm in and Mrs. Kravitz would make that phone call.

The cops would come. Tony and Sal would be long gone. The cops would stand over me, enjoying a smoke, and have a laugh as to who deserved a body bag: the pig landlord or the rat cop.

Faisal came into view, in a sea of unexpected purity. Everything was white, from the countertops and stools, to the white bar. The walls were white, the shag rug on the floor in front of me, white, and on top of it, a plate of clear glass over gnarled driftwood, also white. The schmuck was sitting in a low-set wooden chair, wearing a brown suit, a shirt the color of country mustard, and a thick gold chain around his neck. A black semi-automatic was near his right hand on the armrest.

"Welcome," he said and motioned with his left hand.

"How about I leave the door open?" I answered.

He didn't object. I wanted to keep Faisal talking and engaged. When people stop talking and listening is when they start shooting. I took two more steps. I was in front of him, so he'd never see Tony behind me. I could hit the deck and Faisal might get a shot off and miss, but there was no way he'd get both of us.

I pointed to the pistol within reach. "Nice weapon for an insecure guy."

"You think I'm insecure?"

"Good for a guy if he needs fifteen tries for the ribbon."

Faisal grinned. "And what do you use?"

"Six-shooter." I parted my jacket for him to see my .38.

"Old-timer's weapon."

I smiled. "Only takes one bullet to kill ya."

"And you think you can make the shot?"

"Try me." My eyes drifted to his gun. "It's your brains all over the snow in here."

I wasn't bluffing. I had one advantage over him, other than experience. First, he'd lost his chance by not shooting when I walked in. Second, his ass was so low in that chair he'd be shooting uphill.

I looked around fast. Not one book in the place. Not one potted plant. Not even one of those Boston ferns everyone was crazy about. They required little maintenance. Leave a fern in the bathroom to enjoy the steam from the shower, and the plant could mother itself. Not even one of those.

"Let's talk," I said.

"I'm listening."

"You can either get up and look outside your window, or you can take my word for it."

He said he'd take me at my word. That or gravity had pulled his can so low to the ground he'd need both hands to lift himself up and out of his chair.

"What would I see outside, if I were to look?"

"A car and a person inside it, with a story about a fire on Symphony Road, and the man who paid five-grand to set it off."

He did the little wave of the hand Queen Elizabeth made so popular. I wouldn't know a Bedouin from a Syrian, or T.E. Lawrence in ceremonial robes from a drag queen, but his pudgy face, the squirrel cheeks, the dark hair and eyes, and the arrogant nose annoyed me.

"Five-thousand dollars is a lot of money, and arson is a serious crime," he said.

The gun remained on the armrest. Faisal folded those hands business-like. I could tell he had a lot of practice with the move. I also was aware I had to close the deal soon. I had an impatient gangster behind me, a bellhop down the hall at the elevator.

"You should've thought this through, Mr. Cleary."

"You know my name?"

"Don't look so surprised," he said. "As for your man in the car, there's the matter of credibility, and then there's you, a former cop. As for the allegation of arson-for-hire, I need to remind you of one thing." He held up his index finger.

"And that is?"

"Judges and DA's are elected officials, and their success depends on their relationship with the police. There could be a sudden case of blue flu when your name is mentioned."

"You might be right, but there's also the matter of justice for the person who died in the fire on Symphony Road. This isn't a simple case of a fire for insurance money, but murder or, at the minimum, wrongful death."

"I'm a businessman," he said. "Tragedies happen in life, as do accidents."

I held up my left hand. "Interesting choice of words."

He had returned his gun hand on the armrest. The fingers crept towards the weapon.

"Go for it," I said.

He relaxed, his alligator smile widened. I never had a beef with Middle Easterners. People were upset with Arabs for OPEC and price gouging oil, and before that, the Seven Day War. I paid none of it any mind, but Faisal was different.

"The kid who died in your building was the nephew of a businessman," After a quick glance over my shoulder, I said, "You can come in."

Tony came in gun raised. I expected Faisal to freak out. He didn't. He surprised us with a tawdry grin. Tony told him, "Get up slowly, or you meet Muhammad on the mountain."

"Gentlemen, I don't know what this is about."

"You killed a kid," I said.

"Or left him to die, tied up like an animal," Tony added.

"Is that what the low-life outside told you?" Gun and armrest forgotten, Faisal interlaced his fingers behind his head now. "As I said, earlier, credibility; nobody will take the word of a drug addict and career criminal."

"But you'll admit, he works for you?" Tony asked.

"I felt pity for him and this is how he repays me."

I wondered whether Tony latched onto the Syrian's assumption. The slumlord thought we had Jerry in the car outside.

I ran with the man's mistake.

"More like he pays people off for you," I said. "People, like cops. Perhaps, our friend in the car told us who you tried to hire first to burn down the building."

Tony had had his cannon drawn on The Syrian the whole time. I put my hand out to tell him to lower it. He gave me a curious look. Once Tony relaxed, I moved fast to Faisal's chair and pocketed his weapon.

"I know a shakedown when I see one," the slumlord said. "You want money, is that? Name your price, gentlemen."

The arrogance, the belief he could buy his way out of everything and

194

knowing, in most cases, he'd succeed, I wanted to dent his head with my .38.

"Problem is this, Faisal. You paid off cops and you hired an arsonist. You're right. Nobody cares squat about what a junkie might say, because they're unreliable, and—"

"You think my reach ends with cops? You forget, justice is all about who you know, and what you can afford. I have money and connections. You think I'll take a plea-deal?"

Now, I smiled and I pointed to the window. "Take another look."

He glanced over his shoulder, but didn't move. I penciled in the last detail for him. "The guy in the car down there isn't your bagman, Jerry on Burbank Road."

"You lied to me? How clever of you. I forgot, it's permissible for cops to use deception in questioning a suspect," Faisal said, showing some teeth again. "Only problem is you're not a cop and this isn't a legal interrogation."

"You were wrong about another thing, Faisal," I said. "You can buy your way out of a courtroom, but you'll never escape family justice." I pointed to Tony. "He works for the don."

Faisal inhaled sharply through his nose. "So be it then. You're going to kill me."

Tony pushed me aside and tucked in his piece. Tony grabbed a handful of mustard shirt. "You and I will take a trip and have a conversation."

It was payback, and most guys would be begging for their life. Not Faisal, and that worried me.

"The kid came at me, threatening me," Faisal said.

"Hold on." I pulled on Tony's shoulder. "Threatening you how?"

"He said he'd ruin me. The punk bragged about how he'd laugh and watch my buildings burn to the ground like Nero watched Rome. The kid was a lunatic, demented in the head, so I taught him a lesson."

"You tied him up, and put him in a frying pan?" Tony said.

This wasn't what I'd call a textbook confession, but something wasn't right. Faisal stood his ground against Tony. There was not one bead of sweat on Faisal's forehead.

"Tell me, how does a kid threaten a scumbag like you?" Tony asked.

"The kid thought he was Caesar," Faisal said.

I listened to Faisal explain how the kid said he'd take Faisal's properties away from him, one by one. Vandalism. Scare off renters. Interfere with daily operations. For all I knew, Tony was thinking of Julius Caesar but I thought of Edward G. Robinson from the film *Little Caesar*. As much as I hated to admit it, The Syrian's story might've held a grain of truth. The kid could've been planning his future after his uncle attended his last opera and sang his final aria.

Tony steered the slumlord with a hand on his shoulder. I followed the two of them into the hallway. As we trekked towards the ghostly light of the elevator, my GI Joe instinct screamed again, something wasn't right with this snatch-and-grab. A man about to be taken on a one-way ride was weak-kneed and squealing.

Not Faisal.

In the elevator, my back against the wall, I reached for my .38 without anyone noticing. I told Tony I'd take over for him with Faisal. He said "Okay" and pressed the button for the first floor. Smug as a vulture in a tree watching his dinner die in front of him, Faisal didn't squirm or fidget.

I didn't like this at all.

The Army taught me a lot of things in the theater of death, less so for life back home. There, you'd never forgot the smell of death in the air, or in the fog over the water. Back in the world, death was nothing more than a clock on the wall, the desk in the corner, and the daily commute to work and home. In the field, you learn the only thing you can control was how you breathed and how you reacted. I exhaled and inhaled between chimes and floors to calm and prepare myself.

The bright ding and doors opened. I positioned myself behind Faisal. He was both my shield and hostage should something erupt. I scanned the lobby. Nothing.

I saw through the glass of the front door. Nothing.

I saw the car and Larry's profile behind glass. Nothing.

Tony used his shoulder to pushed the front door open. I backed off and let Sal through next. A breeze hit my face. There was twenty feet between the car and us. Lesser distances have cost me more blood and bullets. We moved.

Larry took his feet off the dashboard when he spotted us.

Sal, on my left, tugged on my sleeve. I didn't look. I listened.

"You said guys walk funny when they're carrying. Look."

I did. Two shadows northeast of us. Silhouettes. One man was above-average height, and medium-build. Second man was taller, thin and birdlike. Both picked up their pace.

I looked to the car and saw the scream behind the glass. No key in the ignition and handcuffed to the steering wheel, a frantic Larry struggled to unlock the door on the driver's side. Tony stopped, read the terrified look on Larry's face. A second before I said "Run," Larry hit the horn hard.

Battle cry or not, everyone ran. The two attackers raised their arms. Shots fired. The assault had begun. Sal, the fastest in the bunch, ran to the trunk of the car. He planned to take the driver's seat. I told Tony, "I'll provide cover."

I didn't shoot first, but Sal did. And not well.

Tony opened the passenger door and climbed in. Larry succeeded with the lock and flung the driver's door open for Sal. Head low, the kid ducked into the seat and snapped the door shut. I shoved Faisal in the backseat and waited outside for Sal to start the car.

Our two assailants came into view under a streetlamp as they shot round after round into the car, about to figure out the vehicle was bulletproof. I recognized them, despite the street clothes.

Kiernan and O'Mara.

Kiernan, gun in each hand, was shooting as if he was at the O.K. Corral. Uneven calibers and recoil made his hands jerk. O'Mara, on the other hand, had level aim. He was hitting the driver's side of the windshield on the beat like a metronome.

Tony tossed the keys to Sal, who somehow dropped them. They were either on the floor or they disappeared inside the leather seating. The car was bulletproof but I was worried about the tires. Kiernan and O'Mara were too busy trying to kill us to think about the wheels.

I decided to buy time. I crouched low and looked for anything I could take and I did. I shot Kiernan in the shin. With Kiernan down, I hoped O'Mara would attend to his partner.

"Forget about me and stop them," Kiernan screamed.

Sal turned the engine over. I hopped in as more bullets from O'Mara slammed into the windows, one concussive thud after another. Tony had already undone the handcuffs on Larry so Sal could use the steering wheel.

Sal shifted and the car growled. O'Mara ran back to his partner. Sal blinded them with the high beams and floored it. The vehicle almost clipped O'Mara. I looked over my shoulder to see them headed for their car, the one with the dirty headlights I'd seen in the South End. No wonder The Syrian was so smug. He must've called them.

Sal worked the wheel like a pro and our car fishtailed onto Washington Street. He ignored the blaring horns of oncoming traffic. With cold eyes he checked the rearview mirror, expecting a chase. Sal read my mind when he said, "Jamaica Way, here we come."

Sal rode the engine like a jockey in the Kentucky Derby through nighttime traffic. He moved into a pocket, weaved when he saw a slot for a better position. His flogged the car for maximum performance. There was the occasional bump and grind of near collisions. We bounced, we veered and we held onto leather.

The floor beneath us hummed. The windows rattled. My bones vibrated.

The last of the streetlights behind us, we entered the oily darkness of the Jamaica Way. Because it was designed for carriages, the four-lane thoroughfare was narrow and terminated into two rotaries.

Their headlights behind us gained speed. Kiernan and O'Mara were ghosts in the night.

We called the enemy ghosts in Vietnam. We didn't have to see them, but we knew they were there. Sal's mask of concentration was one I'd seen in combat. Duck, the biggest man in my patrol, carried The Pig, the M-60 machine gun, twenty-three pounds unloaded, and the most welcome sound in a firefight. Sal delivered that same terrible music, but with squelches and squeals of gear, steering, pedal and brake.

And then he surprised me, he downshifted and slowed the car down.

"Why are we slowing down?" Tony asked.

"Hold on tight," Sal said.

Sal waited until the headlights were almost on us and he gunned the gas and shifted. He hurtled the car down to the first roundabout. We careened around it, rubber tires burning, the smoke behind us.

All of us slammed to one side of the car. Sal placed our car in front of an oncoming vehicle. He flashed the high beams to blind the other driver into slowing down and floored the pedal and cut the wheel back into our original lane. The other car's sonic blast blared past us. Kiernan was still there, on our tail.

"I'm not done yet," Sal said.

He gripped the wheel and entered the second rotary, hard and fast. Faisal dry-heaved. Sal hugged the curve tight and came up behind Kiernan and O'Mara and then cut our lights and took the road to Centre Street, leaving the two cops behind us in the dark.

He let the car settle down into a more normal speed, the way a rider allowed his horse to recover from the race. Tony cuffed Faisal.

"Won't be needing this," Tony said and tossed me my key.

On our ride to the South End, Sal turned on the radio. We listened to the all-girl band Fanny. I dug the hard-driving organ, the vocals of Nicky Barclay and June Millington on the Les Paul guitar, though I don't think Faisal appreciated the lyrics or the title of the song "Borrowed Time."

They dropped me off at my place in the South End. When I got out of the car, I walked over to the driver's side for a word with Sal. "Some free advice, kid. Lose the gun because you can't shoot for shit, but you're damn good behind the wheel."

Sal beamed as if he had made the honor roll. Faisal didn't look so good. Neither did Larry. Tony asked me for my .38. "Why?" I asked.

"Trust me," Tony said and wiggled his fat fingers. "The gun, please."

I surrendered my sidearm.

The car pulled away. I watched the brake lights turn red, then the traffic light blinked green, and they were gone. Call it karma, as I watched the car and the two ghosts inside, Larry and The Syrian, disappear.

Chapter Twenty-Seven: Dead Ringer

I stepped into Winter Hill Gang territory, in Somerville or, as the locals called it, Slummerville.

The Sacco Bowling Alley offered up sights, sounds, and characters. The teal-and-orange color scheme throughout the place suggested the Miami Dolphins instead of the red and white of the New England Patriots. There were lockers and shoes you rented for cheap. The vending machine in the corner had seen more action than Patton's Third Army.

It cost three bucks a string to throw gutter balls, strikes or spares. Three dollars to do it all over again. And for many, it was a deal, a thrill, for others. The rich went to Europe; the middle class took to the tennis courts; everybody else bowled.

I watched two women's teams, Cambridge and Somerville, go up against each other. These ladies were why we'd won World War II. One broad—and I think she'd be offended if I didn't call her that—hurled the ball down the lane as hard and fast as any pitcher in the majors. Her opponent, a petite thing, anted up at the line with enough spunk to either bowl a strike, which she did, or execute a lay-up on a basketball court. Women's Liberation could use three fingers and a sixteen-pound wrecking ball.

The clock above the linoleum counters said Bill was running late. He'd cut me a break this time, inviting me here, instead of some seedy lounge with an even seedier music man tinkling the keys and humming a melody for throwaway change in the oversized glass on top of his piano.

Bowling, the lawn sport of colonists and beer leagues, had evolved into a money-maker within a century. Don Carter was the first athlete in any sport to receive a million-dollar deal; that's more scratch than Broadway Joe made throwing pigskin for the New York Jets or shilling razors for Schick. Bowling even has a national TV show. ABC televised *Pro Bowlers Tour* on Saturday afternoons and Chris Schenkel was the sport's own Howard Cosell, same yellow jacket and distinctive voice.

I spotted him. Bill had come in right behind a dead ringer looking for easy fish. Sacco's had that too, con men and hustlers who rolled in after they'd sharked the pool halls in Central Square. I recognized the type: the ingénue in need of a mentor. They acted as if they were a virgin who'd never touched a bowling ball, an Eliza Doolittle looking for a Henry Higgins. They'd cast a few balls into the moat and act all discouraged. The victim here was sitting on a Lucite bench.

The mark offered advice, stoked confidence, even paid for a few strings, and then the understudy would suggest a wager and that's when miracles happened. There's the first strike, beginner's luck, then two becomes three, the sucker parted from his money like a gobbler separated from his flock on Thanksgiving Day.

"Sorry I'm late."

"What's his name?" I asked.

"Nothing like that. We need to talk."

"Now I feel like one of your dates."

"I've got some bad news."

"You're a cop, Bill. Cops never have any good news."

"I'm serious."

"Fine," I said. "Spill it."

The police department didn't teach officers how to deliver bad news well. Death notifications, for example, were the darkest chapter of any cop's career. Bill and I had both been in the service. We met on the Freedom Bird back to the world. We understood what it meant to ruck up, and deal with a cluster fuck. If I could block out screams and the stench of napalm and burning flesh in Vietnam, I could ignore the surround sound of bowling balls smashing into pins, the whoops and hollers from every owner of a triple-decker in the joint. I saw Bill's eyes. I understood them.

Bad news.

We had one other thing in common. I'd once been a police officer; he still was one. The way we talked to each other was different. There was no need for the steady gaze, the calm voice. We knew and we obeyed that one law for bad news that all cops should follow, and that was to say it face-to-face.

"Kiernan," he said.

"Let me guess, some lawyer found a hole in a law book."

I'd expected as much. Pinto's prophecy that the Commissioner would make an example of one or two officer had come true, except it was one instead of two. He culled Kiernan from the herd, on drugs and related charges, and let the district attorney tack on a dozen more. The DA himself rode the elevator down from his office to convene a grand jury to indict Kiernan on murder one for Luisa Ramírez. O'Mara had been suspended, pending a review, and a cloud moved around him like Charlie Brown's friend, Pig-Pen.

The strategy was as old as the political compromise. Both the Commissioner and the DA wanted wins. No courtesies. No special treatment. The Commissioner would give his blessing for the DA to lean on Kiernan. Threaten the man with the maximum ticket, but tell him he could do less prison time if he raised his snout and ratted out the officers involved. The Commissioner wanted a clean house. The way it worked was simple. The DA would look at his watch and tell Kiernan the offer expired soon. He'd cough, Kiernan would blink and squeal.

The Commissioner would get an envelope with names, dates, and details. The grand jury would be dismissed with the sudden announcement of a plea deal. The Commissioner and Shadow would then do damage control and offer up more dark sheep in the fold and handle the rest internally.

Kiernan was the lever. If he played the loyalty card and said nothing, he'd do time and take his chances that the dealer's compadres didn't shank him in Walpole. The Commissioner and the DA would then turn their undivided love and attention on O'Mara.

Repeat and rinse.

"Just say it, Bill."

"Kiernan's dead."

"Let me guess," I said. "Hanged himself in his jail cell, using bedsheets?" Bill stared at me. I suggested other popular conveniences. "Stabbed with a sharpened toothbrush?"

"He tried to make a break for it before the morning transport."

"He tried to escape, in leg irons, handcuff cover and a martin chain around his waist?"

"Yep."

"Must've been something to watch on the surveillance monitor."

"The camera was on the fritz," Bill said. "He made a break for it and they shot him. All the correctional officers on the scene are saying the same thing."

"Shot him where?"

"What difference does it make, Shane? Kiernan is dead."

"Shot him where?"

"Twice in the back of the head."

"Did he talk to the DA?" I asked.

"Don't know. Word is that he was clipped before he could sing."

"And then there was one. Officer O'Mara."

If the Commissioner had names, he'd close the barn door. The DA was without a case unless Kiernan's partner corroborated the testimony, assuming a judge would allow it.

"More like, and then there were none," Bill said.

"O'Mara is dead?"

"Ate his gun this morning."

"Helped along?"

"It doesn't appear so. He left a note," Bill said.

"Ironic, an actual suicide."

Chapter Twenty-Eight: Loose Ends

Ma had a saying from her ma in the old country for when a child ought to have gratitude. "Count your half pennies." I shouldn't begrudge her the superstition because we came from a people who believed redheads were descendants of cats, and that the cross scored on soda bread kept the Devil out. I'm grateful, though.

Sean the concierge was back at his post on the bottom floor of my office building on Washington Street. I ought to count my pennies. I stitched up the Ramírez case, and there's the promise of a pension from the BPD. Nothing official in the mail yet, so it was distant as smoke in the Berkshires as far as I was concerned.

Sean handed me fresh keys. Business looked good for Saul, enough so that he could afford to lean back and wave at me as I passed his door. All year and most days, Saul tended to customers. He said jewelers were the coconspirators in the creation of memories, whether it was legitimate or extramarital affairs, anniversaries of every sort and kind, and all of life's other secrets and causes for celebrations. Precious gems, gold and silver, he said, were symbols, the ephemera of a moment.

I never understood baubles. A rock was a rock to me, and diamonds meant nothing until a bunch of Victorians made a big deal out of them; the same people who decided pink was for girls and blue was for boys, and created untold complexes for the headshrinkers to cure on leather couches at outrageous rates.

I pressed the button inside the elevator and counted lights and bells. When I got off my floor, I almost slipped and fell because the janitor had waxed and buffed the floor to a high-gloss shine. I was beginning to believe the rumor he drove the Zamboni machine for the Bruins and his work on the ice cost Bobby Orr his knee this year.

The keys from Sean opened a fresh lock from the work order I placed with the manager of the building. I picked up the pile of letters on the floor. Circulars and coupons outnumbered any real mail. I sorted and tossed envelopes faster than the Automatic Letter Facer at the Post Office. The phone rang and I cradled the receiver against my ear, and said my name.

"Calling to extend our congratulations on a job well done with the Ramírez case."

"How did you…never mind," I said, amazed again the man knew I was in my office. "I thought our last conversation was a one-time deal."

"The Commissioner and I are pleased."

"Glad to hear it, but want to know who isn't pleased? I'm not."

"Is this about your pension?"

"That can wait," I said. "I'm talking about this little thing called justice."

"And you don't think there was any?"

"For Kiernan and O'Mara? Sure, even though it's not my idea of due process. I'm talking about the rest of the bunch, the guys who walked and whose dirt endangers the good shields out there. Sully the Bad Cop oughta have his name sullied in every paper in the Commonwealth."

I threw that hook out there to see where it'd land. I'd figured out I was on speaker-phone by the time Shadow said "congratulations." I'd bet the family name and the last potato in Ireland that Pinto or the Commissioner or both were in the room. Suggesting the Commissioner didn't care about corruption among the rank and file was an intentional poke with the Devil's pitchfork.

"I can assure you the Commissioner has noted every name and badge number. The objective here was to put some closure around the Ramírez case. You confirmed our suspicions that her death wasn't accidental, and whether or not individuals within Urban Renewal had a hand in her demise."

"But you suspected cops all along, didn't you?" I said, and added a little steam with it. "Our mutual friend told me in the car, I was tapped because I could visit places others couldn't, and here I am, full circle again with the BPD, dirty cops and with another bullseye on my back."

"Distance was necessary, Mr. Cleary. The Commissioner wanted an honest man, and he got one, and he won't forget it."

The way he'd said it with gravity, pulled me into my seat.

"Okay," I said. "But I need something from you; it's a cop thing, so hear me out."

"This wasn't part of the agreement. I'm not sure I understand."

"Because you're not a cop," I said. "A woman has lost her sister, a nephew will never meet his aunt, and a good woman's corpse was hauled off as if she was a nobody, just another anonymous death in the big city. Do you know what happens to the remains of the homeless and indigent in the Commonwealth of Massachusetts when they die?"

"I do not."

"The Medical Examiner will often refuse the body, citing backlog. In this case, that didn't happen because someone wanted a death certificate that shamed the deceased. We'll never know for certain whether Kiernan and O'Mara were the ones who strong-armed the ME, who was dispatched to Worcester to count snowflakes as they fall from the sky. We'll never know who'd ordered them to spook the good doctor, will we?"

"No, we will not, but the Commissioner has assured me the man will be recalled to Boston and restored to his post in the Office of the Chief Medical Examiner."

"I appreciate that, I do. But here's another question for you. Do you know what happened to her unclaimed body?"

I heard papers shuffle and his voice returned.

"Buried in an unmarked grave. Is it your wish that she receive a proper burial?"

"That's correct, but there's more," I said.

"You do realize exhumation requires a court order?"

"I do," I said. "But you now have a homicide, and you have a living relative, and you have the Commissioner to push the paper in front of a judge, and his name carries weight."

"And why should I comply?"

"How about it's the right fucking thing to do. And one last item I need to clue you in on. When the forgotten die in our great Commonwealth after the ME refuses the body, even though it's his job, and when funeral homes deny the body because there's no money in it for them, it is cops who notify the next of kin. It's a cop who will call every funeral home until they find a taker. It's cops who make sure the deceased has that last shred of respect every human being deserves, burial, and they do this duty, sir, while a cop stands guard over the dead at the scene."

"He wants to do the death notification," a voice I didn't recognize said.

"Correct," I said, and heard nothing until I heard the same voice again.

"Proceed with the death notification…and Officer Cleary?"

"Sir?"

"You're all cop. Thank you."

I needed to tell Toni her sister would receive a proper funeral. She was with her kid and Isabella in Villa Victoria. Nikos had pulled strings and I didn't ask how, but it provided me some comfort when he had explained his rationale. He said the two women and the child would be with their people. His choice of words had smacked of condescension but then I remembered the impetus behind Villa Victoria and understood.

When the very people Luisa Ramírez had attacked set their eyes on Parcel 19 in the South End, a disparate group of Puerto Ricans mobilized to counter Urban Renewal's plan to raze their part of the neighborhood. Mindful of what had happened to immigrants and working-class people in the West End, they vowed it would not happen to them. They held meetings, they pooled money, and they hired architects after putting out an RFP, a Request For Proposal. Villa Victoria was within walking distance from my place in Union Square. I'd seen the two-story townhouses and single-family casitas, the common plaza and the small park.

The newspaper covered the protests. I heard the chants of "We're not going to move from Parcel 19" in English and Spanish from my window and on the television.

They'd hit the Elites where it hurt most, in the pocket. They were organized and could not be deterred, intimidated, or paid off to leave the South End. They said they could build affordable houses, complete with an Arts and Education center, provide low-income housing, including homes for the elderly, and do all of it economically and with every dollar accounted for, and on time.

Which is what they did.

Toni knew her sister was dead, murdered, which was as bad as it gets for news for a family member, but now I had to inform her that Luisa would be exhumed, moved to a funeral home, and then interred again, but this time with a proper tombstone. I thought I'd break it to her with flowers in hand.

I crossed Washington Street. There was a floral shop, sandwiched between the Old South Meeting House and the State Street subway station. It was a small space, a few feet by a few feet, exposed to the elements all year round, and run by a squat and scrappy character with a perpetual case of five o'clock shadow and an apron around his waist. The man guarded his kingdom of flowers like a centurion.

His customers were distant cousins of Saul's customers, too poor for the gaudies under plate glass, but it was the same motivation: to apologize, to impress, and to commemorate an important event or person. Prices were handwritten on a board with chalk. It was a simple operation of point and pay, and Longinus the Roman wrapped the flowers in brown craft paper.

While I was browsing for something among all the choices, I noticed a tall blonde holding an assortment of gerbera daisies. The way her blue eyes hunted for companions to accompany her daisies suggested a cool and rational process of elimination. The merchant asked her if she needed assistance. She told the florist she needed a minute and he came my way. Her smile almost broke me in two, until the sandpaper in his voice put me back together.

"What can I get you, pal?"

I looked down. "Two of those." I pointed to some daffodils.

"Ah, these symbolize rebirth and new beginnings."

I whispered, "Do me a favor, and give the lady over there a daffodil after I leave."

"Hit and run with one daffodil? Why not a rose?" He pointed to some in red, pink, and white.

"That's too forward."

"Forward, in this day and age?" He sighed. "Two bouquets and one solitary daffodil it is, my friend, but if you promise me you'll buy a rose next time, I'll give you the cure."

"The cure for what? I'm fine."

"The cure for loneliness. And no, you're not fine. I can tell from your eyes. You need love in your life." He tilted his head in her direction. "Her name is Bonnie."

"Thanks," I said. I paid him and then bumped into her during my escape. "Excuse me."

"Lovely daffodils there," she said and smiled.

"His name is Shane Cleary, PI," the florist said to her.

"I'm Bonnie, criminal defense attorney."

Chapter Twenty-Nine: Ashes to Ashes

Ninety-four degrees. This Easter Sunday in April marked the hottest day for the month in the city's history since a bunch of nerds started recording weather temperatures in 1872. The word "nerd," Lindsey reminded us, was an invention of Dr. Seuss. He was serenading John and me with literary trivia while we roasted on the sofa.

It wasn't that we weren't interested in whether T.S Eliot thought April was the cruelest month, or if Chaucer took delight in spring rain. John and I struggled to stay awake. We lived for when the oscillating fan blew a breeze over us and melted until it returned. We were straw for the fire. The steady fever from Silvia's kitchen, the combined rage of her stove and oven, had us perspiring, our clothes sticking to us.

I'd chosen a magazine from the table in front of me to fan myself when I noticed the newspaper. It was a copy of the *Boston Herald American*, two weeks old, and the photograph told me why John kept it. The shot was taken not far from the floral stand where I'd bought the daffodils for Izzy and Toni. The newsprint above the image read **The Soiling of Old Glory**.

I took in the scene. A Black man, hands pinned behind him by a Boston city councilor, an enemy of desegregation in the schools, public housing, or anywhere else, was about to be speared with a flag pole by an anti-housing protestor.

I thought, what would Luisa Ramírez say about this hideous montage?

She'd probably teach me something more pertinent about life than Lyndsey's etymology or poetry. She'd remind me of the Boston Massacre, of the day British soldiers shot and killed five colonials. Numbered among the dead, she'd tell me, was a former slave named Crispus Attucks. His death was good press, enough to stoke the righteous flames of outrageous rebellion against King George, but not enough to warrant justice inside a courtroom.

Few people knew the lawyer who represented the soldiers was John Adams, the future president of the United States, and fewer still knew he won every single one of the accused acquittals because he characterized Attucks as less than human and the friends who died with him as "Irish Teagues and outlandish Jack Tars." Luisa would've said all that, whereas John next to me would've pointed to a history book and riffed on a southern expression familiar to him since childhood. "Nobody lies, they tell a story." He'd pause and add, "Except it ain't our story."

I studied the photo, like a cop would. Anti-war protestors loved to wave the flag around, asserting their First Amendment right. This nut from Southie was intent on using The Stars and Stripes as a lance to skewer the Black man in front of him. His stance, the way he'd planted his feet, convinced me that he intended to inflict bodily harm. The racist behind the victim was, to my surprise, ambiguous. His feet pointed away, as in hips turned, which suggested he was trying to move the Black man, a lawyer, out of harm's way. I rethought my conclusion after reading the victim's comment. The attack from behind had hit the Yale graduate with a force strong enough to knock his glasses off and break his nose. The assault from the rear saved his face from the pointed end of the pole in front.

I read the name of the photographer. Stanley Forman.

He'd been awarded a Pulitzer Prize the year before for his sequence of five photographs at Boston fires. All of them were disturbing, though the most heartbreaking one for me was a photo of a woman and child during a blaze on Marlborough Street. What should have been a routine ladder rescue, wasn't.

Lindsey's voice saved me from thinking about photos from Vietnam.

"Did you hear what I said?" he said.

"Sorry." I returned the newspaper to John's table and covered it with some magazines.

John caught what I had done. "That's some shit there, ain't it?"

"Some things never change," I said.

"Unlike my car."

"What do you mean? I had the car washed and included a fresh tank of gas, like you asked."

"Yep, and you were so thoughtful as to replace all the fluids, all seven of them, and I even have new brake pads. I ought to loan my car to you more often. Who knows what I'll get when you return it next time?"

I showed sudden interest in Lindsey's story about the time he met T.S. Eliot on the sidewalk outside of The Coop, a bookstore across the street from Harvard. Eliot had received the Nobel Prize, and Lindsey approached and congratulated the man. I'd heard the story before. The punchline was Eliot's sardonic response: "When they award you the Prize, it is their polite way of saying, you should stop writing."

Tom the poet, at the top of his game, and with a chunk of Swedish money and medallion in hand, didn't know what to do with himself. I couldn't complain. I was flush with money, thanks to Jimmy. Another chunk of money showed up in my bank account, unannounced, and I received a letter from the Boston Retirement System.

About Jimmy.

In the weeks leading up to Easter Sunday, there had been several fires around Boston that kept the newspapers, the Fire Department, and investigators busy. Like celebrity deaths, the fires came in threes: Westland Avenue, a block down from Burbank, went up first; then Burbank itself and then the city's favorite, Symphony Road. All the properties belonged to The Syrian.

I intuited Larry's hand behind the suspicious fires, which meant the don was a merciful mafioso. In reading the statements from investigators in the papers, the recipe fit Larry's MO. The accelerant, gas canisters were left in a smokestack on the rooftop, and tumbleweeds of garbage in the hallways below provided the fodder. Convenient, I thought.

Conveniences also came in triplicate, too. A federal investigator concluded that the first of these fires had been the work of the same arsonist and matched an earlier fire on Symphony Road. This exonerated Jimmy, and he was sprung from the clink.

Multiple fires.

Larry was never pinched or questioned. Convenient. I didn't scratch my scalp too hard to realize the don and Larry must've reached an agreement. I figured it went something like this: Larry would live if he continued to provide the don burnt offerings. In the spirit of revenge against the scumlord, the don was Sherman destroying Atlanta.

Convenience number three. The Fire Department found a body in the building on Burbank Road. It was incumbent upon me to do another death notification, this time with a news clipping to my friend in Florida. The article mentioned an ex-wife, but the newspaper had kept her name out of it. Jerry's obituary depicted him as a pathetic druggie, small-time dealer, and full-time snitch, working for two corrupt cops who had ties to heroin and a certain slumlord.

Faisal had disappeared. No surprise there. I suspected he was in an oil barrel on Deer Island, along with the trash, business associates who were on the losing end of deals with the mob, and other wayward sons of the mafia.

I ran into JC a day after I'd visited Isabella and Toni. He told me a rough-looking character and an old man had claimed the burnt body in the morgue. He said, "This older guy with half a pinky scared the life out of me." I didn't say a word. JC conveyed all of this over a sandwich at Nikos's place.

As for Isabella and Toni, I think I might've detected a tear in Toni's eye after I told her about plans for Luisa's funeral. She apologized for all the times she'd been rude to me. She was grateful, she said, but didn't know how to express it. I could relate. Before I left, she introduced me to her son, Reinaldo. I spent a little time with the tyke, and convinced him that if he planted a stick of Juicy Fruit gum, he'd have a tree in no time, and he'd never have to buy chewing gum again. I'm not sure how much stuck, but I loved the smile on his face and the brightness in his brown eyes.

When I called Toni with the name of a funeral home in West Roxbury, she fretted about the cost, but I told her the director insisted that he'd cover the bill because he remembered Luisa and so should everyone else when they visited her grave in Saint Joseph's Cemetery.

When John and Sylvia invited me to Easter dinner, I mentioned Nikos.

I didn't have to strum the strings about his departed wife. The thought of Nikos at home, alone and watching the religious marathon of *Ben-Hur*, both 1925 and '59 versions, *Barabbas*, *Jesus Christ Superstar*, and *The Greatest Story Ever Told*, depressed me. There was some uplift to the man's mood when I agreed to become his property manager and informed him that he was invited to Easter dinner. He worried that he'd impose.

"No problem," Sylvia said. "The more people, the merrier, and John says bring Delilah. He loves cats and cats love ham."

And that ham.

I could smell it from the living room. After I arrived, I attempted to breach the door to the kitchen and failed, rebuffed by a southern woman who knew how to use a spatula with deadly force. Sylvia recited the menu for me.

Coca-Cola glazed ham with brown sugar and Dijon and sides of collard greens with potatoes, and her famous cornbread.

"Dessert?" I dared to ask.

"What you folks in Massachusetts call a grunt, my people call a slump."

I was too ashamed to ask what any of that meant. I stood there, stupid as sheep.

"See the cast-iron skillet behind me?" I looked, and said I did. "In simple terms, it's a cobbler you cook on the stovetop. And before you ask, it's blackberries with some lemon."

"I didn't know blackberries were available in April."

"Know the right people and anything is possible."

"Never truer words spoken," I said.

"Look at that skillet again. If you don't scoot out of my kitchen now, it gonna land upside your head. Now, go on and get."

There was an hour of conversation, about how the Boston Red Sox had lost to the Chicago White Sox, and then a knock at the door. I opened it to find Vanessa and Sal. She gave me a kiss on the cheek, and walked past the look of shock on my face. Sal was wearing a tailored tan suit, Italian and perfect for spring that was feeling more like summer. The cost for his threads alone amounted to a kid's savings from mowing lawns for five years.

I shook Sal's hand. Sylvia came into the room to welcome Vanessa. Those two had reached some sort of détente. Paris Peace Accords be damned. I watched, stunned, as Vanessa introduced Sal around the room. John simmered on the sofa, uncertain about what to do with the Italian in his living room. John had read Sal, head to toe, and recognized he was more Sicilian than Wednesday was Prince Spaghetti night.

I collected Sal's suit jacket for the bed in the other room. I turned to leave and found Vanessa there. Her hand gripped the doorframe and she angled her body to remind me about what I had passed up. She gave me the silhouette of long slim legs, skirt down to mid-thigh. She went to say something but Sal had eased up behind her and nuzzled her ear. I searched for a spot on the wall. She floated away leaving me with Sal. He looked like he wanted to say something—an explanation, an excuse. I spared him.

"Let me guess: instant chemistry the night the two of you met?"

"Yeah, but I wanted to tell you Tony is downstairs for you."

Tony Two-Times was standing there on the sidewalk. He was dressed in his usual black suit with a four-peak handkerchief in his breast pocket, glossy black shoes, a bright white shirt and screaming tie. He was holding a small box in one hand.

"Waiting long?" I asked.

"Nah. Here, this is for you," he said, handing me the gift. "But don't open it here."

The box had weight. I jiggled it like a kid.

"I wish you wouldn't do that. Bad juju," Tony said.

"Now you've got me curious. What is it?"

"What, and ruin the surprise?"

I tilted my head to look up at the window. "Now, there's the surprise."

"What? Are you prejudiced or something?"

"Not at all." I raised the box. "Let me guess. A gun?"

"I hadda replace the one I took from you a few weeks ago."

"Appreciate it, Tony. I really do, but one question. The one you took won't be connected to someone dying of lead poisoning, will it?"

"It'd be worse for you if a bullet from a cop's leg were to be matched to a

.38, even if said cop was deceased." Tony smiled for the second time since I'd known him. "I dislike loose ends like the change in my pocket. The thing hadda be destroyed."

He reached inside his pocket and the hand came out with a pack of Marlboros Reds.

"Thought you'd quit?" I said.

A cigarette in his face, his hand brought a lighter to his lips. I took the fancy gold lighter from him. My thumb turned the wheel and sparked a flame, and I snapped the lid shut.

"Thanks," he said. "I'll quit one day." Tony held the cigarette away from his mouth. "Sometimes, they calm my nerves, especially when I'm on edge."

"Something upset you?" I asked. "Like whatever the don said to you the night we left Newton, or is it something else?"

Tony exhaled smoke. The cigarette moved with the hand without losing any ash.

"I can't discuss what the old man and me talked about that night."

"Then something else has upset you. I ask because I'm curious."

Tony pointed at me, cigarette between two fat fingers. "Get yourself uncurious then."

"It's Easter Sunday, Tony, a time for new beginnings."

"Yeah, right," he said. "Let me tell you a story to satisfy that curiosity of yours. Ready?"

Like I said, mob guys always talked in code. In their cars, inside the house and outside on the street, as if they thought the pigeons were bugged.

"I'm listening," I said.

"An old king is near the end of his days, and he has these two boys. Both of these kids have an aptitude for leadership, but one of them is anxious to rush his education. He's headstrong and won't listen to the king when he advises him to be patient. Everything in its due course, he tells the kid. This heir apparent doesn't listen, goes astray without anybody knowing it and wanders into a foreign land where he shouldn't be, and none of the king's men could protect him," Tony said. "You follow me?"

"And this other prince?"

Tony tapped his temple. "He's got smarts, and listens to the king. The old monarch has high hopes for him, but he believes in free will, the good Catholic that he is. The king sees a bright future for the kid. But then something terrible happens in the kingdom. One of the princes dies." Tony inhaled and exhaled. "Still with me?"

"Every step of the way."

"The king presents the surviving prince a choice." Tony tapped some ash. "He tells the kid, I can take care of this problem but you have a choice, kid. If you follow one path, it's a life of violence because that's the life of a king, or you could step away from the throne and live a life of peace. The prince's answer surprised the king. Hell, it stunned me."

"Even you, one of the king's own men?"

"Chilled me to the bone." Tony held up his hand. "The truth."

"What did this prince say?"

"Not what he said, it was what he did." Tony wagged cigarette and hand. "The ones who do anything in this life, good or bad, are the ones who don't talk about it. Words mean nothing, unless you're a writer of course, but life ain't fiction. Those who do, they're the ones you need to watch. Get what I'm saying?"

"Actions are everything. Got it."

"A crematorium," Tony said, as an unexpected non-sequitur. "Know how they work?"

"Beyond the basic idea, I can't say that I do."

"The body is inside a casket, something combustible, and placed on a thing that slides the body and casket, like a package, into a chamber called a retort. A door closes and then somebody pushes a button for the furnace. There are flames, above and below the casket. Picturing this?"

"Like a tray inside the broiler or a rack in an oven," I said.

"Exactly, but don't forget there's a door with a window," Tony said.

Tony threw the finished cigarette to the ground and twisted his shoe on it.

I took in a deep breath. "So our prince chose a life of violence."

"He took the bad guy who killed the missing prince, tied him up, and placed him in a special box, and found an oven with a dial instead of a button." Tony

218

shook his head, in disbelief. "Something I'll never fucking forget."

"The box. Special how?" I asked.

"It had a clear cover, like the coffin in the movie *Sleeping Beauty*, when everyone thought she was dead before the kiss of life. Our prince lets this guy lie there to contemplate his crime and, after some time passes, turns up the heat a little so he could see the flame above him, and just enough for him to feel it under him. Turns the dial a little." Tony's fingers turned an imaginary dial, like a safecracker searching for the right number.

"And he stood by the door, so he could watch through the window," I said.

"The guy was kicking and screaming and begging, until our prince turned the dial until there's nothing but the roar of a fire."

"Ashes to ashes, like that house on Symphony Road," I said.

Acknowledgements

Endless gratitude to:

Deb Well, Dean Hunt, and Dave King, who have read and re-read this novel and offered advice.

Shawn Reilly Simmons, my editor at Level Best Books, who steered me clear of errors and improved my writing.

My wonderful Level Best Books family of authors, for whom I am grateful for their support and enthusiasm.

About the Author

Gabriel Valjan lives in Boston's South End. He is the author of the *Roma Series* and *Company Files* (Winter Goose Publishing) and the Shane Cleary series (Level Best Books). His second Company File novel, *The Naming Game*, was a finalist for the Agatha Award for Best Historical Mystery and the Anthony Award for Best Paperback Original in 2020. Gabriel is a member of the Historical Novel Society, International Thriller Writer (ITW), and Sisters in Crime.

CPSIA information can be obtained
at www.ICGtesting.com
Printed in the USA
LVHW042137280422
717483LV00003B/386